NIGHTMARE

OTHER BOOKS FROM ROBIN PARRISH

THE DOMINION TRILOGY
Relentless
Fearless
Merciless

Offworld

ROBIN PARRISH

NIGHTMARE

BETHANYHOUSE

MINNEAPOLIS, MINNESOTA

Nightmare
Copyright © 2010
Robin Parrish

Cover design by Lookout Design, Inc.
Cover photo by Mehmet Turgut
Interior photo credits on page 351

Published by Bethany House Publishers
11400 Hampshire Avenue South
Bloomington, Minnesota 55438

Bethany House Publishers is a division of
Baker Publishing Group, Grand Rapids, Michigan.

Printed in the United States of America

Library of Congress Cataloging-in-Publication Data

Parrish, Robin.
    Nightmare / Robin Parrish
        p.   cm.
    ISBN 978-0-7642-0607-8 (pbk.)
    1. Supernatural—Fiction. 2. Missing persons—Fiction. I. Title.
    PS3616.A7684N54   2010
    813'.6—dc22

                                                                    2010006025

To my brother Ross, who has never once stopped believing in me.

"Whatever else a 'ghost' may be, it is probably one of the most complex phenomena in nature."

Frederic W. H. Myers
Founder, Society for Psychical Research
circa 1882

ONE

"Doesn't matter who you are or what you believe. Everybody has a ghost story."

My father said those words to me as a child whenever I would question his life's work. Scratch that. His life's *obsession*.

I came to learn that he was right. Everybody has had at least one of those moments when their insides say something's happening that's far outside of normal. A fleeting second when something is seen moving out of the corner of their eye. A prick at the back of the neck alerting them to a presence. A location that for no discernible reason fills them with dread.

I had plenty of my own stories of ghosts and the paranormal. As Maia Peters, daughter of the famous Malcolm and Carmen Peters, it was to be expected. I thought I knew everything there was to know about the paranormal. One warm night in New York City, I found out just how wrong I was.

A sign just inches from my face read "YOU WILL BE TERRI-FIED" in a scrawled typeface. The words were blood red, splattered in a sloppy fashion across a plank of rotted wood.

I looked at the sign not with suspicion or doubt, just weariness. It was the third such sign to be thrust in my face since my friends and I had stepped into the line. It might have seemed more authentic had "Ghost Town®" not been printed in the bottom right corner of the faux wood.

"There was always this one closet at my grandparents' house that gave me the creeps when I was growing up," said Jill, rubbing her gloved hands together both to keep warm and—I assumed—out of nervousness. "It was a linen closet in the bathroom at the back of the house, and it was really dark inside. Whenever I looked in there . . . I don't know. It made me feel cold all over."

Jill had been my roommate at Columbia University for our sophomore and junior years. For our senior year, I was paying extra for solo on-campus housing.

Angela, meanwhile, was Jill's best friend since high school. She was similarly coifed with long, straight hair, and talked so much like Jill that I often thought their brains were psychically linked. At Jill's words, Angela shivered slightly but smiled. "I've got one," she said, glancing around to make sure none of the other amusement park patrons in this line were listening too closely. "When I was like nine or ten, sometimes my great-aunt would pick me up after school and I'd stay at her house for a couple of hours until my dad got off work. Her husband was this really mean old guy who'd done all these awful, evil things to her, but he died before I was born. She kept this old recliner in the house that belonged to him, and I hated it. It was ratty and nasty, and it smelled funny. And when I was in the room with it alone . . . I swear sometimes I could see a figure out of the corner of my eye. When I'd turn to look, there was nobody there. But for just a second, it was like this guy was standing right there watching me, and he wasn't moving. It terrified me *to death*, even though I eventually figured it was all in my head."

"Wow," said Jill, her eyes wide and sincere.

"Here's the really crazy part. After a few years, my aunt decided to finally get rid of that chair. And would you believe—after it was gone, I never saw the figure again."

"Ooooh," said Jill, not quite grinning but still enthusiastic. I saw Angela and her glance my direction, hoping for a response.

I think they were frustrated when I didn't react to either story. I couldn't help it; I was bored and distracted by thoughts of the beginning of classes in a few days. I leaned out and inspected the line the three of us stood in, estimating there were at least a hundred people in front of us, waiting to enter the ride. It was going to be a long night.

Jill and Angela were hardly my closest friends, if I even had anyone in my life who qualified. But Jill always paid her portion of the dorm room rent on time and never threw any parties—she just attended them elsewhere with Angela—so I found it hard to complain about the two of them. Even if I wasn't all that compatible with them, personality-wise.

They'd gone out of their way to invite me on this little pre-senior-year jaunt, even though, as Angela had not so delicately put it, "We realize this isn't something you're dying to do, because of . . . well, *you know*."

It was an unspoken but absolute rule in the dorm that no one ever talked about my upbringing. I wasn't ashamed of it, or even made uncomfortable talking about it. It wasn't some big trauma, either. It was just . . . out of the ordinary. *Way* out. And I wasn't interested in looking back. I only wanted to look ahead.

But I *had* impulsively agreed to come along with them, and the pleasantly surprised faces that Jill and Angela displayed when I said yes were all too genuine, and I knew why. I was serious about my studies and my chosen major, and I wanted very badly to be taken seriously. But senior year hadn't yet begun, and as crass as I knew this silly trip would probably be, the truth was, I longed for a little company. My last friendship had ended badly, and I was surprised at how much I missed the companionship and solidarity of having someone around. It was something I'd never expected to need, but once it was gone, I wanted it more than ever.

"So what's your biggest fear?" asked Jill, trying to keep the conversation going.

"Um," ventured Angela, "forgetting to wear clothes to class?"

Jill laughed. "That's not scary, that's just embarrassing! I'm talking about knee-quivering, pee-inducing, 'I-want-my-mommy' kind of terrified. What scares you *that* bad?"

"I don't know," replied Angela as the three of us wormed through the zig-zagging line and I took another peek at the line's progress, trying subtly to distance myself from this conversation. "The thought of being chased through the woods by a crazed ax murderer?" Angela finally answered.

Jill laughed again. "Well, it's a cliché, but it's scary, I'll give you that. Personally, I don't think there's anything worse than a creepy little girl. I mean, think about all those old movies and video games where some bizarre, detached little girl with haunted eyes just stares blankly at everyone while terrible things happen to them. It's like she has no soul. It freaks me out just thinking about it!"

We turned another corner in the line and my eyes found a new sign. This one warned, "YOU MIGHT VOMIT."

Jill and Angela laughed nervously at the sight, but then Angela turned to me. "What about you, Maia? What's the scariest thing you've ever seen?"

My mind slowed down for a moment, and my eyes shifted slowly to Angela as an answer came immediately to mind. "Uh . . . I don't think I should say."

Both girls watched me with sudden caution. Their demeanors betrayed that they knew they'd suddenly trodden into unwanted territory. "Why not?" Angela almost whispered.

The only answer I could give was the honest one.

"Because if I told you, you would wish I hadn't."

I looked away from their stunned expressions, trying to act nonchalant. Finally, after a long pause, I heard Jill exhale quickly in a halfhearted attempt at laughter, but it came out awkwardly and sounded like a nervous cough.

They quickly changed the subject. "Did you hear about that children's advocacy group that's suing Ghost Town because its rides are so scary?" asked Jill.

"That's so stupid!" replied Angela. "I mean, if you're dumb enough to bring your kids someplace like this, you deserve whatever you get."

I'd heard about it, too. It was big news. Having opened just six months ago, Ghost Town amusement park had become the hottest ticket in America. Fright junkies from all over the world were drawn to its state-of-the-art thrills and chills, which were reported to contain the most realistic recreations of the paranormal ever fashioned. I doubted that claim very much, having seen the paranormal firsthand, and knowing it to be nothing like the over-the-top digital effects displayed in Hollywood horror films.

Truth was always stranger than fiction, after all.

But the place was a source of intrigue, I had to admit. Almost as soon as it had opened, Ghost Town had landed at the center of controversy. There were endless reports of attendees suffering ongoing terrors by the things they'd experienced here, some supposedly even requiring psychiatric counseling—which of course only added to the place's popularity. The crown jewel in Ghost Town's arsenal was the Haunted House, which was supposed to be unlike any other haunted house ever built. It aimed to become known as "the definitive paranormal experience"—a guided walk-through tour that promised a face-to-face with the most authentic depiction of ghosts and apparitions ever seen. The Haunted House ride was the most popular attraction at the park, it was the main reason for all of the controversy, and it was the very ride that the three of us were in line waiting to enter.

As our place in line moved up and we read more of the foreboding signs, each increasing in its dire predictions, I couldn't help noticing that Jill and Angela were growing progressively more anxious. Their laughs were more nervous and their jokes cracked at a higher volume.

I was no more nervous now than I was at any other time in my life. I just couldn't be.

Growing up, I'd seen and done things that these two weren't equipped to imagine. I knew it would take more than a fun house to rattle me—a lot more—no matter how technologically advanced it was.

I wondered again why I'd agreed to come along, when I had so much prep to do for school.

Angela and Jill were looking extra nervous now, but fortunately Angela could always be counted on to fill any awkward silence.

"You know that thing when you walk from a bright room into a dark room and you think you see, like, a faint light that shouldn't be in there?"

Jill had her mouth open to respond when I spoke first. I didn't mean it to come out sounding condescending, but there was a clinical tone to my voice. "It's a retinal afterimage. A trick of the eye. An impression of residual light after the light's source has left your field of vision."

"I know," replied Angela, who smiled. "But it's still creepy."

I chuckled without humor, shaking my head.

"Yeah," added Jill, "and if the dark room has a mirror, it's even more—"

Jill's words were interrupted when something lunged at the three of us from the right of the line, emitting a terrifying, otherworldly sound.

Jill and Angela both screamed at the top of their lungs, clutching at each other. It was a spectral form that glowed with a jaundiced iridescence. But it was just a fancy fake, an advanced animatronic with billowing black fabric robes and a face made to look like authentically rotting flesh that had been partially peeled off to reveal the bones underneath. It moved with smooth grace, spiraling around us, on some kind of hidden magnetic track in the ground. Its mouth looked remarkably real as it opened wide to let out its chilling scream.

But no matter how real it looked, it was just another part of the park.

We watched as it raised a single hand to point at the three of us while it "flew" away backwards on its hidden rails, off to scare some other poor souls elsewhere in the park.

My friends were pale white, but laughing now, as were half a dozen others in line on either side of us. I think it took a few moments for Jill to realize that I hadn't screamed like they had. And that I wasn't nearly as amused by all this as they were. I felt like the Grinch who stole Halloween.

"That didn't scare you at all?" Jill moaned.

My arms were crossed and had never unfolded as the "specter" attacked us. I replied, "I saw it coming." I nodded behind Jill and Angela, in the direction the animatronic creature had come from.

Jill and Angela seemed put out by my inability to be frightened, and I suddenly wondered if my lack of outward enthusiasm might be misinterpreted as being ungrateful for the invite. I decided to put some effort into perking up for their benefit.

The line moved again just then, and I caught my first glimpse of the Haunted House as the three of us rounded a corner. "Is that it?" I asked, doing my best to sound at least a little intimidated by the looks of it.

Truth be told, it wasn't what I'd expected. With the out-of-control hype surrounding this walk-through "ride," I had pictured some huge monstrosity made to look like an ornate mansion that Bela Lugosi might come wafting out of in his full Dracula cape. I'd imagined seeing candles and creepy old lampposts layered with cobwebs adorning the outer edges of the attraction, a creaking, rusted iron gate that sealed off the property, and a chimney coughing out black smoke.

Ghost World's Haunted House had none of these things.

The most surprising aspect of it was its size. The Haunted House was remarkably small, made to resemble a ramshackle condemned house with no more than five or six rooms. It looked weathered and old—at least fifty years and seemingly more. It had only one level, and all its windows were boarded up, with no light escaping from inside. There was no precision to its appearance; every part of it looked like the whole structure was barely holding together. The pieces of metal and wood attached to its sides and roof were various shades of black or gray or muddy brown. It looked like something one of the hillbillies in *Deliverance* might have cobbled together up on a lonely mountain.

A basic screen door on the side of the house served as the entrance, resting at the end point of the line in which we stood.

It was all smoke and mirrors, of course, and I imagined that the peeling paint around the windows, the chipped mortar, and rotted wood were some sort of composite materials crafted intentionally to look weathered by decades of decay.

One final sign caught our attention. It read, "YOU MAY HAVE NIGHT TERRORS."

I had to look away in order to conceal a yawn I couldn't quite swallow.

A female amusement park worker in a blood-stained white apron smiled as she handed the three of us complimentary barf bags with the Ghost Town logo emblazoned on them. "Just in case," she said cheerfully.

I saw Angela and Jill glance at one another, their faces betraying a severe unease. The Haunted House was less than fifty feet directly ahead now, and I noticed that it had been intentionally hidden from visitors out wandering through the park by clever use of foliage and the wooden fencing surrounding the line to get in.

No doubt to add to its mystique, I thought.

One of the reasons the line was so long for the Haunted House ride was that large groups could not enter at one time. Ghost Town policy was for no more than four individuals to take the Haunted House tour together, so entrance was staggered as a few tourists were let in every few minutes.

Jill opted to keep our group to just the three of us, so when our turn finally came and the dark kitchen door creaked open by itself, only Jill, Angela, and I stepped inside.

It was almost completely dark in this first room, but the musty smell of mold and mildew saturated my senses at once. The exterior door slammed shut, seemingly on its own, and Angela and Jill jumped. Now it was totally dark *and* completely silent.

After a long twenty seconds of waiting, nothing happened, and all three of us were still standing in the same spot.

"Are we supposed to do something?" whispered Angela, breaking the silence.

As if in response, a deep, gravelly voice that was half whispering and half groaning spoke. The voice was distant, as if coming from somewhere else in the building, yet it was undeniably directed at us as it slowly intoned, *"You . . . don't . . . belong . . . here."*

I heard my two companions holding their breath as a pair of red pinpoint lights appeared in the middle of the room and fixed on each of us in turn, disembodied eyes sizing the three of us up.

I glanced to my left and saw in the darkness that Angela and Jill had sidestepped instinctively toward each other for safety.

The deep, throaty voice spoke again, louder this time, as the two eye-lights burned brighter in intensity. *"GET . . . OUT . . . OF . . . THIS . . . PLACE!"*

A door across the room leading farther into the building was flung open with a bang, and without waiting to be told again, Jill and Angela fled the kitchen to enter the next room. I hesitated, appraising the two red lights, which had fixed on me now and, remarkably, followed me as I walked toward the next room.

It was a nifty effect.

Inside the next room, the kitchen door behind me shut itself silently this time. Angela and Jill were practically hugging each other in the small dining room of the house, around which were six chairs. And in each one of the chairs sat what I assumed were holographic projections of ghostly figures. The clothes or rags they wore billowed and flowed around them as if they were underwater, and the figures themselves gave off a slightly bluish glow, the only light in the room.

The figures were incredibly detailed and three-dimensional, but my opinion of the ride's quality plummeted at the sight. Real apparitions never looked anything like this. These "ghosts" were pure Hollywood magic.

My companions were far more convinced than I was. Especially when the spirit at the head of the table, an elderly man with craggy fingers and clothes that hung from his bones, turned and locked his sunken eyes directly on to Jill. His eyes were filled with hate, and seemed to pierce right through whatever remaining courage Jill was holding on to. His gaze grew in intensity and vitriol until Jill inexplicably shouted, "I'm sorry!"

I still have no idea what Jill was apologizing for, but I knew at the time that it was a knee-jerk response to something Jill found terrifying. The "spirit" looked down on her as if she lived in a gutter, judgment and fury burning in his eyes. The expression was a bit chilling, I had to admit.

The old-man apparition bared his teeth, which were broken and black, to her and opened his mouth wider and wider until it went far past the point at which a human mouth could be opened. It grew bigger and longer, and ever so slowly, he rose from his place at the table and started gliding across the floor toward her.

Jill's hand reached out and grasped Angela's just as Angela was about to slide away, leaving Jill on her own. As the old man came closer to her, but never moving at more than a snail's pace, the other five apparitions at the table rose from their seats and began inching toward both Jill and Angela.

Angela screamed as the old man came close enough to touch her, and suddenly everything went dark and a cold gust of wind blew through the room, whipping up all around us.

I was starting to understand why this place was so popular. But nothing I'd experienced had brought me remotely close to feeling fear. It was all extremely well done, using advanced technologies to astounding effect. But it was too perfect, too scripted down to the last detail, to elicit the desired response. At least from me.

I knew better.

_____

After a bathroom, a brief detour into the basement where numerous things jumped out at us, and a bedroom, where the bed and all the furniture hung from the ceiling, we entered a long, narrow hallway. The house's power attempted to surge to life, but managed only halfhearted blinks and flickers before going out completely. Once all was quiet, something resembling a guttural growl filled the hall, and it began to shake violently, nearly forcing the three of us off our feet.

It was clever, this techno-paranormal wizardry.

I walked at a brisk pace, mostly to keep up with my terrified and sprinting friends, in an attempt to keep them from feeling ridiculous. I felt no fear at anything we'd seen or done. It was all too much like being inside a special effects–filled movie on the big screen. It may have contained a few vague references to the reality of the paranormal—evidence of someone's attempt at real-world research—but there was nothing genuinely supernatural about any of it.

The hallway grew narrower at the far end, and I followed Jill and Angela through a small door, spilling out into yet another dark room. This one was decorated as the house's living room.

I knew we had to be near the end of the attraction, as double front doors lay directly ahead of us. But first, of course, we would have to face whatever artificial "thrills" awaited us here.

From their pale-white faces and wide-eyed expressions, I could see that my friends were ready to get out of there. I knew that in another minute or two, they would be outside in the warm night air, laughing it all off, pretending to have never been afraid at all. But right now I was sure they were sweating.

Which I suddenly realized was odd, because I was feeling a distinct cold sensation running through my entire body, hair to toenails. I had an abrupt chill, but resisted the urge to hug myself, knowing this was probably just a cleverly directed airflow built into the room.

Still, it felt oddly authentic, just like a cold spot. A *real* cold spot, a phenomenon I knew very well.

No lights ever came on in the room, but my eyes had adjusted enough to the darkness by now that I could make out most of the room's mundane details—a dilapidated rocking chair, a crumbling fireplace against one wall, curtains barely clinging to the windows on either side of the front doors.

I was taken aback for the first time when a mist suddenly entered the room and began to swirl about. It didn't come down through the chimney or blow in through a crack in the windows, it passed *through* the wall to my left. Yet this white mist didn't billow or blow, it *flowed* with intention, like living wind. It swirled up all around me like a tiny whirlwind, and I was surprised to find that it was no hologram or trick of lights. It was a tangible substance that I could *feel* touching my skin, ever so lightly.

Only a few times before had I experienced anything like it, and those occasions were genuine hauntings.

Okay, Ghost Town, I thought as the mist swirled through my hair, moving it about. *I don't know how you're pulling this off, but bravo. This is your best trick yet.*

A faint voice whispered in my ear, a female voice. I couldn't make out what it was saying, but if it was a special effect, it was impossibly good, because it couldn't have been coming from speakers hidden in the ceiling or the walls. It was right beside me, in the center of the room.

My heart thumped heavily as I rewound the voice in my head and thought for just a moment that it might have said my name.

I instinctively grabbed my own chest, trying to coax my heart to keep beating.

My breath was visible as I exhaled, almost gasping.

The mist suddenly twisted and flew away from me and then doubled back, bearing straight down on me. Just as it was about to touch me again, it coalesced for a fraction of a second, a three-dimensional white face emerging from the vapor before the entire cloud passed through me.

I froze in place, trying to breathe, but it was as if my lungs had been submerged in ice. At the same moment the fog passed through my body, the very same moment I saw the face in the cloud, I heard the female voice whisper one last time, so faint I knew I must've been the only one to hear it. It was as if a pair of lips were less than an inch from my right ear.

"The nightmare is coming," the voice breathed in a terrified pitch.

The mist dissipated into nothing as floodlights suddenly came up and the front double doors flung themselves open. The ride was over.

Angela and Jill fled out into the safety of the amusement park, but I stood stock still, the sensations and sounds and sights I'd just experienced refusing to leave my senses.

Because the girl's voice I'd heard whispering and the face I'd seen in the mist for a fraction of a second . . . I was certain that they both belonged to someone I knew.

Someone I hadn't seen or heard from in months.

Someone named Jordin Cole.

TWO

"You're Maia Peters, aren't you?"

I stopped in my tracks, my shoulders involuntarily clenching up to my neck. I was crossing the courtyard outside Greene Hall and had almost made it to my dorm in peace when the intruder called out my name. I knew I was being followed from the moment I'd left Forensic Science class, but I was silently praying the whole way to my room that whoever it was would go away.

"Yes," I replied slowly, not turning around to see who'd asked. My eyes danced across the East Campus residence hall entrance, which was just across the courtyard from Greene, and now less than twenty feet away. Its brick walls looked an awful lot like safety and escape just now.

I really hated when people recognized me. Fame had never agreed with me. It wasn't *my* fame they were recognizing, anyway. I was just famous by association. Or perhaps *infamous*.

My Catholic mother and agnostic father—an eccentric pairing if there ever was one—were known all over the United States, and much of the world. And anyone who knew of them, knew of their daughter. Me.

Why couldn't people just leave me be? I didn't relish being a loner, but it was a lot easier than dealing with every wacko who wanted to be my friend just because of my famous parents—or worse, the ones that were only interested in having a good laugh at my expense.

"Jordin Cole. We're in the same English Comp class."

My thoughts froze. Could it be that this girl—a girl whose name I recognized immediately thanks to Jordin's entirely different kind of reputation, despite having no memory of ever seeing her in my English Composition class—had no interest in my parents, or my past? Was she just hoping to copy my notes from class, or something equally harmless and utterly, blissfully normal?

"Mm-hmm," I said tentatively, turning at last but not bothering to hide my skepticism as I sized this girl up. It wasn't that I meant to be rude, but I'd been down this road too many times, and it was growing tiresome.

"I didn't recognize you at first . . . I mean, you look a lot different than you did on TV."

It was true. When I transitioned into the college life, I cut my hair and dyed it a darker color. I changed the way I dressed, and had put on a little weight, too. That last bit was a fact I'd decided I didn't care about. I was more comfortable in my skin now than I had ever been before; being on TV so often made you obsessed about appearances, and now I wasn't anymore. It felt good. I didn't consider myself overly attractive, but I wasn't ugly, either. Looks just weren't a big priority for me these days. Maybe after graduation I'd feel differently, but for now I was focused entirely on my studies.

For her part, there was no getting around the fact that Jordin was drop-dead gorgeous, without even having to try. Sure, she wore designer jeans and a stylish top, and was no stranger to hair or makeup products, but she didn't give off the air of someone who put a lot of concern into either. Jordin was naturally blond, more slender than I was, and had a set of regally white, perfectly straight teeth. She radiated an easy-going, unfussy nature, while simultaneously giving everyone that passed the two of us in the courtyard a taste of that million-dollar smile.

I couldn't figure out if her warmth was pretense or not. Either way, I still didn't want to talk to her.

"Anyway, I was wondering if you might be able to help me, or at least point me in the right direction." Jordin paused, as if hesitant to continue. Finally she plowed ahead. "I need to know if it's real."

I raised my eyebrows, an unspoken question.

"The paranormal," Jordin explained. "Is it real?"

So much for the "innocent fellow student" theory.

Without a word, I turned and walked quickly through the dorm entrance, leaving Jordin Cole alone in the courtyard.

She tried again the next day.

She got in line behind me at the school bookstore. I knew Jordin had to have been intentionally trailing me to find me here.

"Your major doesn't involve people skills, does it?" she said in a conversational tone, as though our prior conversation had never ended. "Which is kind of stunning. I mean, you're a TV star. You have actual fans. I guess most of them have never met you, or they might rethink that."

I glanced at her sidelong. "Do we have to do this?"

"I get it," she said. Her voice was a little louder than I would have preferred, causing several heads to turn in my direction.

"I *totally* understand," she continued, and I was over this already. Mostly because of Jordin's too-casual use of the word "totally." She continued, "If my parents were world-famous ghost hunters with their own reality show, I'd avoid every weirdo who asked me questions about the paranormal, too."

"They're not ghost hunters," I said, almost mumbling, refusing to face her full-on, because it would feel too much like we were having an actual conversation.

"Huh?"

"My parents," I repeated. "They are not 'ghost hunters.' They're not ghost *busters*. The correct term is 'paranormal investigators.' And since you don't have a clue what that means, and I don't really care to explain it, please just go forget you ever met me."

"No, no, I know!" Jordin said, backpedaling and regrouping fast. "I'm just really new to this stuff, and that's totally why I need your help."

"No" was my definitive answer. I wasn't going to get into this, not with Jordin Cole or anyone else. "No, I can't help you with whatever it is you want. I can't get you an autograph, I can't get you on the TV show, and I'm not interested in helping you contact your dead relative."

"I don't want any of those things," she said.

"Then what *do* you want?" I asked pointedly.

"Well, I was kind of hoping you might be willing to consider—"

"What do you want?" I pressed, raising my voice while stepping up to the counter and running my check card through the machine.

Jordin froze, and looked me in the eyes. She seemed to change in front of me, and her hyper-friendly exterior faded.

"I want to *touch* the paranormal. I want to know that it's real. Or not. I don't want to be told. I don't want to read about it. I want to experience it for myself."

"Go to the library," I replied. "Internet search: 'Paranormal investigators, New York City.' Tons of amateurs out there eager and willing to show you around any haunted house in the area you want. Might even let you tag along on a real investigation."

"But I don't want them! And I don't want to visit *any* haunted house," she said. "I don't know anything about this stuff, but I know that no one else has your level of expertise. Your parents are *the* authorities in this field—respected by pretty much everyone— and you were on tons of episodes of the show as one of their best investigators. Until—"

I cut her off. "Do you know the question?"

Jordin blinked. "What?"

"Do you know the question?" I asked again, picking up my purchased textbooks and hugging them in my arms. "Look at every quest, every search, every journey that's ever been under-taken, and at its heart you'll find a question. A question that needs answering. And that drive for answering it is what fuels the quest. The search for the paranormal is no different than any other quest. At its core, there is a question that needs to be answered. Do you know that question?"

Jordin looked away, searching her thoughts. "Why do ghosts exist?"

I shook my head and turned to go. "You go have a nice life."

———

It was three days later before Jordin made contact again.

I was leaving a statistics class when she ambushed me as I walked out of the lecture hall and onto the busy university sidewalk.

"Hey, girlfriend. I figured it out," she said, chipper and pleased with herself. "The question that drives the search for the paranormal."

I stopped under the shadow of a well-manicured tree, satis-fied that we were out of earshot of anyone nearby.

"I'm not your friend," I remarked, unimpressed and once again unnerved that she knew how to find me so easily. "I'm not even on your social ladder."

"What happens when we die?" Jordin continued.

Despite myself, my eyebrows rose. "Not bad. And here I thought you were just a pampered, bored heiress."

Jordin was rich. Beyond rich. Richer than rich. And everyone at school knew it. Some kind of inheritance or something, I couldn't recall the details.

"That's because you don't know me," she replied, shrugging. "And I understand why you don't care to. But I still need your help."

"You may know the question," I noted, "but that doesn't mean you're ready to try and answer it."

"The question . . . it makes sense," Jordin said slowly, thoughtfully. "Do you know the answer?"

I shook my head, unable to mask my boredom with this conversation. "Not really."

"But don't you want to?" Jordin said, confused at my indifference.

"Do you have any idea what a *real* paranormal investigation is?" I retorted, what little patience I possessed dwindling. "We run *toward* the things that most people run *away* from. It's all about cataloging the unexplained. Gathering real, scientific evidence in the worst places and conditions you can imagine. And in cases where real people are being terrorized in their homes, it's about helping them. Are you honestly interested in *any* of those things?"

"Sure."

"You are not!" I shot back.

She hesitated. "Look, my reasons are . . . my reasons. But I *have* to do this. And I want you to help me."

I shook my head at the ground, almost laughing.

"What?" she asked.

"You *really* think you're somehow different than every other 'ghost hunter' wannabe I've ever met, don't you."

"I know I am, sister. Because I'm the first wannabe to tell you that there's no limit to where we could go or what we could investigate."

Ah yes, and here it comes . . .

"I *do* know who you are, Jordin," I said.

"Then you know that when I say the sky's the limit, it's an epic understatement. Anywhere, anytime," she said. "The most haunted places in America—or the world. There's got to be some places out there you always wanted to investigate, but never got to. Or favorite locations that you meant to get back to, but never got around to. I can make it happen. My only request is that you take me with you."

"Quite a sales pitch," I replied, mildly amused. "Practiced it much?"

"I can do this for you, Maia," said Jordin. "I can help you finally find the answer to the question. I *want* to."

"That's . . . *kind*," I replied, eying her sidelong. "But I'm still not interested."

"Because you're serious about your studies here, your career. You want to be taken seriously. You don't want to be known as 'the ghost hunters' daughter.' I get it. But nobody forced you to go along with your parents on all those investigations. And I think that despite this new life you're pursuing, some part of you still wants to know the answer. Find that proof that the paranormal's real. What if I could help you do that? We might even legitimize your parents' lifelong quest."

I didn't even try to hide my curiosity. Jordin was a lot smarter than I first gave her credit for. She was also a lot kookier.

"Okay, say for a moment I got myself some temporary insanity and agreed to . . . to whatever it is you're wanting to do. Paranormal investigation is not some hobby or whim to be undertaken out of curiosity. For the unprepared or the uninformed, it's extremely dangerous. If you're not strong enough, you can lose yourself to what you'll encounter."

She seemed unfazed. "I can handle it."

I frowned. "What are you hoping to find?"

Jordin perked up and whipped out a five-by-five-inch journal. "Stuff like this." She opened the book, and it was overstuffed with newspaper clippings, printed website pages, and dozens upon dozens of photos. Most of them were poor in quality, probably made on a copier or printed on a low-res printer. But it didn't matter; I recognized most of the images as rather notorious photos. There were famous pictures like the Brown Lady at Raynam Hall in Norfolk, Boothill Graveyard in Tombstone, the Cashtown Inn in Gettysburg. Some of the best so-called evidence of the paranormal.

Jordin had collected for herself a record of supposedly real hauntings from the last twenty to thirty years. Amateur photos and reports, predominantly, of paranormal sightings that average people "happened" to unintentionally catch. Many of these sightings were quite well-known among paranormal investigators.

I examined the book for a moment, trying to stay poker-faced. But I couldn't keep it up.

"What?" she asked.

I kind of shrugged. "It's just . . . it's garbage, Jordin. All of this. You're operating on pop culture–fueled notions of what ghosts and spirits are, and it's nonsense. Ninety-nine percent of the stuff in your little book here is nothing at all like what you'd experience in a genuinely haunted place."

She was confused. "What are you talking about? This is some of the best evidence ever captured—"

"Evidence," I repeated, and I couldn't help being amused at the word. I grabbed the book and flipped it open to random pages as I talked. "Lens flare," I said about one photo. "Reflection," I said regarding another. "Blatant photo manipulation."

"But . . ." Jordin backpedaled. "Look at this one. That's one of the best orbs ever captured on film!"

"Your orbs," I said with a tone that refused all argument, "have done more damage to the field of paranormal investigation than all the crackpot psychics and mediums out there combined. They're nothing but bugs or dust that get too close to a lens for it to focus properly, so a light artifact is created on the final image. An *amateur* photographer can tell you this."

Jordin was frowning. She regrouped quickly, flipping to another page. "Look at this one, though. You can't tell me that isn't—"

I snapped the book closed and handed it back to her. "Even the best photos in here—and I'm not saying some of them aren't compelling—are unverifiable. Any one of them or *all* of them could be the product of Photoshop. This is the eternal problem of paranormal investigation. The only people who ever investigate it are amateurs, because no reputable scientist will touch this stuff, and no scientific journal will publish an amateur's findings. It's a catch-22. All of these photos were taken by amateurs because there *are* no paranormal professionals, so it can't be labeled as *evidence*. Amateurs can't be vouched for, and the conditions they research in can't be controlled, so their evidence has no value as scientific currency," I concluded, trying to communicate to Jordin with whatever delicacy I possessed that arguing her case on behalf of science was a hopeless cause.

Jordin was reveling in romanticized notions of what the paranormal was like, but her ideas were an insult to the reality I knew. And I wasn't finished.

"Making matters worse is the fact that a lot of the investigative groups out there don't get along with each other. My parents have done a lot to legitimize the field, and they've never done anything underhanded, but there are other investigators out there—highly reputable ones—who will swear to you on a stack of Bibles that they *know* my parents fake most of the evidence they find. They 'know' it because they believe their own tactics are more scientific, or because they're just plain jealous of my parents' success. Every group claims to be more reliable than all the others, and it just comes down to a big shouting match of 'my word against yours.' It's all a game, and there's no way to win."

As we began walking again, Jordin suddenly tossed the scrapbook she'd spent countless hours compiling into a nearby trash bin. "Fine!" she shouted. "I don't know anything about ghosts or paranormal research. That's why I need your help! Teach me! I don't care if I don't have iron-clad evidence. I just want to experience it for myself."

Again I examined her carefully. "Why?" I asked. "Why are you so eager to do this?"

She held my gaze steadily. "Why did *you* give it up?"

I suddenly felt like a coiled tiger ready to pounce. I knew my stance had taken on a threatening posture as I narrowed my eyes at Jordin, but I didn't care. I hated this girl for realizing that my publicly stated reasons for leaving the world of the paranormal behind were only secondary and superficial.

"We're done," I said.

I had already spun on my heels and begun walking away, flipping through a stack of envelopes I'd picked up that morning in the mail, when Jordin approached me again from behind.

"Not easy affording tuition these days, is it?" she said in her best innocent voice.

I shot her a simple glance but said nothing as I sorted through the mail and continued walking.

"You paying for it all on your own? No help from Mom and Dad?"

I stopped. If it was possible, I liked this girl even less than before. "What's it to you if I am?"

"Nothing," she replied with an innocent face. "Just surprised your parents aren't paying for your studies. I'm sure they could afford it."

My eyes slid downward to the bills again, but my defensive tone of voice never wavered. "Who says they didn't offer?"

"Of course . . ." Jordin put it together. "You *insisted* on doing it yourself. What better way to make a clean break and declare your independence than to put yourself through college, launch your own destiny . . ."

"Don't you have some frivolous shopping to do?" I asked, wanting to be elsewhere. *Any* elsewhere.

"I could hire you, you know," Jordin said. "You need money. I need your expertise. I'm offering you a job that no one else is more qualified to perform. You pick the destinations, based on your knowledge of the field. Anywhere in the world. I'll cover the expenses. We go on weekends or breaks from school."

My ears were burning now. I couldn't believe this girl's audacity. This wasn't my first request to be taken on ghost hunting adventures, but it was certainly the most outrageous. "You think you can get whatever you want with *money*?"

"It's just a job," Jordin replied, keeping exceedingly cool. "*So what* if I'm willing to pay obscene amounts of money, more than the job's worth? It's my money, and I can throw it away if I want. You could pay off your entire tuition—with money you earned entirely on your own, fair and square. And we'd both get something we want. . . ." She paused. "Maybe even something we need."

How I hated this girl. Hated, hated, *hated*.

I wanted nothing more than to smack Jordin Cole across the face. Instead, I clutched my multiple envelopes full of bills tighter, grimaced, and looked Jordin in the eye. "What's the catch?"

"No catch," she said, a sparkle in her eye indicating that she knew she'd hit a nerve at last. "Just one requirement. I want to see a ghost. I want to touch it and interact with it. So when you pick our destinations . . . I'm not interested in going to places that *might* be haunted. I want to go to the places where we're guaranteed to see or experience something real. The most haunted places in the country. Or the world."

"There *are* no guarantees in this," I replied, angry at myself for even continuing this conversation. "The dead don't perform. They aren't here to humor the living."

"Whatever. I just want my chances of actually finding something to be as high as possible."

Again I couldn't help wondering why she was so eager—no, desperate—to go on a paranormal investigation. I'd encountered overzealous paranormal junkies before, but Jordin was different. Smart, confident. She'd quickly realized exactly which buttons of mine to push, and she pushed them like a pro. On the other hand, I still had the impression that all of this might have been nothing more than an odd whim for her, a curious indulgence. A new adventure for someone who was rich enough to have done just about everything else.

I told her I needed some time to think about it, and we parted ways. It wasn't because I *did* need time; I just didn't want to seem eager.

And I wasn't eager, after all. I had lived and breathed this world Jordin wanted to enter so badly for most of my life. It wasn't that I'd gotten sick of it or anything. But investigating the paranormal was always my parents' thing, and while I couldn't deny that it was a rush on those rare occasions in the field when you found something genuinely amazing . . . it was still like something I was born into rather than a path I had chosen for myself. My parents were cool about it; they never pressured me to enter the family business, always willing to accept whatever choice I ultimately made.

So I had left that life behind. There was no "good riddance" or anything on my part. I just kind of . . . graduated. I became an adult, and my passions were now elsewhere.

I waited a few days to call Jordin and give her the answer I had known I was going to give that day she made her sales pitch. Even later, after hands were shaken and terms were agreed to, I still couldn't believe I was going through with it.

But I get to pick the locations. . . .

All right, then. She wants to go someplace already proven to be haunted? Someplace she's guaranteed to encounter actual ghosts?

I'd give her an adventure she would never forget. And it might even be enough to end Jordin's weird little quest before it got out of hand.

I knew exactly where I would take her first.

And hopefully, last.

THREE

I read the introduction to my psychology textbook four times without retaining a single word. The entire tome might as well have been filled with four words, written over and over and over. . . .

The nightmare is coming. The nightmare is coming.

What did it mean?

And what was going on with Jordin? Was that really her I saw Saturday night?

I looked around my solitary dorm room, thankful that Jill wasn't there to talk my ears off. This year I'd splurged and reserved a room at the highly sought after Hogan residence hall, where only seniors were allowed. No roommates in my private room, though I shared a common area and kitchen with a few other girls. I even had my own private bathroom, so there was rarely a time when I ventured outside of my glorious privacy. I preferred solitude as a rule, and thanks to my unusual employment the last year, I could afford the indulgence.

The nightmare is coming.

The nightmare is coming.

I glanced down at my spiral-bound notebook and saw for the first time that I'd filled an entire page with a column of that sentence.

I snapped my textbook shut, unable to focus. This wasn't like me, and it was annoying.

My thoughts were interrupted by a knock at the door. I slid out of my desk chair feeling like a slug and wondering why I couldn't shake off my experience from Ghost Town amusement park. The first day of classes was tomorrow, and I had a lot to do.

I yawned as I opened the door. "Yeah?" I asked mechanically.

"Have you seen Jordin?"

I blinked. Standing just outside my door was Derek Hobbes, with his thin build, wavy blond hair, and impossibly piercing eyes. Those eyes were usually bright and sharp, but today they were clouded by anxiety. Dark circles and a haggard expression made him look like he hadn't slept in days. Maybe weeks.

"Derek?" I asked, a little uncertain that this was really the young man I knew as Jordin's fiancé. His standard college wear of golf shirt and plaid shorts hadn't been ironed, there were traces of dark circles under those keen eyes of his, and he had a day's worth of light-colored stubble coloring his rosy face. I couldn't remember ever seeing him so disheveled.

Derek Hobbes was an undergrad student in Columbia's

Religion Department, preparing to eventually seek his master of divinity degree. He was kind natured and soft spoken, possessing an utterly brilliant mind. Just like his father, he was expected to someday become one of the most influential and respected ministers in America. Everybody said so.

He wasn't my type in the slightest, but he was one of the nicest guys I'd ever met.

"She's not here," Derek said with a kind of desolate panic as he took in my small solo room. "She's not anywhere."

My mind screeched to a halt. Any processing of Derek's words seemed to be happening in slow motion.

"Jordin's missing?" I asked, feeling like a complete dullard. I turned slowly in place, reeling, and ran a hand through my black hair.

I had turned to keep Derek from seeing my reaction to this news, but he interpreted it as an invitation to step inside, so he quietly entered and closed the door. "When did you last see her?" he asked.

Jordin's missing, I thought, my mind and heart both racing. *Jordin's dead.*

"Maia?" Derek tried snapping me back to the present. "Have you seen Jordin?"

My hand was now covering my mouth because I feared I might vomit, so my reply was a little muffled. "Not since last semester . . ." I said, planting myself on the edge of my bed because my knees felt weak. "How do you know she's . . . ?"

His words came out in a practiced rush, making it easy to imagine that he'd told this story several times already. "Every summer before classes start, Jordin takes this group of friends on a back-to-school vacation thing. About six weeks ago, she left with the usual group of about ten or twelve girls, and she took them all up to Martha's Vineyard. A couple weeks after they got there, she stopped calling me and answering my emails. I figured she was just having fun, relaxing and losing track of time—she does that sometimes—but it got to be longer and longer. . . . And before she left, we had this big conversation where we planned this really romantic meet-up at a restaurant near campus the first day we were both back in town for school. But she never showed, and now it's been almost a month since anyone's seen her."

I looked down at the floor, absorbing Derek's story. Jordin had gone missing around four weeks ago. And no one had seen or heard from her since.

Not true. I saw her last night.

My thoughts rocketed back to the here and now as I realized Derek's deeply worried eyes had locked onto mine and were anxiously awaiting a response.

"I don't know what she told you," I said quietly, "but the last trip she and I took, it didn't—"

"Didn't end well," he said, finishing the phrase. "That's the same thing she said. But she didn't say why."

A question was implied, and it was the one question I feared more than any other. I deflated a bit as he looked at me, something akin to accusation in his eyes.

"It was . . . intensely personal. For both of us." I grappled to find the words. How could I explain to Jordin's fiancé—the person she was close to more than any other—that I couldn't possibly tell him what I knew, when it was something Jordin had not chosen to tell him herself.

Derek was about to mount an argument, but I spoke first,

changing the subject. "Has she been reported missing to the authorities?"

"Some of the girls she went to the Vineyard with tried to report it, but they said they didn't get very far."

"Why not?"

"Does it matter?" asked Derek, growing more agitated by the second. "She's vanished without a trace, and God only knows what's happening to her *right now*!"

He immediately looked remorseful, even apologetic, for his outburst. But you could see the worry and frustration boiling up inside him. His anxious expression never wavered.

"You shouldn't assume she's in any kind of mortal danger, Derek," I calmly suggested. "Don't forget that your fiancée is one of the world's richest people. If she got a sudden whim to fly off to Rome on a moment's notice to get you a birthday present, she happens to be one of the few people in the world who could actually do that."

Derek seemed to turn on me, his expression dark. "Mortal danger isn't my primary concern. I'm a lot more worried about dangers to her soul than her body. The things you two were meddling in . . ."

Here we go, I thought. In the handful of times I had met Derek in the past, he'd made it more than clear—in a sweet, passive-aggressive, read-between-the-lines kind of way—that he disapproved of his fiancée's excursions into the paranormal with yours truly. And I suspected that it went even deeper than that. My past, my beliefs, my family's claim to fame. All of it railed against his rigidly held view of the world.

But he'd never come across so belligerent before, so agitated and angry. Until today, I wouldn't have thought him capable of such aggressive qualities.

Cut the guy some slack, Maia. I reminded myself that the love of his life had vanished, and he had to be feeling painfully helpless to do anything about it. That kind of thing would make the saintliest of men turn wild and desperate.

Still, I didn't take kindly to being accused of wrongdoing.

"You can't possibly have any reason to assume that the trips we took have anything to do with Jordin's disappearance," I stated flatly. And then it occurred to me the absurdity of the statement, since I had compelling evidence that there very well could be a connection. Evidence in the form of Ghost Town amusement park.

Not that I was going to tell *him* that. Not yet, anyway.

"It doesn't matter what I think," Derek replied, his ire shrinking to despair. "All that matters is that she's gone."

I watched him, and despite how little I had in common with Derek, I couldn't help empathizing with his pain. It surprised me a bit, because I'm not exactly known for being the sympathetic type. But something about his love for Jordin seemed so pure, so desperate. I really think they needed each other, and were less than whole when they were apart.

Acting on impulse, as my mother likes to criticize me so often for doing, I made my decision then and there.

I was going to find Jordin Cole myself.

"I'm going to find her," I said to myself, not quite realizing I'd said it out loud.

I had no idea what had happened to Jordin, and I didn't know if what I saw at the amusement park was real. But I knew what I felt . . . and what I suspected about the things Jordin was up to right before she vanished.

Which would mean I was at least partly responsible for this entire situation.

"*You* want to help me find her?" asked Derek. "Why?"

I noticed for the first time that he'd been staring at me in shock since my little declaration. My temper flared.

"How many people are lining up to track her down for you, Derek?" I retorted. "You said the police won't do anything. Are you seriously going to question the first person who's willing to try?"

"But you're not a detective," he said, a halfhearted protest.

"Not yet," I reminded him. "I *am* a criminal justice major."

And an investigation of this nature wasn't beyond my capabilities at all. I was a senior at Columbia, studying criminal justice. I had learned more than a few things about law enforcement investigation tactics in my classes here, and after graduation, I intended to get a job as a police detective, and maybe one day the FBI.

It was time to put the skills I'd learned over the last three years to use. See if I really had a future as a detective.

Derek was starting to come around but wasn't quite there yet. "Look, I appreciate your desire to help, but there are any number of things that could have happened to Jordin, and this is very serious, so let me be blunt. Your experience in this arena is relegated to poking around in the dark, looking for things that are nothing more than a trick of the human psyche. It's fear made real by your mind. Ghosts do not exist."

"That's a belief, not a fact," I argued, taking up the charge. "A belief is what you hold to be true despite a lack of tangible proof. A fact is what you can prove. You believe that a soul either goes to heaven or hell—and for what it's worth, I happen to believe the same thing, I was raised Catholic—but *you can't prove it*. Paranormal research is the search for proof of what you cannot see."

Derek suddenly looked sad. "Then I guess that's the difference between us, Maia. My faith is strong enough that no proof is required."

I studied him. "Can you, in all honesty, stand there and tell me that you know what happens after a person dies? In a step-by-step, mechanical, methodical, scientific process? Every detail, every sensation, every action that takes place between the moment of death on the mortal plane and the entrance to eternal life on the immortal plane?"

"You think there are pit stops along the way?" he shot back. "Why can't it be as simple as a direct, straight line? Death . . . to heaven or hell. A to B."

"Maybe it is that simple," I admitted. "I can't say for sure, and that's my point. All I can tell you is what I've experienced. What I've seen and touched and smelled and heard for myself. There are things that happen in the forgotten places of this world. And you can't chalk up every one of those things to overactive imaginations or mischievous demons."

Derek didn't reply for a long moment. "I believe there are many, many supernatural things that happen that we will never be able to know or understand in this life. And I believe in life after death, Maia. I just don't think the things that happen here, in this place, happen because of anything remotely human—dead or otherwise."

"Have you ever considered that the existence of ghosts is not dependent on your beliefs?"

Derek crossed his arms. "Why would a ghost wear clothes?"

The question caught me off guard. "What?"

"Most reports of so-called hauntings feature a dead soul that's seen wearing the clothes he or she wore most often when they were still alive. It makes no logical sense. People die, clothes don't."

"I don't have all the answers!" I cried in a sudden burst. "Ghosts, UFOs, psychics . . . There are scientific, verifiable explanations for these phenomena. We just haven't found them yet. I can't explain why any of these things happen, or why the paranormal even exists. It doesn't matter whether you believe me or not, but I have seen and done things you cannot begin to imagine. If you want my help, don't make light of what I know to be real."

"Why would a ghost wear clothes?" He repeated his question as a triumphant challenge, evidence of his rightness.

I loathed the look on his face and wanted to knock it off.

After a very long moment, during which I had to remind myself to breathe, I answered. "I don't know."

He must have sensed how my mood had soured, so he called off the attack. "Look, I can take *you* seriously. And if you want to try and help me find Jordin, I'm grateful. But I don't believe what you believe, and I never will."

"Fine, don't." I felt like a bull with steam coming out of my nose in hot puffs of air.

Derek's eyes fell to the ground, and I got the impression he was regretting coming on so strong with his opinions. He seemed lost in thought for a long time, staring at the carpet in my room.

If he was waiting for me to break the silence, he was wasting his time. He had caused the tension in the room to rise, not me.

"I'm afraid," he said, his voice almost a whisper. "I'm scared of what could have happened to her. So maybe my faith isn't as strong as I like to think it is."

I was still frowning, but followed him back to the subject at hand. "You mentioned the other girls she went to the Vineyard with," I said, and Derek's downcast eyes looked up. "I assume you've talked to them?"

"Sure, yeah," he replied. "They didn't know anything helpful. Said that one day she just wasn't there anymore. They thought that she'd gone off on her own for a while, but when a week went by and she never turned up, they finally realized something wasn't right."

I walked to the door and yanked it open. "Take me to see Jordin's friends."

Derek looked almost alarmed. "Oh, I . . . uh, I don't think that's a good idea."

"Why not?"

He kind of looked *around* me instead of at me. "These friends of Jordin's . . . They're not the nicest of people. And they don't really like you."

He delivered this news like it was a delicate revelation that could hurt my feelings. It didn't.

"How do they know me enough to not like me?"

"Well, when I talked to them the other day, your name came up because of all the time Jordin spent with you last year," he mumbled, looking as if he wanted to be somewhere else. "They called you Linda Blair, the Blair Witch, and a few other names I don't care to repeat."

I snickered. "Cute."

"It doesn't bother you?"

"I've been called worse," I admitted. Still, there was something to be said for not giving a group of people who disliked you an open opportunity to gang up. "Why don't you pick the least belligerent of the lot and take me to see that one."

He was still reluctant. "It's a waste of time. I told you they don't know anything. I already talked to them."

"Yeah," I replied in my most confident voice. "But I haven't."

Waverly Hills Sanatorium

Louisville, Kentucky

Opened 1910 — Closed 1980

cold, dark, uninviting, and HUGE!

its residents were driven mad by
disease before it took their lives . . .

What if the dead never left?

FOUR

OCTOBER 2ND

"Tell me the name of this place again?"

I leaned back in my seat. The plane had just begun to pull back from the terminal, preparing to whisk the two of us off to Louisville, Kentucky, but Jordin had asked this question at least three times since our arrival at the airport.

"Waverly Hills," I said. "It's an abandoned sanatorium."

Jordin had a brand-new—and alarmingly thick—leather-bound journal in her lap and was writing furiously in it as I talked.

"So . . . crazy people were kept there?"

I glanced at my companion, frustrated at her ignorance. But it was such a common misconception, I found it hard to hold on to the grudge. "A sanatorium is a place where people are treated for long-term *physical* illnesses. The patients at Waverly Hills were treated for tuberculosis, about a century ago."

This would be my fourth investigation at Waverly Hills. I knew it very well.

"And you're sure it's haunted?" asked Jordin, looking up from her notebook for the first time.

"Some reports suggest that as many as sixty-three thousand people died on the premises," I said. "They tried all sorts of things to cure the disease—taking ribs out, removing entire lungs, and electroshock therapy. Waverly Hills is a house of pain and horror. It's saturated with the dead."

Her eyebrows popped up at this. "How big *is* this place?"

"Huge," I replied, glancing at Jordin. "You having second thoughts? I've pulled some strings, using some of my parents' contacts to arrange for us to have the entire facility to ourselves, overnight. Once we're in, we're in. If you want to turn back . . ."

She scribbled in her journal again. "I'm not turning back. I just . . . This isn't quite what I was expecting."

"You said you only want to go to places that are guaranteed to be haunted, right?"

Jordin nodded without looking up, but her expression was less certain.

"Waverly Hills is without a doubt one of the most haunted places in the whole world."

Suddenly she frowned, her expression skeptical. "I've never even heard of it," she mumbled.

"Well, now you have." I looked out my window. It suddenly occurred to me that I'd been thrust into a new role of teacher/mentor. I didn't like it.

We sat in silence for a while as the plane lifted off the ground, and Jordin continued to write. I had hoped to get some time to do a little studying during this trip, but the silence didn't keep.

"Something else has been bothering me," she said softly, closing her book and leaning over a little closer than I liked, like a fellow conspirator. "That day we first talked . . . I got the feeling you don't believe in orbs."

Orbs were a common phenomenon known throughout the paranormal world. They often appeared as tiny white globs of light that flew freely through a given space. The prevailing theory about orbs was that they were disembodied souls trying to manifest themselves visually.

"True paranormal investigation isn't about what you *believe*," I told her. "It's about what you can *prove*. Evidence—pure, scientific, empirical evidence—is the holy grail. It's all about proving that ghosts and the paranormal are real in ways that even the most skeptical pundit can't argue with."

"But has that ever been done?"

"There's some very, very compelling evidence out there," I replied. "Most of it collected by people like my parents. But the world of the paranormal is never eager to reveal itself. My parents' TV show is popular partly *because* they don't accept everything they find as evidence of the paranormal. Whenever they come across something odd, their first move is to find a normal explanation for it. If they can't find one, if they can't prove that it has a logical explanation, *then* it becomes a candidate for paranormal activity."

Jordin considered this. "But . . . *has* real evidence ever been collected? Has the paranormal ever been proven?"

I thought carefully, considering the best response to give. "Any scientist will tell you there are infinite numbers of things in the universe that we *cannot* explain. And no one will argue that proving what happens to us after we die is a question we still can't answer. Whatever label you apply to it—the paranormal, the afterlife, the unexplained—almost everyone agrees that things exist that are outside of our ability to perceive. But defining it, quantifying it, cataloging the exact scientific parameters of what it is and *where* it is and how it functions . . . no, we've never achieved that."

Jordin looked thoughtful. "Then what makes your parents think they ever will? Why keep searching for evidence that might not ever be found?"

I shrugged. "Why do people keep looking for evidence of Atlantis? Or UFOs? Or any other supposedly 'crazy' thing that's never been proven? No matter how many years pass without definitive evidence, people just keep searching. Why do you think that is?"

"I don't know."

"It's because no matter how many times these things are shot down or explained away with logic, it's never a good enough explanation."

Jordin was visibly having a hard time with this. "I don't know what that means."

"We believe because we want to believe," I said. "We believe so strongly that no one can change our minds."

She was frowning. "Are you saying the pursuit of the paranormal is illogical? Irrational?"

"I'm saying that in my experience, it's very human to want to believe that there's more to us than this mortal life. And maybe that desire is inside us for a reason. But don't take my word for it—you tell me. Why are you so eager to experience the paranormal for yourself? What's *your* reason?"

Jordin was instantly uncomfortable, and closed her mouth tight.

I smiled without humor, knowing my point was made. "Whatever your reason, no one ever stops searching . . . because we can't."

———

We headed in a rental car from the Louisville Airport to Highway 21 and eventually to an unassuming single-lane road that took us past a small trailer park and a diminutive collection of apartment buildings and then through a gated entrance. A narrow road snaked back and forth through woods too dense to see through.

One final curve to the left, almost a full U-turn, opened up a full view ahead where the gigantic Waverly Hills Sanatorium loomed like an immense monolith. The massive building, the very ground we drove upon, felt dead.

"Ruh-roh, Raggy," said Jordin, her voice filled with awe despite the silliness of her words.

I wanted to slap the spoiled, silly rich girl in the passenger seat. But I settled for rolling my eyes and choosing not to acknowledge the painful Scooby Doo reference.

I turned my attention instead to what was in front of me. The colossal main hospital building filled the entire windshield as we drove closer, and its dilapidated brick walls, honeycombed with endless rows of huge square holes where windows had once been, were enough to give even the most hardened skeptic pause.

It hadn't changed in the slightest since the last time I was here, more than five years ago.

Waverly Hills Sanatorium was utterly frozen in time, and the setting sun behind the trees off to the left only enhanced the ancient, abandoned feel of the place. It was like staring at a vintage postcard for a place no sane person would ever want to visit.

I glanced at Jordin. She seemed smaller than before, as if she'd physically shrunken. She seemed to sense my staring and turned to look out her side window.

"What are those buildings over there?" she asked in a tiny voice that was trying desperately hard to be nonchalant, and she pointed into the distance beyond the big building.

"Um, well," I had to collect my thoughts for a moment, preoccupied as I was with the cloud this place cast over both of us. "Waverly Hills was originally comprised of half a dozen buildings or so. There were wards and dormitories for men, women, children, and so on. Some of them still stand, but the main hospital is the biggest by far. It's where we'll be spending the night. . . ."

My voice faded in reverence as I stared up at the immense building. The sight of it affected me a lot more than I'd expected it to.

It had been three years since I'd last gone on a paranormal investigation, and I'd had no regrets about leaving that life behind. By pursuing a career in law enforcement, I'd traded off trying to prove the existence of the dead for trying to help the living, and I was happy with the decision.

Yet I could feel the old tingle sizzling across my skin, the anticipation building within me, as I gazed at this exceedingly haunted location. We were going to encounter ghosts this night. I could feel it.

Because they were already watching us.

―――――――――――

I could always sense it as soon as we walked through the enormous, ancient double doors at the front entrance to Waverly Hills Sanatorium. The place was just *wrong*.

The darkness was palpable now that the sun had gone down fully, and the cold air was nearly suffocating in the enormous old building. We were armed only with flashlights, sleeping bags, and snacks for the night.

Hello again, I thought, my heart beating heavily. My eyes darted through the dark, musty atmosphere, searching the crevices and corners. *Remember me?*

I recognized the sensations this place caused from the times I'd been there before, alongside my parents. My lungs seemed to labor to draw breaths, like I was at a high altitude. Yet the cool air wasn't light. It was much, much heavier than what I'd breathed before we arrived.

The walls were coated in graffiti made up of words, names, vulgar phrases, and drawings of skulls. Every surface was either peeling, rusted, or rotten.

I looked at Jordin, who had her hand to her chest. Her face was slightly scrunched up as she absorbed the feelings that seemed to permeate this place.

"This is . . ." She tried to express her feelings, but faltered. "I just . . . I don't . . ."

"Feel a weight against your chest?" I asked.

She let out a shallow, quavering breath, and nodded. Her

eyes were wide and troubled as she whispered, "I feel so sad. It's like there's . . . *misery* here . . . and grief."

I nodded carefully. It was difficult to understand and process, but I didn't want her to miss it. It was too important.

"Most people who come here feel it," I said softly, my eyes darting around the gloom. "So many people died here under such painful conditions . . . the grief and terror they must have felt. I can't explain it, no one can, but it's like the building and the grounds became soaked with those heavy emotions, sopping them up like a sponge."

Jordin looked a little alarmed. We'd barely crossed the threshold into this place, and already we were experiencing things she could never have anticipated. "How is that possible?" she said, her voice louder than normal and echoing down the dark hall that stretched out in front of us.

I shook my head, having no answers. "This is only the beginning. Do you feel the cold?"

She nodded. "I don't like this," she said, still clutching her chest while looking at the air in front of her, trying to see if her breath was visible. "I feel sick."

I cocked my head to one side. "This is what you came here for. Congrats, girlfriend, you've just had your first paranormal experience."

"It feels like I'm gonna have a vomiting experience."

"Come on," I said, taking tentative steps into the darkness. I switched on my flashlight and aimed it down the long, black hallway, until its beam could no longer reach the building's depths.

I led the way as we descended into the night.

———————

Ten minutes later, we wandered the halls as I tried to give Jordin a bit of a tour so she could orient herself amid Waverly's long walls and five floors. Jordin stopped in place and put one hand on her opposite shoulder. She gasped aloud.

"What?" I whispered.

"It felt like someone tugged on my shirt!" She bunched up the shoulder of her shirt to demonstrate what she'd felt. "Right here!"

Her face was pale, and her eyes darted around in all directions.

"Don't be alarmed," I said, trying to keep her calm. I wanted her to get the full experience here, in the hopes that she might be satisfied with this one trip, but if she gave in to panic, it could end really badly. I gazed around the empty space surrounding us. "They're just making their presence known. They're trying to get your attention."

"They have it," she rasped, swallowing hard.

Okay, she's spooked. Back to business.

"So where would you like to start your investigation?" I asked.

Jordin's jittery eyes were following her own flashlight's beam into empty rooms on either side of us, up on the ceiling above and down the hallway ahead. Every now and then she turned quickly to glance behind.

"I want to do whatever you would do if you were investigating with your parents."

"Well, if they were here, right now I'd probably be helping them set up stationary cameras and recording equipment all over the building. . . ."

Jordin stopped walking. The traces of alarm that had outlined her face were gone, replaced by indignation. "You didn't say any-thing about needing to bring recording equipment. How was I supposed to know to do that? I told you I want to do this exactly the way real paranormal investigators do it!"

Her voice had escalated to a shout by the end, and as if in response, a trio of creaking sounds echoed from a room some-where above us, followed by the building's weight-bearing sup-ports letting out a groan that sounded like a long, slow moan of pain.

Jordin's complexion blanched snow-white, like a child who'd been naughty and got caught. I looked around, searching for the source of the sounds. When it died down, I continued the conversation as if nothing had happened.

"I didn't think recording devices would be needed," I explained. "You never said you wanted to gather evidence. You're paying me for a first-hand experience."

Her eyes still examining the ceiling for the source of the creaks and moans, Jordin replied, "But gathering evidence is part of the experience, isn't it?"

I grudgingly bobbed my head in an affirmative, and the two of us began walking again, shining our flashlights all around and talking quietly. "Jordin, you need to understand what gathering evidence means before you commit to it. Imagine long, often boring hours of wandering through haunted places, well into the early hours of the morning, shooting video and recording audio of what more often than not turns out to be absolutely nothing, all in the hopes that some small out-of-the-ordinary thing might be captured on tape."

"I can do that," she replied, indignant.

I wasn't finished. "The problem is, *if* something paranormal is captured on tape, at least fifty percent of the time, you don't know it at the time that it's recorded. Gathering evidence means that all of the recordings you make have to later be reviewed, and it's a *very* tedious process. We're talking about staring at hours upon hours of video footage that never moves or changes angles, and listening to endless hours of audio, usually trying to pick out the tiniest of unnatural sounds from static and silence. It's a huge commitment that's usually unrewarding, and would probably cause your schoolwork to suffer."

"I'll do it," Jordin volunteered. "I'll review all the recordings by myself. My course load is light this semester anyway."

I sighed, wondering if she truly had any inkling where these early steps might lead her. But her countenance was not one of impulsiveness. She appeared resolute, her shoulders set.

She really wants this, I thought. *She wants it bad.* And again I wondered what was behind that need.

"Teach me everything, Maia," she said. "Everything. *That's* what I'm paying you for."

"All right . . ." I said, steadying myself. I allowed my senses to reflexively become alert, listening, feeling for anything and everything that might be out of the ordinary. My words came in whispers, as if to keep from disturbing the silence, but mostly out of reverence and respect to those who'd died here. This wasn't some museum or roadside attraction. It was a mass graveyard.

"First lesson," I said as we walked carefully through the black hallways. "True hauntings are nothing like what you see in the movies or on TV. There's no CGI effects, no creepy soundtrack, and actually *seeing* a genuine apparition with your eyes is the rarest of occurrences."

"Hmm" was Jordin's only reply.

"Second lesson. There are three classifications of hauntings. Residual, intelligent, and poltergeist."

"That movie freaked me out," Jordin admitted.

I shook my head, frustrated at how quickly she fell back into a pop-culture frame of reference. "It was an escapist flick that had no basis in reality. Poltergeist hauntings are typically subconscious manifestations of intense emotional trauma in the *living*. They're almost always caused by the living, inadvertently, and usually have very little—if anything—to do with the dead. But they can be very dangerous."

Jordin was openly surprised. "Have you ever seen a poltergeist?"

"Four times," I told her. "It's uncommon, but less so because most people mistake it for a ghost."

"And the other two kinds of hauntings?"

"Those occur more frequently. *Residual* hauntings are the most common type of all, but they're the hardest to classify, because no one really knows what they are. They're like recordings of past events, playing themselves out over and over again. The 'ghosts' in these instances are usually full apparitions, but they're unaware of the presence of the living. There's no intention or responsiveness about them.

"If you've ever heard someone describe a ghost that doesn't know it's dead, the residual haunt is what they're referring to. Some people don't even consider these haunts to be spirits at all, but some kind of mental or spiritual imprint left behind after death. It's as if the traumatic event that lead to their death caused some leftover part of them to become unstuck in time, and the act of that death—or sometimes even just mundane acts from the dead person's life—becomes an echo, playing on a loop that we can perceive. They're not dangerous, but they are fascinating to witness, and they rarely have any idea that we're here."

"So there's probably a lot of residual ghosts here at Waverly, because of how they died?"

"Without a doubt," I replied. "But the most unpredictable type of haunting, the third classification, is the *intelligent* haunt. This is what most people think of when they think of a ghost: a disembodied soul who's completely aware of their surroundings, their memories . . . and any living people they come in contact with. Why they linger is a huge mystery. It's unknown if they're *stuck* in one location—almost always the place where they died—or they're simply unwilling to leave. But they come in every temperament and variety, just like the living: they can be playful and harmless, or they can be wicked and vengeful. They're the most erratic type of haunting, and accordingly, the most hazardous to your health. But they're the most sought-after type for paranormal investigators, because anything with intelligence can find a way to communicate, and with communication comes the possibility of collecting real evidence."

"Okay. So, three types of hauntings," Jordin repeated. "Got it. Anything else?"

"Well, there is a fourth type, actually . . . but we won't be going near any of those."

She stopped short. "What is it? Tell me."

"Demonic," I replied, matter-of-fact. "Not all investigators consider those cases to be hauntings, since no humans are involved. But like I said, it doesn't matter, because we're steering clear of known demonic haunts."

Jordin shivered. "You're sure there's nothing like that here?"

I nodded, confident. "Countless investigators have spent

hundreds of hours in this place, and no one has ever reported an encounter with anything terribly threatening."

She didn't look reassured.

We stationed ourselves in a central hallway on the notorious fifth floor, where the highest rate of paranormal activity was regularly reported, and where I had once seen and heard some very strange things myself. The walls around us were again tagged with layers of multicolor graffiti, courtesy of locals and visitors who felt the need to leave their own mark on the place.

But it was the dead who had left the most of themselves here. The fifth floor was the ward where patients were sent when the disease affected their minds, the place where the mentally disturbed lived and died.

Tonight, instead of actively searching for activity, we waited for it to come to us. I sat cross-legged on the floor with my Advanced Psychology textbook, studying for my first exam of the semester by flashlight. I was only half listening as Jordin prattled on.

As much as I wanted Jordin to feel like she'd gotten her money's worth on this trip, there *were* limits to my patience. To my dismay, she seemed incapable of maintaining silence for very long. And I began contemplating the fact that despite her grandiose wealth, even Jordin Cole might not have enough money to get me to go on another of these trips. It was the first small feeling of encouragement I'd felt since we'd arrived.

"We've been here for six hours," said Jordin.

"Mm-hmm," I said absently, snuggling deeper into my sleeping bag to stave off the freezing cold.

"This place is creepy as all get-out," she said, rubbing her arms nervously. "I still feel sick to my stomach."

"You mentioned that."

"It smells funny, too."

"Yep," I replied with a sigh.

Jordin glanced over, watching me study as if I were oblivious to our bizarre surroundings. A tinge of impatience seemed to strike her. "So is anything else going to happen, or what?"

I looked up at last. "Whatever's in this place, it doesn't operate on our timetable."

She frowned, her shoulders slumping. "I didn't think it would be so . . . dull."

I grinned. "Welcome to paranormal investigation. Hours of tedium, punctuated with seconds of skin-peeling terror. Just how it is."

———————

I watched Jordin in amusement an hour later as her eyes tried very hard to close themselves. She wasn't used to staying up all night and it showed.

But I had my reasons for requiring that we stay awake at least until four a.m., which was still forty-five minutes away.

Then, from the darkness down the long hall to our right, came a voice.

"Jordin!" I hissed, throwing my sleeping bag open.

"Hm?" came Jordin's groggy voice.

"Get up!" I whispered.

Her eyes blinked wide, and she saw that I was already standing. She quickly grabbed her flashlight and joined me.

"What is it?"

"Shh!" I whispered.

In the distance, the sound of a muffled cough could be heard.

I instinctively ran toward the sound, trying hard to keep my feet from clomping on the cement floors. I was fifty feet down the hall before I thought to look back and see if Jordin was following. To her credit, she was right on my heels.

We slowed to a stop as we heard the sound again, and I threw a warning hand in Jordin's face. Both of us fell completely silent while the coughing went on for almost a full minute, as if someone in some distant room was having an asthma attack. It was still far away, somewhere down at the farthest end of the facility. I wasn't even sure it was on this floor, but we had to go after it.

I'd never heard coughing at Waverly Hills before. I'd heard voices, seen shadow people, picked up on lots of strange smells, and experienced a dozen or so other odd occurrences. But this was new.

It made sense, though. Waverly Hills was a sanatorium for tuberculosis patients, and fits of coughing were one of the most prevalent symptoms.

My heart pulsed hard, my face felt flushed, and sweat prickled at my scalp beneath my thick black hair, even in this bitter cold. The rush had me.

Who had spoken? Who was coughing? Was it really a ghost? Was it something else?

Was I about to come face-to-face with a disembodied soul? Would I be able to interact with it, touch it, and communicate?

Could it tell me what it's like on the other side of the veil? Could it explain what happens when you die?

The sound grew as we neared the end of the hallway, more

than three hundred feet from where we'd started. It had to be coming from one of the patient rooms on either side of us, or the last room straight ahead at the end of the hall.

There was a scream. It was muffled, but it was there, and it was close to us.

We ran the last few feet and I pointed into the room on our left.

"Put a light in there!" I whispered. I did the same to the room next door.

On the left was an old elevator, closed up and not functioning.

As soon as our flashlights illuminated the rooms, the coughing and screaming stopped. All fell silent.

I shined my light throughout the large, empty room, checking every corner, every wall, the ceiling and floor. Nothing.

I ran over to the room Jordin was in and repeated the procedure. There was nothing.

"You're absolutely certain we're the only people in here?" she said, raising her voice to full volume now that the commotion had passed.

"There's no way to be a hundred percent sure! It's a huge building situated on a massive plot of land. It wouldn't be that hard for someone to sneak in, even under controlled conditions."

She let out a long sigh.

I kept talking. "But if the sound we heard *was* coming from someone alive . . . then where did they go?"

Jordin looked around the room anew, her spirits rising. "The sounds were definitely coming from somewhere down here. *Had* to be in one of these two rooms," she agreed.

I nodded. "I don't think it could have gotten past us."

Jordin was grinning all of a sudden, no doubt feeling the rush of having experienced something genuinely unexplainable. "So what are you thinking? Residual haunt? That thing you said where a place stores a recording of something that somebody did while they were alive?"

I walked outside and examined the doorpost. It was marked as room number 502.

Of course. I should have remembered. . . .

"I know this room," I explained. "The story goes that one of the nurses working here hung herself in room 502. She was pregnant but either she lost the baby or aborted it, because it was found at the bottom of the elevator shaft not long after the nurse was found dangling from the rafters."

Jordin looked around the room again and rubbed her arms, feeling a palpable chill.

———————

I felt like nothing more than a glorified tour guide as we made our way down to the slanted tunnel nicknamed the Body Chute. I suggested the stop after we left room 502, explaining its history to Jordin.

The hospital administrators decided that with so many people dying daily of tuberculosis under the facility's roof, it could be detrimental to morale to see bodies constantly being taken away through one of the main exits. So the tunnel was put to use, allowing the bodies to be removed via a railcar.

A popular urban legend suggested that when the number of bodies grew to be too overwhelming, the hospital staff decided to forgo the railcar and just let the bodies tumble down through the tunnel. I had studied the history of the place enough to know that this was just a spooky story told to unnerve people into thinking that many of the ghosts of Waverly Hills were victims of this mistreatment and were still here to take revenge.

We stared down into the corridor to the point where the light was swallowed by darkness, stretching into infinity. Jordin grabbed a small piece of broken-off brick from the floor and sent it sliding and rolling down the tunnel. We heard it much longer than we could see it as it rattled on and on against the cement floor.

A new voice called out in the distance, a man's voice.

Jordin and I froze again, listening hard to get our bearings on the new sound. We couldn't make out what the voice was saying, but as we listened, it spoke again.

"Is that you?" the muffled voice echoed down the hallway behind us.

Jordin let out a nervous laugh, pumping her fists in triumph. "This is un-stinkin'-believable!" she whispered.

I shushed her, listening hard. The voice was speaking again.

"Caroline?" the feeble, worried man's voice called out. "Honey, is that you?"

"Yeah! Yeah, it's me!" called Jordin in reply, still exuberant and celebrating that the whole place had suddenly come alive. "This is Caroline!"

I grabbed Jordin by the front of her shirt and shoved her up against one of the heavily graffitied walls just outside the Body Chute. Jordin was on some kind of endorphin high, but as she opened her mouth to protest, I cut her off.

"Stop it!" I hissed. "*Do not* provoke an intelligent haunt. Don't taunt them, don't play with them. Don't ever!"

"I thought you said it was a residual!" she asserted.

"The first one was," I said slowly. "*This one* reacted to us. It called out after you threw the rock into the tunnel. It's intelligent."

I let go of her shirt, and for a moment I wondered why I'd reacted so strongly, almost violently. Then I remembered that haunted locations like this could get to you sometimes, transferring emotions from those who'd died here into you. Plus, Jordin had all but insulted the poor soul who'd died here, and that sort of thing just didn't sit well with me.

Jordin frowned as she straightened her shirt back out, trying to process something. "But . . . your parents provoked spirits sometimes on their TV show. I've been watching it a lot lately. It was their way of trying to get the ghosts to do something, communicate in some way."

"Yes, they provoke sometimes," I grudgingly admitted. "*I* don't like it. It's disrespectful."

"But if it—"

"Don't ever forget," I whispered, "we are trespassing on their turf. *We* are the ones who don't belong here. We're here to observe only."

Jordin looked around in frustration and raised her voice. "But if we can't interact with them, then what's the point?"

"Interact all you want. But treat them with respect. And the point of this, since you asked, is to prove they exist."

I couldn't understand why Jordin's brow was still wrinkled. "What if that's not enough?" she asked.

I had no answer.

The male voice did not call out to us again all night.

When four a.m. arrived and the activity seemed to be settling down for the night, I declared that we were done, and we began rolling up our sleeping bags. While Jordin had originally insisted on our staying the entire night, the last hour's excitement had wiped her out and she put up no arguments at the mention of getting a pair of hotel rooms before we flew home.

Once we were back in the rental car and out on the highway again, she turned to me and said, "So where are we going next?"

I'd been afraid of this. Paranormal investigation is a field in which closure is a very rare commodity. The nature of how it works—positioning oneself to observe highly random paranormal events—all but prevents you from ever feeling like the job is complete. Usually you wound up feeling instead like you stopped only from exhaustion, and often right when things were just getting interesting.

That lack of closure made it a very addictive activity, particularly for newcomers. It was a difficult business to walk away from, which had made it all the harder for me to return.

I knew that no matter how many times I took her investigating, it would always run the risk of never being enough, since there would never be any resolution to the experience. There was no evidence strong enough to convince the whole world that ghosts exist.

I looked at her, frowning, and tried to think of a way of cutting off that craving in her before it grew too strong. "You said you wanted to touch the paranormal. You just did, Jordin. More than most people ever will."

She was silent for a moment before she quietly said, "But I didn't find what I'm looking for."

"And remind me what that is?" I tried to coax her.

"Pick the next place, Maia." Jordin's expression hardened as she stared out the windshield. "We're going again."

FIVE

Carrie Morris had tired eyes.

I was trying to give Jordin's roommate time to sort through her memories, using kind-but-firm questioning techniques I'd learned in class. But I'm not known for my patience. And this chick wasn't going out of her way to hide her disdain for my presence.

The three of us sat on a sidewalk bench in the courtyard outside Hogan Hall in the cool morning sun. Carrie was on one side of me, and Derek—who hadn't said a word since introducing the two of us—was on the other.

It turned out that the group of friends Jordin routinely went off on this "annual vacation" thing with were all members of the Columbia volleyball team, of which Jordin was once a proud member. But not anymore.

"So you saw Jordin Thursday afternoon, August 5, on the beach . . . ?" I tried to prod her. "You're sure that was the last time you saw her?"

"Yeah," Carrie replied, watching other students bustle about, bobbing one knee up and down in agitation. "She kept saying how she wanted to go to England, she was planning a trip to England, she talked about it all the time. So when she disappeared, we figured she'd finally gone."

England. Jordin's interest in England didn't surprise me. I knew all about it.

"So you didn't suspect anything was wrong right away. How long was it before you went to the police?"

"The next Wednesday, I think."

"Derek said they didn't take you seriously."

Carrie yawned. "Well, this officer gave us a big condition that had to be met before a person could be declared missing. We were in the middle of explaining to him how long Jordin had been gone when he recognized her name. He said it was probably some kind of 'rich person eccentric impulse' and suggested we 'contact her estate.' "

Every time she quoted from someone else, Carrie made annoying little rabbit-ear quotation marks with her fingers.

I turned to Derek. "Has Jordin ever done anything like that? Disappeared for an extended period of time without warning?"

He shook his head, and I caught the wary look in his eye, though he was trying to hide it. He didn't want to appear ungrateful for my help, but he was indulging me without a lot of confidence in my abilities or in this particular witness. I supposed that as a future pastor, it was a good thing that honesty came so naturally to him.

Whatever. I wasn't here to pacify him. I was sure there had to be more details I could wring out of Carrie. My mind spun, thinking through the kinds of questions a detective would ask.

"Did you notice anything unusual about Jordin before she disappeared?"

Carrie glanced at me warily. "You mean more than ever? She's always been weird, even more so since she met *you*."

When I said nothing—I was trying to practice reading Carrie's expressions and body language, and ignore her belligerence—she went on. "She used to be a fun person, you know. Carefree. Spontaneous. Really funny. And an amazing athlete. Then you came into the picture, and she quit the team and stopped hanging out with us. We had to *beg* her to go with us on this year's trip."

"And when you say 'go with us,' " Derek quietly interjected while examining a nearby tree, "you of course mean 'pay for.' "

Carrie squinted at him but made no response.

"Why didn't she want to go this year?" I asked, trying to stay on point.

"Guess she had 'more important things to do,' " Carrie replied, popping out the quotation marks again. "But she may as well not even have been there, because we barely saw her. Well, she *would* always turn up in her room each morning, but we could never find her in the evenings when we wanted to go out."

Well, sure. That wasn't surprising at all.

"What about her behavior? Any sudden mood swings? Did she complain of any odd pains?"

It was entirely possible, though I had no intention of voicing the possibility aloud, that Jordin had fallen ill and was languishing in a hospital somewhere. Or, the much worse possibility . . .

And that was a suspicion, I told myself forcefully, that had nothing at all to do with what I'd seen at Ghost Town amusement park.

"She was having nightmares."

My ears perked up. "Nightmares?"

Carrie nodded, remembering more as she spoke. "Yeah, she always seemed tired during the day, and she kept mumbling about this nightmare she was having over and over. . . ."

I carefully filed that away for later.

"Also," Carrie went on with a rather satisfied glare at Derek, "I think she'd just gotten a tattoo."

Derek looked as if he'd been jolted out of his daydream. "I'm sorry?"

"That morning before she disappeared, she kept rubbing the back of her neck like it was sore," Carrie explained. "I got a glimpse of it when she turned around, and it looked like some kind of tattoo. I remember thinking it was kinda rude of her to go off and get one by herself, since that was something all of us could have done together. You know, to commemorate the trip."

"Jordin would *never* get a tattoo," Derek whispered under his breath.

I leaned close to him. "You're sure?"

"She hates them. It's a sin to defile your skin that way."

"So, she hates them, or *you* hate them?"

Derek didn't seem to like my tone of voice, and turned away from me.

So I turned back to Carrie. "What did this tattoo look like?"

"Her hand was covering it so much, she kept rubbing at it,"

Carrie said, trying to remember. "I never really got a solid look at it. But it was pretty small and I think it was black."

"And no one said anything to her about it?"

She shrugged. "If Jordin wants to talk about something, she'll bring it up herself."

Derek rose from his seat, apparently done with this. As he walked away, he mumbled something so low, I only caught part of it. Something about ". . . forbid you should be an actual *friend* . . ."

Ten minutes later, after reluctantly giving my cell number to Carrie in case she thought of anything else, I caught up to Derek and suggested heading for the school library. I needed to get online and didn't really want him poking around my dorm room while I sat at my laptop.

"I assume you *have* contacted Jordin's 'estate' already?" I commented.

Derek was slow to respond, his thoughts seeming to linger elsewhere. "If you call her housekeeper Linda her 'estate,' then yes, I did. Jordin's never been comfortable living in her parents' old house alone. She mainly holds on to the mansion for sentimental reasons. When she's not in school, she keeps a small condo in downtown Manhattan. Linda's the only employee still working at the Cole house, and she hasn't seen or heard from Jordin in almost a year. Which isn't out of the ordinary."

Derek opened the front door to the library and held it open so I could enter first. Still he never made eye contact with me, his features distant and filled with impatience. I thought how glad I was that today wasn't the first time I'd met him, because I'd be getting a very poor impression of him if it were.

I found an empty computer in the library and began a quick search for tattoo parlors in Martha's Vineyard. It was a long shot, but it was all I had at the moment.

The search pulled up more than three dozen tattoo parlors.

"What was that about back there?" I asked, keeping my voice just above a whisper to be respectful of the other library patrons.

Derek sat to my left in a chair he'd borrowed from a nearby table. "What was what about?"

I knew that he understood exactly what I was asking about. I kept reminding myself that Derek wasn't himself—he was agitated, worried about his fiancée, and barely keeping control of his feelings of helplessness.

"You seemed to hold Carrie in a bit of contempt," I said.

Derek feigned shock. "I'm a pastor in training. I'll have you know I bear nothing but compassion and love for everybody in the world."

I waited until he sighed and continued.

"It just . . . frustrates me sometimes," he explained. "Because she's wealthy, Jordin tends to attract people who want to be around her but have very little interest in actually being a friend to her. Sometimes I think I may be the only real friend she has. Although for a while, she seemed to consider you one, too," he added as an afterthought.

That was a strange notion. During our adventures, I'd never thought of us as close. At best, I merely tolerated her.

Derek seemed to read the confusion on my face. "I think it's because you didn't fawn over her the way everyone else does. You told her what you really thought. You never worried about offending her, and she found that . . . invigorating."

My eyebrows popped up. "Was that a compliment?"

Derek frowned, running a nervous hand through his close-cropped hair. "Just because I don't agree with your . . . shall we say, 'unique occupational history' . . . doesn't mean I think you're a bad person, Maia."

I almost smiled, but I think it came off instead as an unintended smirk.

"But you've spent way too much time meddling in things that shouldn't be meddled in," he added. "It's a dangerous way of living, and it's going to burn you eventually if you keep at it. I used to wish I could make you—and Jordin—see that."

My smile turned sour, and I quickly lost interest in hearing any more of his beliefs about the paranormal. He had no idea what he was talking about.

"There are dozens of tattoo parlors within driving distance of Martha's Vineyard," I said, back to business. "We'll have to contact each one of them individually."

"You really think this is that important?" Derek asked. "I know my girl, and I don't buy for one second that she would ever get a tattoo."

"Because she's *never* done something you wouldn't approve of," I shot back. Instantly I wished I could take the words back.

Derek ground his teeth, though he was working to hide it. "Your excursions with her would be the sole exception."

I sighed. "Look, if she really did get a tattoo, and if the person that gave it to her was one of the last people to see her, then it could be important, yeah," I said. "But if you have any other leads, I'm listening."

He didn't reply.

"All right, then," I said. "Now, most tattoo parlors don't

require identification for the procedure. So they're not likely to recognize her name. Which means we'll have to give a physical description of Jordin and hope it rings a bell with someone. The more specific we can be, the better. Jordin's a tall, lovely blonde. I'm sure they see plenty of those, so we need to give them details that aren't as common."

Derek looked at me, thoughtful. I thought he was going to ask me something else about tattoos, but he had other things on his mind. "Carrie said Jordin was never around in the evenings in Martha's Vineyard. Was she . . . was she doing what I think she was?"

"Probably. Martha's Vineyard is very old," I acknowledged. "It has tons of locations believed to be haunted. Jordin must've been sneaking out each night to investigate. By herself. She was still chasing the paranormal."

"What was she thinking?" Derek's expression turned hard-edged, but he was silent for a long time. Finally he said, "She was really obsessed with this stuff, wasn't she?"

I remained silent. That was one question I wasn't eager to answer.

———————

I fell asleep quickly that night, feeling content that the day had been well spent. We hadn't found Jordin but we'd narrowed the search, and I believed it was only a matter of time until we turned up some new information about her.

And cracking a missing persons case while still in college would look *killer* on my job application.

I woke up around midnight when someone rapped loudly on my door. Worried it was Derek with dire news about Jordin, I quickly jumped out of bed. But when I opened the door, nobody was there. The lights were on out in the hall, as they always are, and I could hear other residents behind their closed dorm doors, listening to music or talking and laughing. But no one was in the hall.

I figured someone was just being stupid and trying to get a rise out of me. I went back to sleep.

By two a.m., I was dead asleep again. Yet for no reason I could identify, I sat up with a start, opening my eyes wide and looking around my room.

At the foot of my bed stood the outline of a human figure. I had all the lights out and the curtains drawn, so I couldn't make out any features. Just a silhouette.

I was startled, but quickly my experience in the paranormal kicked in, and I studied the apparition as best I could, staring at the spot where its face should have been. Part of me wondered if it might be Jordin, come to bring me another ghostly message.

Then I blinked once, and the figure was gone.

I was sure it had happened, that it was real and not a dream. Yet the more time that passed after I lay back down, the more I was inclined to think I was just over-tired and seeing indistinct shapes in the shadows that my mind tried to form into a familiar pattern.

I eventually fell asleep again.

Less than two hours later, I awoke once more.

Surrounding my small bed were five dark, hazy figures.

My first thought was that this whole night was probably some kind of hazing. Someone in my dormitory had learned about my past and cooked up a prank as some kind of senior year rite of passage.

But then I realized that I could see *through* all five figures.

As before, they vanished almost as fast as I laid eyes on them. But at the same moment my bed raised up off the floor by an inch and then slammed back down. Every muscle in my body clenched, and I didn't know if I should get out of the bed or stay put.

Loud, clomping footsteps echoed across my small room's floor. My bedside lamp flew off the nightstand and shattered against the front door on the other side of the room. Books from my desk flew open, their pages fluttering. My small television, mounted atop my chest of drawers, came to life and began changing its own channels. Faster and faster the channels went by as I watched, until the TV finally let out a giant spark and fizzled out.

The room fell completely silent, and I sat up a little straighter. My familiar surroundings had just become hostile territory, and I didn't feel safe. For ten, twenty, thirty seconds I remained still and the room stayed quiet. It seemed the activity had ended.

I finally decided to get out of the bed, swinging my legs out over the side, when every single object in my room—every piece of furniture, every book, article of clothing, snack food, every appliance—leapt into the air like a jumping bean and came back down. I couldn't hold back a scream as I crawled backward on my bed until my back was against the wall.

Sheets pulled out from under me, flying into the middle of the floor, followed by my pillows.

I sat there and waited, somehow knowing that wouldn't be the end.

I heard an inhuman laugh, and everything in the room jumped again.

And again.

And again.

Suddenly I knew. The rhythm. Everything was slamming in time to my heartbeat.

My heart gave a thunderous bang against my ribs at the realization, and everything in the room jumped again.

Again and again it happened, keeping up with my heart rate, which now pulsed faster with fear. *Bang. Bang. Bang.* Quicker and quicker and then I could hear people shouting, wondering what was going on. Someone even rattled the doorknob at one point, but the door wouldn't open.

And I hadn't locked it.

With one final heartbeat, everything jumped higher than before, and I was tossed from the mattress to the middle of the floor. I crashed, burning my hands and knees on the carpet.

I lay on my stomach, almost unwilling to turn over for fear of what might happen next. But when something touched my ankle, I spun over lightning fast.

Something like a very cold, wet hand was crawling up my bare leg, but I saw nothing.

Suddenly, objects all around my room tore themselves free from wherever they'd been at rest and began flying around in all directions. One after another after another. My backpack, my desk chair, my keys, my laptop. Around and around they flew, crashing into one wall and then flying up into the air to go crash into another.

I put my hands on my head and curled into a ball, trying to keep from being injured, but it wasn't long before things started brushing past me or just flying into me. There was so much happening now, a hurricane of energy and rage, destroying everything it touched, and slamming items both blunt and sharp into my skin. I heard my own screams and cries muffled within the storm. And all the while, the freezing hand continued its slow climb up my leg, past my knee now. I tried to grab it, to claw it away from me, but you can't take hold of nothing.

Someone was beating on my door from the hallway outside, trying to get in and save me, but I couldn't reach the door. I couldn't move. I just lay in a fetal position in the middle of the room, screaming for it to end. My heart was racing so fast, I knew it would soon give out.

I heard terrible, loud crashes and disembodied cackles of laughter. I could feel hot, wet, sticky spots pouring across one hip, a shoulder, and the top of my head. I was bleeding.

The tempest reached a powerful crescendo, sounding as if the entire building were coming down. And then without warning, everything simply stopped. The violence ended, the chilled hand vanished, and everything was still.

One second passed, and I heard the tiny sound of my cell phone vibrating against the floor. Aside from the beating on my door, the only other sound I could hear was of someone crying.

It took me a moment to realize that the person crying was me.

I was trembling violently as I opened my eyes and looked around. The entire room had been destroyed, stripped down to the studs in the walls. All of my furniture, all of my belongings, reduced to debris.

I was hurt, but I couldn't tell how badly. I wasn't even sure I was still breathing. But I had to be alive, because the heavy beating of my heart had become painful to my chest.

My phone was situated right next to me on the floor. A blinking light indicated an incoming call.

I placed a shivering hand over the phone and put it up to my ear.

I tried to say hello, but my voice wouldn't obey my command to speak. Instead I let out a weak croak.

When the voice on the other end spoke, it reached my ear as a whisper from a voice I didn't know.

"The nightmare is coming, Maia," it said, and my blood turned to ice. "Forget Jordin Cole, or it comes for you next."

The Stanley Hotel

Estes Park, Colorado

Opened 1902

Stephen King made it famous!

SIX

Snow was falling in Estes Park as our rental car crested the top of the hill and our destination came into view.

"I assume you approve?" It was a question I asked carefully.

It had been hard getting much out of Jordin since we'd met up back at JFK Airport in New York. Her attitude couldn't have been more different than the way she'd behaved on our first trip, two months ago. She hadn't said one word on the plane, refusing even a complimentary beverage. She sat in her window seat, her gaze tracing the roadways and farms and other structures and signs of civilization far below.

She was so withdrawn and pensive that I began wondering what could have happened to her. And not knowing her all that well, it occurred to me she might be brooding. Wallowing in something.

As much as I enjoyed the opportunity to study without her endless chatter, the silence had grown uncomfortable, the tension surrounding her rising from the moment we got in the car and made our way out to Estes Park.

I was sure that if anything could jar a reaction out of her, it would be the gorgeous vistas of the Rocky Mountains surrounding Estes Park, which nearly every visitor agreed was one of the most beautiful places on earth. But she hadn't spoken at all, still looking out her window as I drove carefully through the snow-covered streets, winding up the hill toward our stop.

When she said nothing, I tried again. "Do you know where we are?"

No reply.

"Jordin . . . this is the Stanley Hotel."

Finally she blinked. Slowly she swiveled her head to face me. "*The* Stanley Hotel?"

I nodded.

"Where Stephen King wrote *The Shining*?" Jordin said, her enthusiasm rising.

"Well," I pointed out, "he didn't actually write it here, he was just inspired to write it by his visit. After the comments you made about Waverly Hills, I figured a more famous landmark might scratch your itch."

Jordin sat up straighter in her seat and leaned into the middle to peer out of the front windshield at the lovely white building that lay straight ahead. "Wow . . . I've always wanted to see this place."

I almost smiled, proud of myself for pulling Jordin out of her funk. Until I remembered that this meant her nonstop talking would likely return, as well.

"How many times have you been here?" she asked.

"This is my fifth," I replied. "Used to come up once a year with my parents—they had an open invitation."

I turned back to the windshield to take in the full view of the grand old hotel with its white siding, stone foundation, Georgian architecture, and six flagpoles jutting out at a severe angle over the large covered front porch, and once again I found myself enjoying a small tingle of the old adrenaline. Every time I'd been here in the past, I'd witnessed unquestionable paranormal phenomena—and every time, it was a different experience than before.

The car wound carefully through the snow-covered driveway up to the front entrance, where we deposited ourselves in the foot-deep snow with our bags. A bellhop quickly descended the front steps and snatched our things before I could stop him. I always preferred to do things for myself, but I had to remind myself that I was on an all-expense-paid business trip and could let my "employer" pick up the tab on anything and everything. Which Jordin seemed only too happy to do.

The yellow rays of the sun had already faded to orange by the time we neared the front steps. It would be dark soon, and I knew Jordin would be ready to get started the minute the sun was gone.

It was understandable. Even a novice like Jordin was familiar enough with the building's reputation to know that the Stanley was very special.

Someone brushed a curtain aside in a room on the fourth floor. I sensed the movement and looked up, but all I saw was a shadow, a person's silhouetted face staring back at me. As soon as I focused on it, it dissolved and the curtain fell back into place.

I automatically tried to dismiss what I'd just seen, assuming it was a trick of the light. But something about it made my eyes linger on the window for a long moment.

"You coming?" asked Jordin, already on the bottom step.

"Yeah," I replied, still studying the window.

Jordin led the way up the front stairs, and we went inside. As we waited to check in at the charming front desk, which was stained a deep welcoming hue and had a marble countertop, I decided it was time to lay down some ground rules.

I spoke softly. "I need you to keep in mind that this is a vastly different scenario than what we did at Waverly Hills. For one thing, we're not the only people here—there's a full staff and a couple hundred other guests—so we don't have free reign. I know you're anxious to get started but we need to wait until midnight. I was able to get permission for us to investigate tonight on the condition that we will respect the other guests and we won't go poking around in places where guests aren't allowed. With one or two exceptions. Jordin, are you listening?"

She was fishing out her journal from inside her large pocket-book as I spoke. "Yeah, yeah. Leave everybody else alone, don't make any big noise. I got it."

We settled in and I tried to entertain myself by watching the hotel's channel 42, which played Stanley Kubrick's version of *The Shining* on a continuous loop, twenty-four hours a day. But I was really just waiting for the hotel to fall asleep. We needed the depths of night for our best exploring.

As if sensing my own rising anticipation, Jordin knocked on my door the second the clock struck midnight, a very full backpack hefted over one shoulder.

"Where do we start?" she said, her zeal for the hunt already in plain view.

I didn't mind that she'd abandoned formalities. I was ready to get on with it, too.

"Let's try the ballroom," I said. "It's where one of the most frequent reports originates. The grand piano in there sometimes plays all by itself."

Jordin shifted her backpack and led the way down the narrow white hotel corridor. She seemed distracted. "Anything weird happen to you yet?"

I glanced her way. "Like what?"

"When I got in my room, I opened my suitcase and laid out some fresh clothes on the bed. I went to the bathroom and showered, but when I came out to put those clothes on, they were back in my bag. It could've been the maid—except I had the door locked. And chained."

"Hmm," I said, intrigued but trying to sound noncommittal. It wasn't that unusual of an occurrence, but I knew that something like that happening to Jordin so quickly after we arrived could spell trouble later on. Something in the hotel might have taken a special interest in her. If so, further activity would not be confined to her room. It would follow her wherever she went.

I eyed her bag. "What equipment did you bring?"

"Everything you recommended," she replied without turning around. "Digital camera, digital voice recorder, video camera."

"A good start," I remarked approvingly.

"Start?" she echoed, nonplussed. "What else is there?"

"Loads. Thermal imaging cameras. Temperature gauges. Electromagnetic frequency detectors. Full-spectrum DSLRs."

Jordin stopped and retrieved her journal from her bag while we waited for the elevator to arrive. "I should be writing this down," she muttered.

We rode down the elevator in silence, and then walked a short way down the main floor hall to the ballroom. The lights were on inside but I found the wall switch first thing and turned them off.

Something about the large emptiness of the ballroom always gave people chills. Nearly everyone who entered it was taken in by the sensation.

"Why does it have to be dark?" Jordin asked.

"Hmm?"

"I've been reading up, and a lot of reported paranormal activity doesn't even happen at night. So how come you always investigate after dark?"

"Because it's scarier," I deadpanned.

She stopped. "What?"

I laughed. "There's nothing that says you're *required* to investigate at night. A lot of investigators don't. There are lots of reasons to do it this way, though. Primarily it's a logistical issue, especially for populated locations. It's just easier to gain wide access to the most haunted locations at night, when there are fewer people around—or none. The absence of the human element makes it easier to record EVPs and capture imagery that's authentically paranormal. In a field where it's almost impossible to investigate under controlled circumstances, investigating at night increases what little control you do have over the environment."

"Remind me what EVP stands for again?" Jordin asked.

"Electronic Voice Phenomenon. Disembodied voices that the human auditory range can't hear, but recording devices can."

It was unnerving to be in the big, unfriendly room, but where most would have been timid about entering, I was surprised to see Jordin stride right out into the open space without a care. I could only imagine what was going on in her head, considering how sullen she'd been earlier. I felt like she was making an effort to rein in the exuberant rookie I'd investigated with at Waverly Hills.

She made a beeline for the piano, which sat silent across the room.

"Cold spot," she reported. "It's very cold over here."

I joined her by the piano, confirming that it was indeed colder than the rest of the room.

Cold spots were a common phenomenon when paranormal activity was present. No one really knew why, but apparitions almost always drained the warmth out of the air.

"You should be recording," I whispered.

"Ah!" Jordin exclaimed. She dropped her pack softly on the ground and pulled out her video camera. To her credit, it was ready to go and all she had to do was turn it on and press *Record*.

Jordin held the camera while spinning slowly in place for a few minutes, shooting video, mostly of the piano and eventually moving to the bench, where she sat down.

"Why do electronic devices pick up sounds the human ear can't?" she whispered.

I wasn't sure if Jordin really expected me to provide a sure answer, but I replied anyway. "I don't know. Maybe they have a better auditory range than the human ear."

Jordin suddenly turned the camera to face the floor and began inspecting it. "Oh man . . ."

I glanced her way, half expecting this. "Battery?"

Jordin looked up in surprise, her long blond locks giving off a dull gleam in the dark. "It was fully charged, I know it was! I checked it before I left my room!"

"Sudden battery drain," I explained. "It's pretty common during investigations. There are theories as to why."

Jordin was all ears. "Like what?" she whispered eagerly.

"The most popular thought is that when a spirit wants to make itself known to human senses, it'll draw on any energy source around it to manifest. Including electrical batteries, if they're handy."

Jordin screwed up her eyebrows. "I'm not sure that makes any sense."

"Neither am I, to be honest, but it's just one theory. You brought some spares, right?"

She blinked. "These cameras all take special batteries that are supposed to last for hours! You didn't say anything about bringing extras!"

I picked up her digital voice recorder and spoke into it. "Note to self: always bring extra batteries to an investigation."

Jordin scowled at me, placing her recorder back on top of the piano.

We stayed in the ballroom for another twenty minutes, but all was quiet.

"So why is the Stanley so haunted?" asked Jordin as we were packing up to leave.

I frowned, not in frustration but from searching for the words. The truth was, I didn't know. No one had ever been able to determine why the Stanley was so haunted, aside from the fact that it was built on very old land that had passed down through many generations. Before the Stanley was built, Native Americans lived all throughout the region for unknown numbers of years. Most of the sightings seemed to indicate the presence of immigrants from the eighteenth and nineteenth centuries.

F. O. Stanley, who built the hotel, and his wife, Flora, were believed to be behind most of the sightings. History records that the two of them dearly loved the area for its beauty. Mr. Stanley was all but healed of tuberculosis thanks to the clean mountain air and how much his morale improved just by being there. Maybe he just never wanted to leave.

Hours later, we had hit several known hot spots throughout the hotel with little success. But I wasn't ready to give up yet.

We were returning to our rooms so Jordin could plug in her batteries to recharge when we got our first hit of the night.

It was past three a.m., so the lights had been dimmed in the brightly colored guest corridors, the walls adorned with ornate wallpaper and dotted with large antique black-and-white photographs. We were walking quietly to keep from disturbing the other guests when Jordin stumbled and dropped all of her equipment.

"Shhh!" I whispered over the enormous clatter. I thought of my phone conversation with the owners a few weeks prior when I promised them we would be discreet during our investigation.

Jordin collected her things and stood with shaky legs beneath her. She stood next to a floor-length mirror, and her eyes were huge as she looked into it. She glanced over her own shoulder, as if she expected to see someone there, and then she turned back to stare into the mirror again.

"What is it?" I asked.

"I saw a man!" she whispered back, her voice fragile and frantic. "In the mirror! I saw him in the mirror!"

I eyed her suspiciously.

"It was a man. An older man, and he was wearing . . . like, an old-fashioned suit."

The smallest of chills brought goose bumps to my arms. Despite all my experience, I still did not like mirrors. Something about looking into them with the chance of seeing something other than yourself looking back unnerved me and I tried, as a rule, to avoid them.

"Where did you see him?" I whispered, joining her to stare at the mirror.

"In the mirror!" Jordin replied with over-the-top obviousness, pointing to the spot we were both staring at. "I glanced at it as I passed by, and he was standing *right there* looking back at me!" She pointed at a small alcove that housed one of the hotel room doors.

"He was only in the mirror!" she said, and her whole body jerked suddenly. She rubbed her arms, which had turned pale. "But as soon as I looked, he disappeared. He was just gone."

"What else did you notice about him?" I asked uneasily, as I tried to look deeper into the mirror.

"I don't know. . . . He was bald, but with, like, a comb-over. And one of those old-timey mustaches that curl up on the ends?"

"A handlebar," I said slowly, realization dawning in my mind.

"Yeah. And he had real beady eyes, and he was wearing a pinstripe suit. With a vest."

I took a deep breath and let it out slowly, the hairs on my arms standing on end.

"You just described the earl of Dunraven," I said softly. "Lord Dunraven was the original owner of this entire area, back in the 1800s, and he's been rumored to haunt not just the Stanley, but most of Estes Park."

Jordin's eyes grew even wider, and the two of us stood in stunned silence for a long moment.

I broke the silence first. "You just laid eyes on your very first full-bodied apparition."

Jordin offered a trembling smile, and I recognized the thrill of adrenaline that had to be coursing through her right now. It was giving her a noticeable buzz.

"So why does this guy haunt the town?" she asked.

I picked through my memory to relate Dunraven's story in concise words. "He wanted to use his land as a private game reserve, so he's probably unhappy with what's become of it."

"Huh," said Jordin dully, and I noticed a new expression on her face I hadn't observed before. "I forget that ghosts were people like me and you, with the same emotions and wants."

I watched her. "Does that mean you've made up your mind about the existence of ghosts? Is that what this is about for you?"

She didn't answer at first. I was sure she knew that I was trying to get her to concede that there was no further need for these adventures of ours. "I'm not here to prove the existence of ghosts, Maia. Even if I were, I know I wasn't imagining what I saw in that mirror. So what else is on the agenda?"

I sighed. "Next we make sure we have plenty of batteries for our flashlights, 'cause we're going to need them."

———————

"Shh," I whispered. "Did you hear that?"

In the silence, I realized with slight alarm that my heart was pounding hard in my chest. I wasn't frightened, I was sure of it. I didn't usually get scared during investigations. Excited, thrilled, even emotional sometimes, sure. But you just couldn't do this job if you let the fear in.

Yet here we were on a fairly routine investigation, my heart hammering and sweat beginning to rise on my face and head despite the chill of our location.

Jordin shook her head, then stood in silence, waiting. I was glad to see her flick on her voice recorder without my needing to remind her this time.

The sound came again.

"I heard *that*," she said, and I could see that her breathing had also increased.

We heard it a third time.

Somewhere in the distance, maybe right down the hall from where we now stood, a child's voice was giggling.

We were nowhere near the guest rooms anymore. We had descended down to the basement tunnels—a special allowance I'd been granted by the hotel's owners, thanks to my credentials. Besides, it was the middle of the night. This area was locked off, and I was the only person besides the owners with a key to get in, so no one could have possibly been down there but us.

It giggled again.

"It sounds like a little girl," Jordin whispered.

I nodded in agreement, listening, standing perfectly still. After a moment, I motioned for Jordin to follow, and the two of us moved slowly down the dark corridor, which had actual mountain rock exposed right up against the foundational walls. I tried to track the sound to its source.

"Hello?" I called, and Jordin jumped at the sound, though she tried to cover it.

"*Hell-o*," came a muffled, singsong response, from one very happy-sounding little girl. Her voice was stifled, like she was behind a wall, or maybe inside it. It was like she was playing somewhere nearby, unconcerned with where she was or what time it was and just wrapped up in her own little world.

"Hello?" called Jordin, following my lead. I didn't mind. Initiative was good, when it was properly placed.

"Hell-*oooo*-oooh," called out the playful little voice.

"Who are you?" I asked.

No answer.

"*Where* are you?" asked Jordin.

"Right here, silly!" the girl happily replied. She giggled again and began humming a lullaby.

Jordin and I exchanged a stunned look.

Jordin almost smiled as she whispered, "That is the craziest thing ever."

The two of us spent the next hour searching through the tunnel for any sign of a little girl—alive or otherwise. It made so much more sense to assume that a girl staying at the hotel had wandered down here alone in the middle of the night and was calling out to us from the other end of a ventilation duct or something.

But we found no evidence to support that. The basement was

utterly bare, aside from pipes and wires and the hotel's hot-water heaters, and there were no ventilation ducts to carry the sound from another room. It was like an ancient cave down there, and we made absolutely certain that it was completely sealed off, making our way through the darkness into every last square inch of the place.

There was no child to be found, though she called out to us again every fifteen minutes or so.

Once again, the Stanley had not disappointed.

"Wait, what time is it?" Jordin asked, halting suddenly in the dark.

Did she already notice . . . ? I wondered. "Three thirty-two."

Jordin had been sharp this trip, I had to admit. She'd come pretty far in a short time.

"We've had major activity since three," Jordin noted. "And didn't the same thing happen back at Waverly?"

"Three a.m. is believed to be the hour when spirits—and dark forces in particular—are most powerful," I said. "And as you've already seen, it's often true."

"Why?" she asked.

"It's called the witching hour," I replied. "Some call it the *demonic* witching hour. Its significance comes from the fact that Jesus is believed to have died at three p.m. on Good Friday. So the exact inverse of that hour is when dark spirits most often choose to manifest. It's a perversion of Christ's death on the Cross."

Jordin shivered. "Wait a minute . . . 'dark forces' . . . Are you saying this little girl isn't a little girl at all?"

I shrugged. "It's not a universal rule. I've been to plenty of places where nothing happened at all at three, or most of the activity occurred at other times of the day. Or things happened at three that were quite harmless."

"But . . . you said we weren't going to deal with demonic hauntings," Jordin protested.

"We're not. Though demons are definitely the darkest of entities."

"What other kinds of dark entities are there?"

"Angry spirits. Malevolent ghosts," I said, and decided it was time to call it a night. "Come on, I'm ready for some sleep."

As we were walking back to our rooms, Jordin seemed to become sullen again, like she was during our travel to Estes Park. I was tired and couldn't handle her mood swings anymore.

"What?" I said, a little louder than I should have in the dim, quiet corridor.

Jordin looked up as if suddenly remembering I was next to her. "Huh?"

"What's with you? You've been temperamental all day long."

"Oh," Jordin replied, almost whispering. "I, uh . . . Derek and I had a fight. He's my fiancé."

Great. I'd just ventured into territory I had no desire to get into. Jordin's personal business was *way* outside my interests. I was here as her employee—I didn't need to be her confidante.

Despite this, my mouth betrayed me and formed the words "What happened?"

Jordin grimaced. "I told him about you. About *this*. Our ghost-hunting trips."

"We're not 'ghost hunting,'" I said mechanically.

"Right, right, I meant our *paranormal investigations*."

"And Derek doesn't approve?" I asked, though it was obvious.

"I can't remember if I told you before," she said, stopping in the hallway, "but Derek's a religious studies major. He's planning to go to seminary in a couple of years and eventually start a church of his own."

She didn't have to say any more. It all made perfect sense. *Of course* her fiancé didn't approve of his future wife carrying on with a "ghost hunter." Such things were taboo for most of evangelical America. If it got out after the two of them were married that his wife had once been obsessed with the paranormal, it could do major damage to his reputation.

I'd never met this Derek, but didn't at all think less of him for being concerned about his social status. If anything, I empathized. My own reputation was a daily concern for me; I often worried that my past might keep me from ever being taken seriously by my peers as a law enforcement professional.

I had to wonder how much Jordin really loved her fiancé if she was willing to risk his future by going on these trips with someone like me. Or maybe her reasons for doing it were just so important they blinded her to all other concerns.

Another thought occurred to me, and I had to suppress a tiny laugh.

"What?" she asked, not offended and ready to join in on the joke.

"It's just an odd picture...." I tried to explain. "A minister... married to one of the richest women in the world. Who happens to be defying his wishes and his beliefs by investigating things he probably thinks are dangerous and better left alone."

Jordin nodded knowingly. "People never quite seem to 'get' me and Derek. I know we're an unlikely pairing."

"Hey," I said, "I'm the product of an unlikely pairing. I'm not gonna judge. So, what, were you childhood sweethearts?"

I was half joking, but she replied, "We were, actually. Best friends since kindergarten, in love since high school."

"So," I said, trying to get a better picture of the two of them in my head, "do you . . . share his beliefs? His worldview?"

Jordin almost seemed surprised that I'd asked. "Oh, of course, totally! That's one of the reasons we met and fell in love—we went to the same private Christian school growing up."

"Huh," I said, without humor. "You don't strike me as a typical Christian."

"What's a typical Christian?"

I paused. "In my experience, they tend to be very closed-minded. But you're not."

She sort of shrugged. "I suppose that's true. About some things."

Okay. Kind of makes sense, I decided. *More than it did before, anyway.* Jordin and Derek's union would certainly present its share of challenges when her money was someday combined with his ministry. I couldn't imagine a scenario where that would end well.

But it really was no stranger than my own parents—a devout Catholic married to a strict agnostic. There were always those who beat the odds.

"But he doesn't believe in ghosts, right?" I asked. "I mean, you said you had a big argument. It had to be about that."

"He doesn't think it's all in my head or anything," she said, quick to defend her beloved. "He's never condescending. He's not that kind of guy. He thinks the stuff we're investigating is real.

But he doesn't believe in ghosts. He thinks it's . . . something dangerous."

I knew exactly what that meant.

"So if Derek doesn't want you to be doing this, and you love him as much as you say you do, why are you defying him?"

I was pretty pleased with myself for finding a way to ask the same question I'd been asking of Jordin since this whole thing began. But she was too clever to let me get away with it.

"I told you . . . it's none of your business, Maia. No offense," she added quickly.

I sighed. "Well, you're going to have to tell me sooner or later, 'cause as long as we keep taking these trips, I'm never going to stop asking."

"Fair enough," Jordin replied. "When I'm ready to talk about it, I'll tell you."

SEVEN

Derek found me at St. Luke's Hospital the morning after the attack, around eight-thirty. I was poring over a book on criminal psychology that one of my dorm mates—who also offered to let me crash on her bottom bunk—had been kind enough to let me borrow. Even in my condition, I was trying to work ahead for my first class of the semester, which was scheduled to begin that afternoon. And I was determined to be there.

Word had spread overnight about the girl in Hogan who was hurt in the night, but in the absence of facts, fiction was distributed without qualm. The most prevalent story was that some kind of bomb had gone off in my room, utterly destroying it but miraculously leaving all the other rooms on my floor untouched.

I was covered in scratches and bruises over nearly every square inch of my skin, but thankfully nothing was broken. I'd had more stitches than I could count, in numerous places, but all things considered, I was very fortunate. And at least my face had been spared aside from a few mild scratches, so as long as I wore warm clothing and kept the wincing to a minimum, no one would be the wiser.

What really hurt was knowing that I'd lost everything I owned—everything I had brought with me to school, anyway. Many of my clothes were salvageable, and thankfully I'd backed up my laptop hard drive on a USB flash drive that didn't get destroyed. Otherwise, there was very little that was irreplaceable, but the thought of losing so many personal belongings still stung.

The ER doctor—an alarmingly short man with perfectly groomed hair and fingernails—decided to keep me until morning for observation, because I had a big, ugly egg on the top of my head.

Derek arrived just after an unappetizing breakfast, and once he was sure I was okay, I told him everything I could remember. Knowing full well what he would think it was.

"It was a demonic attack!" he whispered to me conspiratorially as a nurse left the room after taking my blood pressure for the millionth time. "I told you, you shouldn't be nosing around in the paranormal all the time! You've opened the door to something and your life is in danger!"

I normally welcomed a good intellectual debate, but I didn't feel up to it this morning, so I changed the subject back to our attempts to find Jordin. Last night's attack only strengthened my resolve to find her.

"No luck, I take it?" I asked, referring to the tattoo parlors in Martha's Vineyard.

He shook his head.

"Me neither. Most of the places I talked to were kind enough to look back through their records for a small tattoo at the top of the neck, but . . . their records . . ." My voice drifted off as a new thought came to mind.

"What?" he asked.

"Her journal," I said, thunderstruck. "When we were traveling, Jordin recorded all of her experiences in a journal, and if she was planning to keep investigating without me, she probably kept writing in that journal all summer. Possibly right up until her disappearance. Did you ever see it?"

"Never," he replied, his features pained, probably at the thought of another part of Jordin's life he knew nothing about. I could only imagine what terrible fears he might be fighting against right now, like wondering if he ever really knew Jordin at all. I hoped he wouldn't give in to those worries.

The doctor showed up a few minutes later to go over some of the results of the tests and give me the good news: I was being released. No permanent damage had been done, and as soon as I signed some papers and changed my clothes, I was good to go.

When he was gone, I picked up our conversation where we left off. "We need to find that journal," I said with conviction. "Maybe one of those girls she went to Martha's Vineyard with—"

I was interrupted when my phone rang. I didn't recognize the number, so I asked Derek for privacy before answering.

"Hello?"

"Um . . . is this Maia Peters?" asked a timid female voice. I didn't recognize it.

"Yes," I replied. "Who is this?"

"It's Carrie—Carrie Morris. We talked yesterday? About Jordin. You gave me your number. "

"Oh," I said in shock. I hadn't actually planned on her calling me. But she was and she didn't sound well. I said so to her.

I thought I heard Carrie's voice trembling as she spoke. "I, uh . . . I'm scared. I think something's really wrong."

"Okay . . ." I said, thinking fast. "Do you want to tell me what's going on?"

She let out a shuddering breath. "Could you just come to my dorm? Please?"

Somehow it sounded like a setup, and I didn't feel like playing any games. Still, something about her voice . . .

"When would you like me to—?"

"Right now, if you can," she said, sounding close to tears. This was no joke.

I sighed. Apparently restarting my own life, heading to class, and finding a room would have to wait.

"What dorm?"

———————

I knocked hard on Carrie's door, ignoring the stares I drew from other girls in the hallway on their way to class. Apparently girls in this dorm didn't look like they'd lost a fight with a bear. I hoped whatever it was Carrie needed to tell me would at least be quick. Class time was soon approaching and I didn't like being late. It made a very poor first impression.

Carrie opened the door wearing a bathrobe. Her eyes were puffy, her cheeks moist and red. The sight of her this way stopped me in my tracks. I couldn't quite believe this was the same girl I'd met yesterday.

"What's going on?" I asked as she stepped aside to let me in, closing the door behind me.

Carrie walked around me to sit up at the head of her bed, leaning back on pillows. I wasn't sure whether I was supposed to join her by sitting down or what, so I stood awkwardly at the foot of the bed, trying to ignore the pain all over my body and wishing I'd taken up the doctor on his offer to prescribe some quality painkillers. I had been thinking that I didn't want anything in my system that might dull my senses just now, but the nagging pain turned out to be equally distracting.

"I've been having nightmares," Carrie said, her voice an emotional squeak. "For about a week now."

"What kind of nightmares?" I asked, more out of an impatient desire to get to the point than to express sympathy.

"I'm in this empty, dark place . . . and I'm lost . . . I'm being chased by a dark figure. It's so vivid, so real. Sometimes it's hard to think during the day because it keeps coming back to me."

I glanced at my watch. "I'm sorry to hear that, but I don't understand why you called me."

Carrie had been staring far away as she recalled her dream, but now her weary eyes, filled with fear, came into focus.

She stood from the bed and walked so close to me that she violated my personal space. I was about to take a step back when she turned her back to me.

"When I got out of the shower this morning, I found this." She tugged at the back of her bathrobe until the collar fell down a few inches.

A small, dark black symbol was on her skin right at the spot where her head met her neck.

My heart skipped a beat and then returned with a heavy thud against my rib cage.

"It's not a tattoo," Carrie whispered, barely able to choke the words out through sobs. "And it won't come off."

I had never seen anything like it. It was complex for such a small mark, with intricate shapes extending in labyrinthine directions, crisscrossing over one another like a very complicated knot.

It was a long minute before I could think of something to say.

"You're sure you have no idea how it got onto your neck?"

Carrie just shook her head, trembling with the effort of trying to keep calm. Finally she spun back around to look me in the eye. "Is what happened to Jordin . . . happening to me? Am I going to disappear or be abducted or something?"

"I don't know," I answered honestly. All thoughts of my first class had just been shoved far out of my mind. "Come here. Sit down."

I guided her unsteadily to the edge of the bed, where we sat down side by side. My mind was racing through possibilities, scenarios, all thoughts centered around a forensic analysis of what was happening here, and I couldn't stop glancing at the mark on Carrie's neck.

"Do you think someone could have broken into your room in the night and put that on you while you were asleep?" I asked.

She wiped the tears from her eyes. "I'm a really light sleeper. I would have heard someone breaking the lock long before they ever touched me. Besides, the door's fine." She pointed at the door

I had walked through just minutes ago. It was true; the door and the lock were perfectly intact, with no sign of tampering.

"Why didn't you tell me about this yesterday?" I asked, thinking of how she had been the one to first reveal to me that Jordin was having nightmares the entire week before she disappeared. Didn't Carrie think it might be relevant that she herself had been having nightmares for a week?

"I don't know. I guess I didn't want to believe that Jordin's nightmares and mine could be related."

I don't know why I felt compelled to do what I did next. Instinct took over.

"I need to ask you something that may sound strange," I said.

"All right."

I took a deep breath and blurted it out. "Have you ever been to the Ghost Town amusement park?"

If Carrie was confused or annoyed by this question, she didn't show it. She was still trying not to cry. "Some friends and I have been wanting to go for weeks," she said in a small voice, "but we haven't made it yet."

My mind continued to spin. "What about Jordin? Has she ever been to Ghost Town?"

Carrie took a moment to think. "I don't know. She didn't mention it if she had."

I shook my head, clearing it. "Never mind, it was just a hunch. Okay, whatever's happening to you seems connected to whatever happened to Jordin—I think that's safe to assume. But it doesn't mean you're going to just up and vanish like she did."

Carrie didn't look any more reassured. I did something thoroughly out of character and put my hand on her shoulder. It was awkward, and I couldn't seem to relax it enough for it to feel natural to me, but Carrie's reaction indicated that she drew strength from the gesture.

"I'm going to figure this out, okay?" I said. "We're going to find Jordin, and we're going to figure out what this thing on you is. In the meantime, I want you to go to Health Services and have a doctor check you out. Have them look at that . . . mark . . . on your neck, and make sure it's not infected or anything." I stood up and took out my cell phone. "If you don't mind, I'd like to take a picture of it."

Carrie nodded and wordlessly pulled her hair up while I quickly took a close-up shot of the ugly black marking on her neck.

I had already opened the door to go when I turned back to look at Carrie, another thought jumping to mind. She still sat on the bed right where I'd left her, as if frozen and afraid to move.

"Do the words 'the nightmare' mean anything to you?" I asked.

Carrie looked up at me, fast. Her eyes were huge. "That's what it says—the figure in my dream!" she whispered, her voice quivering again. "Over and over! It says, 'The nightmare—'"

" '—is coming,' " I finished with her, the two of us saying the phrase in chorus.

Silence hung in the air between us, lingering with a thick, indescribable dread.

Early that evening, after informing Derek of what had happened in Carrie's room, I went back to use a computer in the library since my own had been destroyed. Besides, I was grateful for an opportunity to work without Derek's prying eyes watching. This particular search was something I just wasn't prepared to discuss with him. Not yet.

I typed the words "The nightmare is coming" in the browser's search pane, placing the entire phrase in quotes, and I was surprised to see several hundred entries pop up. I scanned through a dozen of them rapidly, learning that most of them were written by people who had visited Ghost Town amusement park. Their stories were similar to mine, with strange specters appearing to them at various random locations throughout the park and saying the foreboding phrase. But no two experiences seemed to be the same, and none of them matched mine.

Next I found a message board that was dedicated to the phrase, and most of the people that posted there were collecting utterances of the words at the amusement park, chronicling the times and locations that it happened. The consensus seemed to be that it was all some kind of interactive experience meant to excite fans and build curiosity about the amusement park. That wasn't what I was hoping to find.

So I ran a search for the exact phrase "Ghost Town amusement park."

The park had its own website, of course. But after spending a few minutes surfing through some of its features—a dedicated page all about the Haunted House, a look at some fan-written reviews of numerous attractions at the park—I found it didn't contain any info that was all that helpful. I looked for a staff application page, wondering if Ghost Town was hiring new employees, thinking that might be a possible justification for Jordin's appearance there. It made no sense to me that super-rich Jordin Cole would get a summer job working at an amusement park, but I wasn't ready to consider any explanations yet that ventured outside of what was natural.

Coming up dry, I decided to try a different tack. I typed some new terms into the search bar: "Ghost Town," "funded," and "owner."

Several news stories came up from about a year ago, announcing the forthcoming opening of Ghost Town in New York. I clicked on the first one. It was an article from the *Times*.

The article identified the primary investor in Ghost Town to be something called DHI, though it failed to explain just what DHI was.

I typed the three-letter acronym into the search bar and several possibilities came up. There was the Door and Hardware Institute. Definitely not that one. DHI Water and Environment. Doubtful. There was an advertising firm, a hair loss clinic, a home building conglomerate.

I was about to give up when at the bottom of the page I spotted Durham Holdings International. The link gave no indication of what kind of business Durham Holdings was, so I clicked on it.

Up came a snazzy website that described DHI as an international investment firm, with partners in industries of all kinds, from around the world. I clicked a link labeled "Assets" and scanned the long list of company names.

There it was. "Ghost Town LLC."

I spent the next half hour reading up on Durham Holdings International, absorbing all that I could. I walked away knowing that the company had been started by one Howell Durham, a world-renowned wild game hunter and venture capitalist, and that his company's interests were extremely diverse but mostly based around new product development. I was disappointed to discover that its corporate headquarters were in Copenhagen, which eliminated any chance that I would be able to pay them a visit. From a world away, DHI was virtually untouchable.

All the while, a nagging thought kept tugging at the back of my mind.

What if I was making too much out of nothing? Did I really see and hear what I thought I did that night at the Haunted House? What if it was just a psychosomatic response?

The thought kept intruding on my research to the point that I finally decided to give in. Abandoning the web, I stood to my feet and exited the library.

I had to know.

Ghost Town was located out on Long Island, just east of Queens. It'd be a trek, but I wouldn't be deterred by this; it was only six in the evening when I jumped on the train and I knew Ghost Town would be open much later than most amusement parks. This place was one of a kind, and scaring patrons was easier to do late at night than during the day, so its operation hours stretched deep into the night.

The place wasn't quite as packed as I remembered it from the other night. That was a Saturday; this was a Tuesday, and with summer over, visitors seemed less enticed.

A taxi from the station dropped me at the entrance, and I paid the thirty-five-dollar admission fee, though it pained me to turn that money loose for the sake of confirming what had probably just been a kooky coincidence. But I did it, and made a straight path for the Haunted House.

My theory was simple. If I walked through the tour again and the events inside unfolded exactly as they had before, then that meant the attraction was nothing but smoke and mirrors, and my overactive imagination was seeing patterns and connections to things in my own life that weren't really there.

If it played out differently, however, then . . . then that thought led to dark places I didn't hope to explore.

Despite the park's diminished attendance, the wait in line for the Haunted House was almost as long as before. At the entrance, I was admitted with a pair of teenagers who looked like they were on a date. They screamed and held each other tight at all the predictable places. I tried to ignore their over-the-top reactions, focusing instead on watching the attraction's events unfold with a clinical detachment.

Most of it occurred exactly as before. The red eyes in the kitchen. The dining room apparitions. The creepy hallway.

When I got to the living room I made a point of being the first one in so I could take up my position in the center of the room before the teenagers did.

Just like before, the room was dark and a mist entered the room. But this mist was different. It was a much brighter white and it seemed to dart from one side of the room to the other. Just when one cloud would disappear, another would dart past, going a different direction. It happened again and again, and my eyes traced its origins to a system of ducts hidden near the ceiling on all four walls.

It was programmed, precise, very well executed, and . . . unquestionably artificial.

As the double front doors opened and I followed the teenage couple out into the cold night air, I felt a numbness fall over my skin. It wasn't a supernatural sensation; it was my own emotions allowing the horrible truth to sink in.

I'd seen Jordin Cole here three nights ago, and whatever she was, she wasn't part of the attraction.

So what was she? What happened to her? And if she really was a ghost, how did she wind up in this park, of all places?

And then, the worst thought of all entered my mind.

I was going to have to tell Derek.

The Myrtles Plantation

St. Francisville, Louisiana

Built: 1796

The most haunted house in America?

EIGHT

Baton Rouge, Louisiana, provided a surprisingly warm and welcome respite from the frigid winds of New York. In fact, it was downright sticky as we exited the Baton Rouge airport and headed north to St. Francisville, the first of three stops on this trip.

I still couldn't believe I'd let Jordin talk me into this one. It was spring break, for crying out loud. We had a whole week, and I could have been sunning at the beach or catching up on studies or visiting my family. Instead, Jordin offered to pay me triple for a week-long adventure at multiple haunted locations far away from New England.

There was just no sating this girl's thirst.

So I chose three of the most haunted locations in the deep

South and plotted a trip that would give us time to spend at least one night at each.

The Myrtles Plantation was first on the itinerary. Once a stately plantation home, it was now a converted bed-and-breakfast nestled in the backwoods of rural Louisiana. I had briefed Jordin about the place on the plane, and though she'd never heard of it, she had stopped questioning my choice of haunted locations. The place overflowed with legends, and it's anybody's guess how many were true.

Surrounded by five thousand acres of cotton fields, the Myrtles was supposedly built over an Indian burial ground. ("Why are so many places built over Indian burial grounds?" was Jordin's comment when I told her about this.) There was a large mirror in the foyer in which many have claimed to see the images of people who died on the grounds—an unpleasant thought for me.

The most famous Myrtles legend concerned a slave girl named Chloe who was owned by the plantation's owners in the early 1800s. Over five hundred slaves lived and worked and died on the plantation, but Chloe was by far the most famous. Reports of how and why she died varied greatly, but the story told most frequently said that Chloe had had her ear cut off for spying on the plantation owner, who kept her as his mistress and then later killed her for accidentally poisoning his wife and daughters. But whatever happened to her, it was probably pretty awful, and she was the apparition seen most often on the property, a mournful figure wearing a green turban.

At one time, the owners tried to downplay the rumor of hauntings, hoping not to scare customers off, but in recent years they'd begun to embrace the legends, welcoming paranormal enthusiasts as regular guests.

We drove through the short white picket fence that surrounded the place and past the tall white guard house, and I pointed out the many statues throughout the property. Long strands of gray Spanish moss hung from the canopy of trees surrounding the plantation as we drove up the dark, narrow driveway. The white main house ahead was so lovely, Jordin mentioned how impossible it seemed that a place this quaint and welcoming could be haunted.

"And I thought it would be bigger," she added as we unloaded our gear and luggage from the car.

I couldn't criticize her for that. I'd told her so much about this place, and it had such an infamous reputation, it was easy to overestimate how big it might be. The Myrtles was a small plantation house, made up of just twenty rooms total, including the guest rooms.

The two of us slowly made our way up the short stairs that led to the picturesque north porch. It was still midafternoon, so there was no need to rush to check in. Blue wrought-iron railings with intricately patterned details surrounded the porch and extended all the way up to the overhang. Seven or eight white wooden rocking chairs sat empty on the humongous porch, rocking themselves by inches due to a mild wind blowing.

I was glad I'd brought warm-weather clothes with me. My sweater and jeans I'd worn on the plane from brisk New York were already making me sweat. Changing would be the first order of business when we got checked in.

We got to the front door, but Jordin hesitated, looking back over her shoulder at the surrounding grounds.

"Have you ever met a witch doctor or voodoo priestess?" she asked.

I shook my head.

"Me neither. I guess being in Louisiana, the feel of it, just made me wonder. How about witches? Or Wiccans? Ever met any?"

"Only once or twice. Made me uncomfortable," I confessed. "All the rituals and stuff—too dark, too weird. Seems to bring them close to dark forces that no one should get close to."

"I think the most paranormal thing I ever did was play with a Ouija board at a sleepover when I was eleven."

"Bad idea," I said. "I can't believe they still sell those things. As if they're harmless board games! They're incredibly dangerous. You wouldn't believe how many people have used them to accidentally invite dark entities into their homes."

Jordin didn't argue. "It was definitely creepy, though we never had anything bad happen afterward. But my dad was furious when he found out. Called it a witch board, said it was of the devil."

"Guess he wouldn't care much for his daughter going out ghost hunting, then."

Jordin looked away. "No . . . he'd probably say we're playing with fire. Just like Derek."

I still hadn't met Jordin's fiancé, and the two of us hadn't discussed him since what Jordin had told me at the Stanley Hotel. It was a touchy subject, and even though she gave me an opening, I tried to steer things in a safer direction.

"Does he remind you of your dad? Derek?"

Jordin's face was a mixture of sadness and elation. "Yeah. He really does. I guess that's a good thing. They say you always pick a mate that reminds you of your parent."

"So what did it tell you?" I couldn't resist asking.

"Hm?"

"The Ouija board."

"Oh, um . . .." Jordin's eyes darkened and her voice dropped to a mumble, "it told me my parents were going to die."

_____

The friendly staff at the Myrtles checked us in quickly and showed us to our rooms. Jordin had gladly put up enough funds to ensure that we would have the building entirely to ourselves overnight, with no other guests and even the front desk clerk being paid extra to take the night off.

Jordin also gave them enough money to allow the two of us to have our own private rooms on the ground floor, and when she mumbled something about needing to rest after the long plane ride, I silently agreed and shuffled into my own room. Best to get a good nap now to prepare for the long night ahead. And talking about Jordin's parents had seemed to cast a gloom over us both, so I was glad for the break.

I was about to lie down on the comfy-looking bed, having drawn the curtains closed and turned off all the lights, when I saw in the sunlight still stubbornly filtering through the bright-colored curtains that my door was still open.

I could've sworn I'd closed it, but gave it little thought as I pushed it closed again. This time I locked it.

Finally, I gave myself to the gloriously soft bed and hand-crafted quilt on top.

_____

Three hours later, I awoke to the sound of crying.

I opened my groggy eyes and noted that while the sun was still out, my room had grown a bit darker as I slept. So deeply asleep had I been that it took a few seconds to remember where I was.

Then I saw it. The door to my room was cracked open. Again.

Even though I'd locked it.

Beyond the small opening between door and post the distant sounds of painful sobbing drifted into the room.

My first thought was that it was Jordin, in her room several doors down the hall. She must have still been upset about speaking of her parents dying. I rose slowly from the bed and slipped out into the hall, my barefoot steps tapping lightly on the hardwood floors as I glided toward Jordin's room.

But Jordin opened her door before I could reach it and cast a significant gaze at me as she, too, listened intently to the sound. Oddly, it seemed no louder at this end of the hall than it had from my room, even though I had been certain that it was coming from this direction.

When we were close enough to speak, Jordin whispered, "You think it's her? That slave girl, Chloe?"

I shook my head, having no answers for her. "Grab your digital recorder."

Jordin spun on her heels to zip back into her room.

I stood very still and listened from my perch in the hallway, trying to get a bead on the direction of the sound. It showed no signs of stopping. It was a pitiful, soft wailing.

It suddenly hit me just as Jordin returned with her recorder in hand and already on.

"It's outside," I said.

Jordin listened and nodded eagerly in agreement, so the two of us located the nearest exit and walked around the building until we got closer to the sound. We rounded a last corner to face an empty wall of siding. Nothing was visible, but the sound was very close now.

I quickly pulled out my phone and snapped some photos of the area, set to the highest resolution my phone would allow. I didn't stop to review them; there would be time for that later. I just kept snapping until my phone ran out of memory.

"I don't see anything," said Jordin, and though her words came out in a whisper, the grounds had been so quiet aside from the sobbing that I nearly jumped when she spoke.

Apparently I wasn't the only one. Because just like that, the crying stopped and all was quiet.

"I think you scared it off," I observed. It seemed as though Jordin's statement had gotten the ghost's attention and caused it to flee the area. "Come on, let's head back inside. We won't see or hear her again anytime soon. If that really was her. Now she'll be watching for us."

Jordin hesitated, staring all around. "Sorry if I frightened you," she said quietly as she searched the landscape for any signs of the apparition.

I was a bit surprised at Jordin's soft-spoken words. Maybe there was hope for her as a genuine paranormal investigator yet.

―――――

Dusk approached rapidly, and since we were already outside, I directed us to the gazebo. The Myrtles had a man-made pond with a small island in the middle. Sitting atop that island was a tiny white gazebo, and it was the site of a lot of reported activity.

"So what's the story here?" Jordin asked, her eyes peeled and her digital recorder already going.

"The Myrtles is steeped in Civil War history," I replied. "A Confederate soldier is sometimes seen or heard in this area."

We circled the gazebo slowly from opposite sides, and then entered to meet in the middle.

"Snap to, soldier," Jordin called out. "A Union battalion just arrived! Grab your gun and fall in!"

I threw her a wicked look.

"Chill out, Maia," said Jordin. "I'm not teasing it. Just trying to get a real response."

We didn't stay there long.

———

Once we were done at the gazebo, I tried to give Jordin a tour of all the hot spots, and there were many.

The former slave shack was popular with tourists. Despite its dilapidated exterior, it was used as a private cottage for visitors and was outfitted with modern furnishings inside. We did some recording and moved on to the graveyard. The Myrtles had its own graveyard out on the surrounding land, and most of the headstones were more than a hundred years old. It was a truly creepy location, deathly quiet, but we didn't find anything. We swung through the cobblestone courtyard where Chloe was often seen leaning up against an exterior wall. Again we found nothing and had no other sign of Chloe that evening.

———

Long after nightfall, the two of us wandered back through the double front doors, diffused with opaque glass, into the main house, with video cameras, flashlights, and digital audio recorders in hand. We checked out the ladies' parlor and the gentlemen's parlor, expansive and lavish sitting rooms on the first floor. The walls were covered with costly artwork, and each room was filled with antique furniture. The empty space in this bed-and-breakfast was nothing like a traditional hotel. It was more cramped, and though there was room to move around, it seemed that every inch that could be spared was devoted to an endless collection of historic objects and luxurious furnishings. Beautiful multicolored rugs covered the hardwood floors, and elaborate candelabras hung from the ceilings of nearly every room.

After spending a few minutes in the dining room, we made our way up the old wooden stairs, covered in a long row of red carpet, and slowly went through the empty guest rooms. It didn't escape my notice that aside from a few subdued comments or ghostly provocations, Jordin had not been her usual chatty self all evening. I again wondered if talking about her parents' death that afternoon had dredged up bad memories that wouldn't go away.

And I couldn't help wondering if her parents' death had something to do with Jordin's obsession with investigating the paranormal.

Around midnight, we were walking the halls when we thought we heard footsteps in one of the guest rooms ahead. I turned to one door, sure that the sound had originated from there, while Jordin approached the door opposite me.

Before opening her door, Jordin caught herself. "You're probably right. . . ." she whispered, and spun around to join me.

Both of us were facing my door when a creaking sound came from behind us.

I turned quickly but Jordin rotated far more slowly, being the closer one to the source of the sound.

"Did you . . . ?" I whispered.

She shook her head. "Never touched it."

The door Jordin had been about to open now stood fully open.

"Um," Jordin began, her voice high and jittery, "would you call that an invitation to come in or a warning to go away?"

I threw her a look to indicate that I didn't know and then plowed straight into the now-open room. I held my video camera high, doing a full 360 of the room. It wasn't until I'd finished that Jordin joined me inside.

The room was similar in size to the room I was staying in, decorated with quaint historical accoutrements, like a portrait of a stern-looking man hanging on one wall and identical antique flower vases situated on opposite ends of an ancient hardwood bookcase.

I sat down on the edge of the room's queen-size bed. "Is anybody in here?" I said out loud. "Are you trying to reach out to us?"

Jordin sat in an antique rocking chair opposite the bed. She held her audio recorder aloft with one hand while pulling out a digital still camera with her other. She began snapping photos of every view of the room she could manage.

"It's colder in here," she whispered.

I agreed. "Air's heavy, too. Breathing is a little harder."

Jordin decided to try her hand at communicating. "Can you do something to let us know you're here? You could move something here in the room, or tap on something, or even touch one of us."

There was no response.

"What's your name?" I asked the dark, oppressive room.

Jordin let out a small gasp.

"What?" I asked.

"It just—" Jordin's eyes were wide and she was searching the entire room, breathing faster. "It felt like someone touched my hair. Like they wanted to see what it feels like."

"Maybe they did."

"Is this level of activity normal?" she asked. "Seems like we've had really good luck on every investigation we've had."

"No," I said, "this isn't normal. I mean . . . we *are* intentionally visiting places known for their extensive paranormal activity. But we've had exceptional results. If I didn't know better, I might think paranormal activity itself was up—way up—across the board. Either that, or . . . well, never mind."

"What?"

I squirmed a bit. This wasn't a theory I was eager to put forth. "Sometimes certain people can attract high levels of activity. Like, maybe it's not the place that's haunted—it's the person."

Jordin looked shocked. "A *person* can be haunted?"

I nodded. "But if either of us were, we'd be noticing it all the time. Not just during investigations. Has anything unusual happened to you lately? Like at home?"

"Not that I've noticed."

"Me neither. So that leaves us with the raised activity theory—"

My breath caught in my throat as my eyes fell on the portrait on the wall.

Jordin followed my gaze. "What?"

I stared long and hard at the portrait before answering. I had to swallow before I could get any words out. "The man in that photo," I whispered.

"What about him?" Jordin whispered back.

"He's . . . kind of . . . smiling," I said, unable to believe my eyes. In all my experiences and travels, this was something I'd never seen before. The edges of the man's lips were curled up just slightly.

"So?"

"He was frowning when we first came in."

Jordin did a double take and rose off of her seat to examine the portrait up close. She took several photos before responding. "Are you sure?"

I nodded. I was as sure as I was sitting on that bed. But she didn't have to take my word for it. I turned off my video camera and rewound the footage to my circle in place of the room when I entered.

"Look," I said, pointing at the camera's LCD viewer. The camera never stopped moving, but the image of the portrait was perfectly clear. The man was definitely scowling.

Jordin let out a shuddering breath and rubbed her arms. "Look at that!" she whispered. "That's *crazy!*"

Much as I hated to adopt her terminology, there wasn't another word that did it justice.

Crazy, indeed.

The next morning around eleven, I was woken up by Jordin knocking on my door. The knocks became louder, and it wasn't until I feared she might break the door down that I finally roused from the comfortable bed.

"You have to hear this!" she said, and billowed past me to sit on the edge of my bed.

"Sure, come on in," I yawned, apparently to myself.

I sat next to her on the bed and only then realized that Jordin was holding her digital voice recorder in her hand. Her eyes were huge and her complexion pale.

I was a little nonplussed that she'd already begun reviewing the evidence we gathered last night, having hoped that she would wait until we were back in New York to analyze the data after gaining a little distance from the experience.

The minute I was seated, she hit the *Play* button, having already cued it up to what she wanted me to hear. She had the device turned up so loud that our ears were hit by an unpleasant level of static. But behind the white noise, a deep, throaty voice could be heard.

"I like the blonde," it growled.

Now my eyes went wide as I glanced up at Jordin. I was startled for two reasons.

One, managing to record a disembodied voice that was so clear and easy to understand was all but unheard of. Most recorded voices were garbled at best, and took the trained ears of numerous investigators to come to a consensus on what they might be saying.

And two, I was a brunette. So the voice could only be describing Jordin. Possibly even threatening her.

"That's one of the best EVPs I've ever heard," I said, suspicious that the recording had been tampered with or our surroundings had been compromised when it was recorded. "Where was it taken?"

I was pretty sure I knew the answer to that question before she said it.

"The room with the portrait," she replied.

It was an amazing piece of evidence if it was legitimate, but Jordin appeared unhinged.

"Does this freak you out?" I asked.

She looked at me like I was crazy. "It doesn't freak *you* out?"

I'd heard tons of EVPs but I'd never had one that spoke of me personally.

"I don't feel safe here," she admitted.

I nodded, understanding. "No problem. It's about time we headed for our next destination anyway. You still want to keep going?"

"Absolutely," Jordin replied, though she tried unsuccessfully to suppress a shudder as she said it.

Jordin checked us out while I loaded the rental car. We split the duties to expedite our departure. The longer we were there, the more Jordin looked like she might throw up.

When she came out to the car, I made up an excuse to duck back inside, claiming to have forgotten something.

Jordin remained in the car as I approached the front desk and asked about the conditions of our investigation last night.

The kind woman at the counter—the Myrtles's caretaker and historian, whom we'd arranged our stay with—smiled and assured me that Jordin and I were left completely alone on the premises overnight, just as requested. She winked as she noted that she wouldn't have made such a concession for anybody else, but that my reputation—and that of my parents—made it possible.

I was sure she would ask about the kind of night we had, to make me ask such a question of her. But she merely smiled and told me I had an open invitation to return anytime.

I had a feeling that if I ever took her up on the offer, Jordin would sit that trip out.

NINE

"I don't understand why you're not writing this down," said Derek, his voice growing louder with every word.

He and I sat across the desk from police sergeant Bill Rutherford, an abnormally large, muscular man whose dour, blank expression never wavered as Derek related his story to him. It felt like trying to talk to a pit bull.

"Her name is Carrie," said Derek, nodding at a blank pad that sat on Sergeant Rutherford's desk. "Carrie. Morris. And she's missing. Just like my fiancée. Jordin. Cole."

Rutherford had listened carefully to our tale: that less than twelve hours ago, Carrie Morris had gone missing the night after she found a strange symbol on her neck—Rutherford had mumbled something that sounded like "gang-related" when

I showed him the picture on my phone—just like Jordin Cole before her.

Derek had insisted on reporting Carrie's disappearance to the police, but I believed this exercise to be a waste of time. For one thing, we'd already been blown off by a wire-thin elderly woman at the university registrar's office, who had politely recited "dropouts are very common, particularly at the beginning of the school year" as if she were reading it out of a textbook. Apparently it wasn't university policy to consider every person who dropped out without telling their roommate or went off on a drunken road trip to be a missing persons case.

After hearing that, we hadn't bothered with school security, assuming we'd hear the same line.

So we ventured out to the local police department, at Derek's insistence and over my protests. I knew in my heart that there would not be a natural explanation for Jordin's and Carrie's vanishing. After a strange symbol appeared on their necks. After they'd had a week's worth of vivid nightmares. Something else was at work here.

But Derek wouldn't hear it.

"We'd like to file a missing persons report over this," said Derek when Rutherford remained silent, looking bored.

Rutherford let out a long, worn-out breath and began rummaging through a file drawer in his desk. "Fill out one of these for every person you want to report, then take 'em to the officer at the front desk," he said in a lifeless monotone. "Just be sure to notify us when your friends show up again."

Derek blinked. "Uh, no. No, no. She's not going to 'show up,' because she's *mis-sing*. As in, abducted. Taken by someone who's still out there and who needs to be stopped!"

I got up out of my chair. "Come on, Derek." I put a hand on his arm and dragged him out the door while he continued to glare at the police sergeant behind us.

When we were out in the front lobby, Derek located a seat in the waiting area where he could properly fill out the forms. He flopped down into it angrily.

"I know you think all of this is pointless," he complained, "but it wouldn't have killed you to give me a little support in there."

I sat across the aisle from him. I know I could have apologized, but I said nothing, letting him get it out of his system.

Like campus security, the police department apparently dealt with a lot of so-called "missing college students" who had a tendency to turn up drunk or high after attending some party that got out of control.

Derek was still steaming as my thoughts went elsewhere. He glanced up from his papers. "So why didn't you?"

"Hm?"

"Why didn't you say anything to help me out?"

I sighed. "Because one day I hope to work with these people, or people like them, and I'd rather not do anything to annoy them before that day comes."

Derek's shoulders slumped, understanding entering his eyes. "Oh, right. The cop thing, I forgot. Okay. I guess that's fair. I wouldn't want to take *you* to a job interview at a church. No offense."

I almost laughed. Almost. "The symbol is the key," I said. "That symbol on the back of the neck. There's got to be more to it."

"I've never seen anything like it," Derek said.

"Yeah . . . But somebody has. I think that should be our next step. But I have one more thing I want to do first."

"What?"

I barely heard him, thinking again of what the woman at the registrar's office had told us. "Come on, let's go."

———————

It was late that afternoon by the time my first task was complete, but it was well worth the effort spent.

First we returned to the registrar's office and asked if they could give us an estimate of how many students had withdrawn so far in the first week of school. When the registrar lady tried to give us the runaround, Derek did something wholly unexpected. He seemed to sense what I was up to and abruptly turned on the charm. And for a moment, I could see what Jordin saw in him. I saw what others saw in him when it was whispered around school that he was on the fast track to become one of the most influential ministers in the nation.

He was capable of incredible magnetism and charisma, a form of which he used to charm the registrar woman into giving us the information we were after. I wouldn't have believed it if I hadn't been there when it happened. He had her hanging on his every word with a smile by the time we left.

As we were leaving the office, I couldn't help asking, "You learn that from your dad?"

It was his turn to chuckle now. "All the men in my family have what we call the 'Hobbes Family Charm—you can turn it down, but you can't turn it off.' "

I rolled my eyes at his little family motto. Charming *and* cocky. Yep, I could see that being Jordin's type.

Derek's father was the pastor of some megachurch out in Texas. I didn't know which one, but he was extraordinarily popular, and quite influential, appearing often in the media as a guest panelist

or advisor on a wide range of moral issues. He had a huge following, which made me suspicious of him, but from the handful of
times I'd seen him on the news, he didn't strike me as a phony. He
actually seemed like a pretty down-to-earth guy. Someone you'd
enjoy watching the big game with, or debating some hot topic with
over a nice dinner. Derek had a lot of the same qualities.

"The registrar said that about ten students gave written notice
of their withdrawal or transfer, but none have dropped out. It's just
too early," he said, back to business. "*But*, I took the initiative to ask
about last spring and this summer semester, and she said twelve
students dropped out or simply stopped coming to class. You
thinking that these dropouts may not actually *be* dropouts?"

I shrugged. "It's just a theory. Needs confirming."

"Library?" he asked.

He caught on quick.

"Library," I said.

———————

Three hours later, we'd found evidence in police reports,
college surveys, and one noteworthy newspaper article from a
reporter in Boston that provided all the confirmation I needed.
Whatever had happened to Jordin and Carrie, it was happening
at major metro colleges all over the mid-Atlantic seaboard. Over
three hundred in the past six months.

I clicked back a page on the computer screen to look again
at the *Boston Herald* article. Written by one Pierre Ravenwood.
Seemed to be an editorial more than an actual report, and it was
buried on the back page of the Local section. But this reporter
seemed to have pieced together the strands of the same strange
happenings that Derek and I had stumbled onto. The article

mentioned the rash of dropouts at major universities across the East Coast, and suggested that the dropout rate was significantly higher there than at other colleges throughout the country. Ravenwood's article stopped just shy of suggesting that these "dropouts" weren't dropouts at all, and slyly joked that it was "almost as if some complex conspiracy were at play."

After quickly running a search for his email address, I sent Pierre Ravenwood a brief note:

> One of the "dropouts" mentioned in your article is a friend of mine. I have reason to believe that she and the others who've disappeared are in terrible danger—if they're still alive. If you have the means to investigate a company called Durham Holdings International in Copenhagen, I think you should do so. This "complex conspiracy" of yours may come into focus if you dig deep enough.

There. That seemed to sound good and juicy. Just the kind of thing an ambitious reporter wouldn't be able to ignore. I hesitated, but then as an afterthought ended the email by adding:

> The nightmare is coming, Mr. Ravenwood.

I thought it might be hours or days before I heard back from him, but I received a reply before I even logged off.

> I already suspected a connection to DHI. The question is, what do you know about it? Can you meet me in person to discuss? I promise to keep you an anonymous source if that's your wish.

I had just replied with an affirmative suggesting he call to set up a meeting when Derek reappeared. His head popped up over the cubicle barrier separating my computer station from the one next to it.

"Found it," he said.

I'd had him working on a separate task related to the second thing I wanted to do today.

"Columbia has a visiting professor in the Department of History and Archaeology. Sounds like exactly what you're looking for. Apparently the guy's pretty famous. Name's Dr. Ronald Eccleston."

I looked at my watch. It was four o'clock already. We'd both missed our entire day's class schedule, which still bothered me, even though the last few days—not to mention what happened in my room Monday night—had proven that I was caught up in something a lot more important than my studies.

"Where is he now?"

"Last lecture of the day," Derek reported.

"Where?" I asked, quickly rising from the desk.

―――――――――

We made it to Eccleston's classroom just as he was wrapping up his lecture. Not wanting to interrupt, we waited out in the hall for the room to clear, which took a surprisingly long time, as Eccleston seemed to have quite a few admirers who felt the need to offer their praises of him after the class ended.

Once we were satisfied that the last student was gone, we headed inside. Eccleston was still up at the front of the large room, which had stadium-style seating and a huge old-fashioned blackboard that stretched across the entire front of the room. The professor had written across a good three-quarters of it during his lecture, and was now taking the time to erase all of it himself.

A classy leather briefcase sat open on the room's desk, beside a black golf hat. The professor himself wore an all-black suit and tie that made him resemble a Mafia hit man. He looked like he might be in his late forties, which meant a slightly sagging stomach and a light gray goatee that was so full it looked like fur.

"Dr. Eccleston?" I began, approaching him from the side entrance to the room.

"Yes," he said absently, not turning around to acknowledge us, "thank you, dear. I'm glad you enjoyed the lecture, but I really have no more time for personal requests today, thank you." He had an American accent, though he spoke with the unnecessarily formal diction so often used by a lot of highly educated professors.

He was still erasing the chalkboard as I drew near, Derek right behind me. "I'm sorry, sir, we weren't in your lecture today. I was just hoping—"

"If you weren't in my class," he interrupted, his back still to us, "you really have no business being in here, now do you, dear."

All right, I admit it. I didn't like the way he kept calling me "dear." It probably seemed like a quaint, charming little affectation to him, but it rankled me.

"Look, Professor," I started again. "I don't have time for your—"

"Sir," Derek jumped in, seeing the irritated look on my face. "If we could just have a moment—"

I rolled my eyes and walked up to the professor until I was standing right over his shoulder.

"Now listen here," Eccleston said, his voice turning

authoritative. As he finally turned to face us, he was saying, "I've already told you I can't—"

But he saw something he wasn't expecting when he faced me. I'd pulled out my cell phone and called up the photo I took of Carrie Morris's neck. When Eccleston turned, the tiny screen was right at eye level.

He startled for a moment but then his eyes focused on the image on the screen and grew wide for just a brief second as he took it in. He glanced at me, then back at the symbol, and then at me again, and Derek, as well.

When he spoke, he was no longer looking at me as the famous professor. All formalities had been dropped, and his tone was one of urgency. "Who did you say you are?"

Eccleston's temporary office was a spacious room almost the size of a classroom itself. But where I'd expected to find plenty of "old world" wooden furnishings, huge armchairs, walls covered in books, and a smoking lamp or two, instead it was more like a state-of-the-art computer lab.

Not what I'd expected from a world-renowned art historian.

"Have a seat, please," he said, throwing off his sports jacket and placing his hat and briefcase askew on his primary desk. He walked to the wall and retrieved a rather large and impressive laptop computer. But instead of sitting down behind his desk, he sat in another chair next to us so that we could see what he was doing.

We'd spent the ten-minute walk to his office explaining where I'd taken the picture of the symbol, and I could see that his sci-entific curiosity had gotten a jolt of excitement at the prospect of a new puzzle to solve. The fact that someone as versed in symbology as this guy was, was *this* excited over what I showed him told me that this was no ordinary symbol.

"Ms. Peters, would you kindly email the photograph from your phone to me?" he asked, and then followed the question with a spelling of his email address.

I did as he asked, and then Eccleston got to work on his computer, quickly retrieving the image from his in-box and opening it in some kind of imaging program.

"Have you ever seen anything like this before?" Derek asked.

"I don't believe so, no," said Eccleston, who had eyes only for the prize on his computer screen. "Look at the finely detailed engravings around the edges. . . . It's not symmetrical at all, yet it has a certain balance to it . . . just spectacular—it really is quite spectacular for something so small, isn't it?" He seemed to be descending into his own little world now. "And to achieve that kind of perfection on human skin, of all canvases . . ."

I started to fear that he'd forgotten we were there, so I spoke up, trying to clarify his statements. "So you don't recognize it, then?"

Eccleston glanced at me, his eyebrows raised in excitement. "Oh no, I didn't say that, dear. This mark has telltale cultural indicators, just as all symbols do. I'm certain I can identify it, but it will take some time. . . . It almost looks alchemical in origin, but it's much more complex. . . ." He was talking to himself again.

Sensing that our presence was more a courtesy extended by Dr. Eccleston than anything else, and also that we were likely to just slow him down, I stood and nodded toward the door. Derek agreed and followed me.

"So you'll call us then, when . . . ?" I called out.

"Yes, yes! Of course, my dear, of course," he replied, leaning in so close to his computer screen I was sure it had to be doing harm to his eyes. "Fear not—I have your phone number right here, at the bottom of the email you sent. . . . I'll let you know the moment I decipher it."

Good enough for me.

———————

We were exiting the building when my phone rang. My hopes jumped instantly that Dr. Eccleston had already had a breakthrough, but it wasn't a number my phone recognized.

"Hello?" I said as we continued to walk.

"Maia?" said the caller in a hollow, despondent sort of way.

I stopped walking and nearly dropped the phone on the sidewalk. I recognized the voice.

"Jordin?!" I shouted.

Derek tripped over his own feet and scraped his knees on the pavement before jumping back up.

"The nightmare is coming," whispered Jordin. "Follow the symbol, Maia! The symbol holds the answer."

The line went dead. My heart gave a profound thud against my chest, skipping a very long beat, and then I gasped for air like I'd been underwater for a full minute.

The world blinked and swam, and before I knew it, Derek had grabbed my arm and helped lower me to the ground, where it was all I could do to keep from losing myself to the darkness.

St. Louis Cemetery #1

New Orleans, Louisiana

Opened in 1789

are there more dead here per square
inch than any other place in the world?
(need to research)

TEN

MARCH 5TH

"We shouldn't stay here long," I said as we walked through the white brick fence surrounding St. Louis Cemetery. It was already after eleven, and streetlamps from out on the sidewalk were the only source of light. It was a sultry New Orleans night, and sounds of parties and general revelry met us from nearly all sides.

Jordin looked at me teasingly, holding her usual video camera in one hand and her digital voice recorder in the other. "Surely you're not frightened by this place?"

I didn't share her humor. "This *place*? No. The vandals and grave robbers and thugs who frequent it in the dark? Yes."

Jordin turned serious, almost alarmed. "Then why did we come?"

"Because it's haunted."

"It's tiny," she complained. "Just one city block."

"Which is exactly why it has so much activity," I told her. "There are more than *a hundred thousand* people buried here, mostly in above-ground crypts. This tiny city block is a concentrated paranormal nexus."

Right on the edge of the French Quarter, St. Louis Cemetery was one of three different graveyards in New Orleans to go by that name. The one I'd selected was by far the smallest, but also the oldest and most famous. It was filled with above-ground granite tombs of wildly differing architectural styles and sizes. All of them had once been white, but now most had faded to gray thanks to decades of mold and mildew.

It was unlike any location we'd investigated yet, because it was outdoors and completely open to the public. I'd already warned Jordin on the drive in that there was no way to seal it off for our investigation, which meant that we had to contend with sneaking around the above-ground burial vaults in the dark knowing that any shadowy figures we might chase could very well turn out to be flesh and blood.

"Come on," I said, leading the way into the interior.

"Where are we going?" Jordin asked.

"You asked me the other night about voodoo, so I want to show you something. The most famous tomb here belongs to Marie Laveau, a powerful and influential voodoo priestess who lived in the 1800s. It's said that people saw her wandering the streets of New Orleans after her death, and some claim to see her still."

"Okay," Jordin said, playing along. "How come you seem skeptical?"

"Marie Laveau was a genuine historical figure, and she really was known as the Voodoo Queen. But does she haunt the cemetery? I've seen strange things happen here, but no more so in front of Laveau's crypt than any other."

We arrived at the tomb, and I again noted that it was fairly unremarkable, hardly the most beautiful or ornate in the graveyard. It was tall and narrow and white all over, with a bronze plaque affixed to its bottom left corner identifying it as Laveau's crypt.

"What's with all the junk?" Jordin asked.

Surrounding the tomb's base were "offerings" to Laveau—beans, tiny statues, candles, and even coins. Much worse was the graffiti covering the tomb; it was the same mark, over and over, but in different colors and sizes. Three x's in a row, again and again and again.

"Just a bit of local color," I replied. "Tourists ask for Laveau's help with some great desire. The tradition says that if you knock three times on the head of the crypt to wake her up, draw three x's on the crypt, knock three times again, and state your wish, she may grant it."

"That's ridiculous," Jordin said with an odd look on her face. Almost like she knew it was absurd but *wanted* it to be true.

"Is all this about your parents, Jordin?" I blurted out. I half wished I hadn't and half wondered why I'd waited so long to say it. "Just tell me, all right? I won't judge you."

She sighed, long and hard. "Yes, okay? Happy now? I want to talk to my parents. That's it."

I couldn't help being curious. Her dogged determination to touch the paranormal was something I had pondered again and again since we'd met. But I wasn't so heartless as to touch upon a painful subject with a person I hardly knew.

Until now. I don't know what made me ask it this night. Something about her expression when I talked about Marie Laveau granting wishes. In that moment, I just knew.

"It's probably impossible," I said quietly.

"I don't care!" she replied, tears swelling in her glassy eyes. "I have to try. They died when I was *thirteen*. You don't know what it's like, Maia. . . . I mean, have you ever lost anyone?"

I grimaced, trying to think. "I lost my grandmother a few years back. But we weren't close. How did they die?" I tried not to be indelicate, but she was finally talking about it, and I wasn't going to miss the chance.

"Car crash. But you have to understand . . . they died *together*. I didn't lose just one of them, it was both, at the same time. My mom and my dad, gone in an instant. Imagine just becoming a teenager and finding yourself completely alone in the world. No one to take care of you. The two constants in your life, snuffed out during one of the most difficult stages of life. I'd give anything to see them again, talk to them. Touch—"

Jordin's words were cut off midsentence when she let out a sharp gasp. She raised her arm and pointed over my shoulder.

I spun and looked, but saw nothing.

"What?" I asked. "What was it?"

"There was a shadow!" she whispered. "As soon as I looked at it, it took off *crazy*-fast! That way!" She pointed farther up the row, and I stepped out into the open to get a better look. I couldn't see anything moving.

"Are you sure it wasn't a person running by?"

"No, it was just a shadow!" she said, resolute. "It moved by itself! Only it wasn't up against a wall or anything, it was right out in the open!"

"Like it had its own mass and weight?"

She nodded eagerly.

"Show me," I urged her, and we ran.

I had a very good idea what we were probably chasing: Jordin had seen a shadow person, a phenomenon I was well acquainted with. They were, simply put, a form that ghosts sometimes took when trying to manifest. Shadow people had three-dimensional physics completely unlike real shadows and moved independent of their surroundings. Some investigators believed them to be demonic in origin, but I'd never seen proof either way.

We looked left and right down the aisles and rows as we ran toward the far end of the cemetery, but it was hard to make out one shadow from another. If a shadow person wanted to disappear, it would be easy enough with all of the real shadows cast by the crypts—some of which were well over ten feet tall.

"Unless it moves again, I don't know that we'll ever find it," I whispered.

Jordin's eyes grew big as she exclaimed, "Ooh! Ooh! I almost forgot!"

She pulled off her backpack and whipped something out of it with great flourish and pride. I recognized it instantly.

"Nice!" I said with sincerity, and took the item as she offered it to me.

ROBIN PARRISH

"A little surprise I ordered a while ago and had shipped to arrive to us this morning," Jordin said with a grin.

It was a thermal imaging camera. It worked just like a regular video camera, only instead of recording what the human eye sees, it recorded any and all sources of heat. It was shaped vaguely like the handle of a gas pump, but with a shortened nozzle where the camera's aperture was. Behind that, above the grip, was a generously sized screen that showed everything the camera picked up. Red meant hot, blue meant cold, and there was a rainbow of temperatures in between.

They were also terribly expensive, so much so that most amateur investigators couldn't afford them.

I'd worked with these devices before—my parents owned one—and found them invaluable. If there was a shadow person here, the thermal imager would pick it up without a doubt.

I turned it on and did a slow sweep of our surroundings. Unsurprisingly, the marble vaults all registered as dark blue—cold and lifeless. This was a good thing if our friend should return; it meant his red-hot outline would show up on the imager in sharp contrast to his surroundings. There would be no missing him.

I held the thermal imager out in front of us, and we began exploring the area. I kept my eyes glued to the screen while Jordin moved in front, guiding our path.

"Maia, do you believe in curses?" she asked, in a small-talk tone of voice.

I felt a bit of whiplash. Just minutes ago Jordin had been angry at me for figuring out her secret. Now she was making chitchat about curses the way other girls talk about their favorite brand of makeup. Was she for real?

And even though I wasn't looking at her, I noted how much effort Jordin was expending trying to sound casual when she asked the question.

"You mean like hexes and gypsies and stuff?"

Jordin paused, as if reconsidering this line of conversation. Then she let out a breath. "Do you think it's possible for a *person* to be cursed? You said the other day that certain people can attract ghosts."

I thought carefully about my response before giving it. "My parents have met with clients who had above-average amounts of encounters with the paranormal, who believed themselves cursed. My dad doesn't put much stock in those kinds of superstitions, preferring to find a scientific explanation for everything. I would probably side with him on this."

"Because it isn't something . . . scientifically verifiable?" she probed. She continued walking in front of me, not making eye contact.

"Why are we talking about curses, Jordin?"

She shook her head. "I used to know someone who thought she was cursed, but it was a long time ago."

"Who?" I asked.

"Just an old friend."

I saw something on the thermal imager. "There, look!"

The outline of what looked like a man of above-average height and normal build stood some fifty feet away, but there was no way to tell if it was facing our direction or away from us. The surroundings registered blue and black, but the shadow person was a mixture of distinctly yellow and orange.

We both looked up. To the naked eye, there was nothing. The

shadow person, if that's what it was, was camouflaged perfectly by the graveyard's darkest crevices.

Jordin took another look at the viewer and launched into a sprint toward the shadow person. I followed close behind, trying my best to hold the thermal camera steady enough to see if the figure moved. But it was too hard to run flat out and keep the camera trained on one spot, and before I knew it, the figure was no longer on my screen.

"Where'd it go?" I whispered as we pulled up at the spot where it had been standing. I turned the camera 360 degrees, trying to spot the shadow person again.

"I think I saw it go this way," Jordin said, pointing to the right.

We turned down the aisle she indicated and followed at a walk this time, catching our breath and taking the time to inspect each side row on both sides of the aisle. If it was a real, living person we saw on the camera, they were very good at hiding. If it was a shadow person, they were even better.

By the time we reached the end of the row, I had a feeling the apparition was gone for good. There had been no sign of it by infrared, flashlight, or any other means. So we returned to wandering the small courtyard aimlessly, hoping to get lucky again.

Ten minutes later, Jordin tried making small talk once more.

"So have you ever seen—" She stopped and I heard a sound as if Jordin had tried to gasp but her lungs clenched halfway through.

I spun and saw that Jordin was frozen, like a movie that had been paused. She wasn't twitching; she wasn't even breathing. Her color had drained completely away.

All of this I took in instantly, and then I turned to follow Jordin's line of sight off to the right. But I saw nothing save white crypts in the darkness.

"What is it?" I whispered.

She gulped in a lungful of air. "I saw a face! But *just* a face—there was no body!"

I shivered.

I ran ahead of her and looked where she was looking. "Are you sure?"

"*Yes!*" she shrieked. "It peeked out from behind that crypt. Like it was hiding but wanted to get a look at us." She placed a hand over her heart as if trying to force it to beat slower. Her complexion was still alarmingly pale.

We ran to the crypt together and walked all the way around it. There was no sign of whatever she had seen. I didn't catch anything on the thermal camera, either.

"It's colder here," I whispered, my throat tight, my muscles tensed.

She rotated slowly and nodded in agreement.

I looked at the objects in her hands. "Did you get it on video?"

Jordin's eyebrows jumped a foot into the air. "Oooh, maybe!"

She knelt to the ground and quickly rewound her recording. It only took a moment. She stood again and we watched the replay together.

A chill ran down my spine as the image came up. The face was tiny and barely visible in the dark, and would look a lot better on a larger screen whenever we got around to reviewing the evidence, but it was there. It had a pale gray tint, and you could only see about half of it—the other half was obscured in shadow. But the eyes gave off a slightly yellow glow, and it was unnerving.

"That doesn't look human," I observed, as burning bile slid up my throat.

Jordin didn't reply.

———————

An hour later, we took a break and sat on the ground to recharge with some snacks Jordin had brought along.

"Can I ask you something personal?" Jordin said.

I sighed. *Oh, yay. Let's talk about me.*

"Okay."

"Why are you helping me?" she asked.

"You hired me, remember?"

She smirked at me. "That's not a good enough reason. You have such passion for this. A lot more than I'm paying you for. So tell me the truth. Why are you really helping me?"

"Isn't it obvious?" I turned to her with great sincerity and replied, "I'm a giver, Jordin."

That's the first and only time I can remember making Jordin Cole laugh out loud.

———————

Half an hour later, we jumped up from our seats on the ground when I spotted the shadow person again. But I lost it before we could even get to our feet, and wasn't sure which way it had gone at the end of the row.

I instructed Jordin to go left while I went right.

I had just rounded the next corner when my heart pounded like it was being hit by a sledgehammer. I put a hand to my chest and almost fell to my knees, instead bracing myself by leaning against the nearest stone crypt.

Something isn't right, I realized, finally seeing it. There had been moments when my heart had beat irregularly hard on almost every investigation Jordin and I had been on, but only now did it enter my consciousness that a pattern was emerging.

I didn't feel scared. I rarely allowed myself to be frightened during investigations. But what I was feeling now left me gasping for breath like I was drowning. My chest was so tight it was painful, and the intensity of the pain only made the panic more intense.

This wasn't fear beneath my chest. It was something a lot worse.

————————

It was earlier than usual when we ended the investigation. We'd teetered on feeling unsafe for most of the evening, but a group of wildly partying frat guys that passed by on the sidewalk outside pushed us over the edge. Jordin muttered something about being spent for one night, so we returned to our hotel just before two. After we'd been there over an hour and I was sure Jordin would be fast asleep next door, I called a cab and had the driver take me to the closest emergency room.

I knew there would be a long wait. I'd never been to an emergency room when there wasn't. This one was almost two hours, so it was nearly dawn by the time a doctor saw me.

They ran about half a dozen tests on my heart, with all sorts of contraptions, and roughly ninety minutes later, the verdict was delivered.

A palpitation. I'd had a heart palpitation.

I couldn't believe it.

I couldn't fathom sleeping that morning after I returned to the hotel, choosing instead to hit the shower while agonizing over this news. All I could think about was what this meant to my career goals. How could I be an effective police detective with a heart that could collapse into full-bore arrhythmia at any time? It wasn't something I could hide; it was bound to betray me in the field.

I'd be a joke, laughed out of every job interview I dared to undertake.

Tears soaked my towel almost as much as the shower water did. How could this be happening? It was a total emasculation of everything I wanted to do with my life!

What was causing it? Was there an effective treatment? I would have to wait until I got home to find out; the doctor in New Orleans was reluctant to offer long-term options, suggesting that "any number of reasons" could be to blame. He said it was a "somewhat mild case" and preferred to let my primary care physician in New York handle the full diagnosis and treatment. So seeing him would be job one when we returned home.

But that was still three days away. There was one more stop on our little tour of the South, and it was a location less known to be haunted than the last two. But I knew this place all too well, and it was not a haunting to be undertaken lightly.

I worried that it might be too much for me to handle in this condition. Was it wise to investigate the paranormal with a weak heart? I'd already had several flare-ups while in the field, which could have been caused by being startled or alarmed. Did I really want to tempt fate?

By morning, I'd decided that this little heart thing wouldn't defeat me, wouldn't control me, and wouldn't define me. I was still Maia Peters, and I was going to find a way to get past this.

ELEVEN

After Jordin's phone call, I'm happy to say I managed to avoid blacking out entirely. Making a fool of myself out in the middle of the school grounds, with dozens of people passing by, was never high on my priority list.

I vaguely recall Derek saying things like "Jordin?!" "Is she okay, Maia?" "Is Jordin alive?!" in a frenzied voice. I don't think less of him for it. I'm sure he was concerned that I was okay but just couldn't help himself at hearing me talk to his fiancée on the phone.

After a few minutes of deep breathing, I was more or less steady again. I talked him out of taking me back to the hospital, but I was going to die of embarrassment if we didn't get away from the crowd that was starting to form. I heard whispers begin to imply that I was drunk. Or worse.

So Derek guided me to a quiet corner in the back of a fast-food place just one block away. He insisted on getting us both sodas—I think he was concerned I might have low blood sugar or something—but was unrelentingly cheerful as he set off to do it. More than five times as he all but dragged me inside the tiny restaurant, he'd said to himself, "She's still alive!" or "Thank you, God."

While he stood occupied in line at the front counter, I took the opportunity to pop a pill. I also grabbed a few napkins so I could write down some thoughts. My head was swimming with possibilities, and I needed to connect some of these dots. Derek returned while I was still lost in thought and placed my drink in front of me.

"You're sure it was her?" he asked, for the third time.

"I'm sure, Derek."

"Can I see your phone?" he asked.

I saw little point in arguing and handed it over, though I knew he would find nothing useful. I'd told him while I was taking deep breaths on the ground that I had pressed the *Talk* button on the phone without looking at the caller ID. And once the call was over and I was back on my feet, I looked back at the "recent calls" list and saw that no call had been logged. In fact, it didn't even look like my phone had been activated in the last hour. So no phone number had been recorded for the call, and there was no evidence that my phone had even been in use. Jordin may have been speaking to me through my phone, but it wasn't with the help of Verizon.

Derek mashed buttons on my phone like a mad man, as if

trying to will it to reveal its secrets to him. "How can someone call you and not actually activate your phone?" he asked.

I took a deep breath. I couldn't put it off anymore. It was obvious that, whether Derek would like it or not, something very *not* normal was responsible for what was happening all around us.

I gently took the phone out of his hand and pocketed it. "I need to tell you something," I announced, not quite meeting his gaze as he looked at me with anticipation.

Here goes, I thought.

"I saw Jordin the night before you came to my dorm looking for her."

Derek nearly stood up out of his seat. "What?!"

"Breathe, Derek," I said. "It's not what you think."

"Why didn't you tell me!"

"You wouldn't have believed me—"

"What does that mean?"

I began to see that this wasn't going to go well. "I saw Jordin at that new Ghost Town amusement park. But she wasn't *there*. Not physically. She appeared to me—and only me—in the form of an apparition. A ghost."

Derek's posture froze. He didn't register disbelief, amusement, or anything else as he continued to stare at me. It was like someone had taken a photo of him, freezing him in place.

Finally he leaned back in his seat and contemplated my words deeply, looking me in the eye. I knew he had to be wondering if I was serious or if I was crazy in the head. Was I enjoying a sick joke? Had I really uttered aloud the words he thought he'd heard?

"A ghost," he repeated softly, as if afraid someone else in the restaurant might overhear him saying such a ridiculous word. Or maybe he'd lowered his voice because of the anger I saw bubbling beneath his surface and he'd trained himself to keep such things suppressed.

I nodded, bracing myself for the onslaught. I was mad, or I was cruel, or I had been dreaming. Any or all of these accusations were about to be shoved down my throat.

He cleared his throat and looked at me as if he was about to counsel me with his best pastorly advice. "Tell me exactly what happened."

"It was the end of the Haunted House. Except what happened wasn't part of the tour. I was surrounded by this white mist that I can only describe as possessing intelligence, because it moved around me in ways that no naturally occurring airflow could. And for just a second, I saw a face in the mist, and it was Jordin. She called me by name, and she said to me the very same phrase that Carrie Morris heard in her dreams. The same phrase that was used as a threat right after my room was turned upside down. The same phrase that Jordin whispered to me ten minutes ago on the phone before asking me to help her. *The nightmare is coming.* Then she and the mist vanished."

Derek stared at me for a very long time. He neither frowned nor smiled, though he did run his fingers through his hair at one point. But he never took his eyes off of me, as if waiting for me to crack and reveal that it was all a joke.

"Why didn't you tell me?" he repeated, and I could barely hear his voice.

"You wouldn't have believed me," I said again. "You still don't, do you?"

He frowned. "I don't know you to be a liar. If you say you experienced something, I have no reason to presume you didn't. We just have different frames of reference for what an experience like the one you described really is. If you say it happened, I believe you. But that doesn't mean what you saw is really what you think it was."

I tried to swallow his words. "So . . . you believe I saw her, you just don't believe it was really her?"

He hesitated. "I don't know. I don't believe in ghosts, so if it really was her you saw, there has to be another explanation. But at least now I know why you're so obsessed with helping me find her. And don't misinterpret that as ingratitude. You're doing a lot more than helping—you seem to be the epicenter of all the action."

I couldn't argue with that. Though I had no idea why everything was happening to me.

"Aren't you ever going to ask me *why* I don't believe in ghosts?" asked Derek, leaning back in his seat.

"No," I replied. There was no need.

"It's more than just my religious beliefs," he barreled on, ignoring my response. "It's illogical. There are so many things about haunting reports that make no sense. The clothes thing or why ghosts are always stuck in one place and not able to move on?"

"I respect that your particular areas of interest give you a uniquely colored worldview," I said slowly, with more patience than I was feeling.

Derek offered his best grim smile. "Which is a really nice way of saying, 'I could explain it to you, but your rigid beliefs will prevent you from accepting anything I say.' "

I stopped for a moment and stared at him in mild curiosity. He was surprising, this one.

"Maybe we should just agree that I see the world one way and you see it differently," I tried, attempting diplomacy.

But Derek was restless. "What is a ghost? Define it."

"A ghost is regarded as a disembodied soul. The idea has been around since—"

"—since ancient times, I know," he finished. "People have reported encounters with the dead for millennia. I'm a religious studies major."

I crossed my arms and examined him. "All right, then, you know so much about my opinions. . . . I know what you think, too. I know exactly what you believe all hauntings really are. Demons."

"Absolutely," he replied. "And that's why Jordin shouldn't have been dabbling in this stuff. It's dangerous—and not just physically."

I pursed my lips and narrowed my eyes. "That's not good enough," I said.

Derek was caught off guard. "What?"

" 'Demonic activity' is not a compelling enough answer for all of the things happening under the umbrella of 'paranormal activity.' I'm sorry, but it's not. And you're not qualified to say otherwise."

I knew Jordin wouldn't have wanted the two of us to get into this, and she would have advised either one of us, separately, not to start something with the other. But backing down from a challenge isn't my style.

"I'm not *qualified* to have my own opinion?" Derek retorted. "I thought everyone was entitled to their own opinion."

"Sure, but if you have no personal experience with the subject matter, then how is your opinion in any way valid? Christians base a lot of their opinions on what they're taught and precious few on anything learned through firsthand experience. Even this stuff you're telling me right now about ghosts being nothing but demons, you're just regurgitating opinions—from your dad, probably, no offense—you've been told all your life."

Derek leaned back in his seat, listening to my argument with great interest and a wry smile. Clearly I wasn't the only one who enjoyed a challenge.

"I respect my father more than I respect any other person alive," he began. "But he would be the first to tell you that I am my own man. Because he was the one who pushed me to be an independent thinker, to *own* my beliefs and know why I believed them. And believe it or not, he and I disagree about quite a few things. Doctrinal issues, mostly—"

I put up a single finger. "Have you ever encountered a ghost? Yes or no?"

"Not that I'm aware of," he replied.

"Then how can you be so sure they're not real?" I asked, pressing my point. "I mean, even as a Christian, I don't see the disconnect for you. Christians believe in life after death. Why can't they believe in ghosts?"

"Christians believe," he said, speaking with authority, "that death results in your soul being routed to one of two places—heaven or hell. There's no room for dawdling on earth in between."

"But that's the thing," I said. "We *don't know* the mechanics of how it works. Nobody does, because no one has died and come back with indisputable evidence of what it's like. So many people with near-death experiences have reported seeing the bright light beckoning them to 'cross over,' but nearly every story like that implies that in order to move on, you have to *decide*. You have to choose to 'go toward the light.' "

Derek sat up straighter. It wasn't hard to imagine that he'd been wanting to get this topic out in the open for a long time. "Why would a person be allowed the choice to stay here—even if only for a little while—if their final destination is eternal punishment in hell? Criminals don't get to choose the day and time of their judgment.

"Or if their final destination is eternal paradise in heaven," he continued, "why would they *want* to stay behind here on earth, a place that in comparison to heaven is wretched at best?"

"All right," I replied, my wheels spinning, "say that's all true. Die and go directly to heaven or hell, don't pass Go, don't collect two hundred dollars. Who's to say, then, that those escorted to heaven after they die aren't allowed to come back and visit from time to time? Don't look at me like that—I'm serious! I can accept that hell is a prison, but is heaven a prison, too? Redeemed souls check in, but they don't check out? The Bible offers precious little information when it comes to the workings of heaven and eternal life. How can we say with absolute authority that occasional visits to the mortal realm aren't allowed?"

Derek squinted his eyes. "We can't," he conceded.

A moment of silence passed as I enjoyed my brief triumph. But he rallied with a new approach.

"Tell me something. What belief system do you subscribe to? Spiritualism? New Age?"

I grimaced. Why did everyone always assume that if you were open to the existence of ghosts, you had to be a Spiritualist?

"In my experience, people who trust in those kinds of belief systems tend to practice very dangerous things. Rituals and such, that—whether knowingly or not—often invite unwanted things into their lives."

"Unwanted things," Derek echoed. "Like demons."

"For example."

He almost smiled. It was the first time I'd seen his eyes light up since Jordin had gone missing. "That's a starter for a whole other conversation right there," he said. "But before we get side-tracked . . . You never answered my question. What do you believe in?"

"As it happens, my mother raised me Catholic."

Derek noticed the distinct phrasing. "So you don't practice?"

"Not since I became an adult. My mother required it of me, regularly taking me to mass, enrolling me in catechism and all that. My father thought it was nonsense, but he knew better than to argue. He's agnostic, and the two of them settled long before I was born on letting each other cling to his or her own belief without trying to change the other."

"But your mother believes what you believe—about ghosts. Doesn't she?"

Has he seen my parents' show? I wondered. The differing views of my parents were a unique aspect of the show, and one that made it so popular. "My mother was born and raised in Mexico City, where Catholicism mixed freely with mysticism and superstitions like the Day of the Dead. I suppose you could say she's fashioned her own beliefs that take into account both the teachings of the Bible and the paranormal things she's seen and experienced for herself."

"And is that what you've done?" Derek asked. "Formed your own belief system by picking and choosing the tenets of various theologies that you find most fashionable?"

I was sure I'd just been insulted, though I couldn't quite put my finger on the exact spot where it'd happened. "It will no doubt surprise you to learn that I believe the same things that you believe, about the Bible and God and Jesus. I just believe . . . a bit *more*. And don't act like I'm unusual or something—there are plenty of Christians in the world who believe in ghosts.

"Even the disciples believed in ghosts. That was their first thought when they saw Jesus walking toward them on the lake. And also when He was resurrected. I know that one by heart. He said, 'Touch me and see; a ghost does not have flesh and bones, as you see I have.' He doesn't lecture them on whether ghosts are real or not. He's alive, that's what matters. And that's just the New Testament. Don't get me started on Saul using the Witch of Endor to conjure up Samuel. Are you telling me Samuel was a demon?"

Derek stared at me with slitted eyes for a very long time. "I don't know," he finally admitted. "But Saul's choices were evil. Nothing good came of it."

It was my turn to lean back in my seat. "I don't like a religion that doesn't leave room for questions. *Don't* sit there and tell me that ghosts are an absolute impossibility when the very text your entire belief system is based on not only doesn't rule out the notion that they exist, but actually refers to them more than once as if they're real."

Adrenaline was coursing through my system as I finished my little speech, and I almost felt bad for Derek. He looked as though I'd slapped him across the face.

"My biggest question," he whispered, "is what's happened to Jordin."

As if in answer, my phone rang. I checked the screen and this time it was a real call.

"Hello?"

"Ms. Peters?" said Dr. Eccleston. "Is your friend with you? I need to see you in my office at once."

"What is it?" I asked.

"I deciphered your symbol. I believe you're going to be very surprised at what I found."

I looked at Derek meaningfully. "We'll be right there."

———————

On Eccleston's computer screen was something remarkable. It was a perfect rendering of the complicated symbol from the back of Carrie Morris's neck, which the professor had somehow extracted from its original image and manipulated in three dimensions.

"I kept thinking," explained Eccleston, "it was so complex, it was like looking at more than one symbol at a time. And then it hit me. . . ." His index finger reached out and stabbed a single key, and the symbol on the screen rotated ninety degrees sideways to reveal three distinct black shapes, stacked on top of each other. All three were fashioned out of a similar iconography. "It *is* more than one symbol," he finished, clearly proud of himself. "Three, to be exact, intertwined and overlapping each other like a tied knot. The image you supplied was so small, it took some creative extrapolation to see all three symbols in their original state. There are several lines—like this vertical one down the center, and this outer curve—that overlap perfectly. Once I realized this, I recognized all three immediately. Then it was just a matter of modeling—"

"What are they?" Derek interrupted. "What do they mean?"

"They are ancient alchemical symbols," Eccleston replied with a hint of reverence in his voice. He tapped another key and they swiveled back to a front-on view, but slid apart so we could see all three more clearly. He pointed to each in turn as he explained. The first looked like a lowercase *m* with a strange little curl at the end. "This one is commonly known as the zodiac sign for Virgo. In alchemical terms, it essentially stands for *distillation* or *separation*," he explained.

He pointed at the second one, which was a circle with a vertical line running down its center. Breaking off from that line to the left was a horizontal line, which was looped with a second circle. "This one is less common than the other two. It appears to be a representation of lodestone. Lodestone is a natural magnet, so I believe that in this context, it represents the magnet's ability to bind one thing to another."

Eccleston's finger hovered over the final symbol. It was the simplest of the three, merely an inverted triangle with a horizontal line passing through it. "This is the alchemical symbol for earth."

The two of us were silent as his explanation sank in. It made no more sense now than it had before the professor had untangled the symbols.

"So what does it mean?" Derek asked.

Eccleston shook his head. "Well, the fact that it was found on human skin is significant. The ancients believed that symbols were more than just a language; they thought that the symbols themselves held power. Where did you say you saw this on your friend, again?"

"The spot on the back of her neck where her neck met her skull," I replied.

"Where the neck meets the skull . . ." he muttered. "Hmm."

We both looked at him. "What?" asked Derek.

"Well, this place that you describe on the back of the neck . . . It's long been theorized by pagans and parapsychologists that that could be the seat of the human soul."

The human soul . . .

I crossed myself involuntarily as a terrible thought began taking shape. I couldn't believe I was even entertaining such an idea, but the more I thought about it, the more it added up. Every piece of this crazy puzzle suddenly fit perfectly.

He allowed us a moment to process this before continuing. "If I didn't know better, I might think someone was using this trifold glyph trying to *bind* a human soul to something."

"Bind it to something?" Derek asked, not catching on. "What do you mean?"

But it was all coming into focus for me.

"Well, grammatically the word 'bind' is used when something is tethered or anchored to a specific thing or place."

That was it. I understood. I knew what was happening.

"A specific thing or place—like the earth," I said, my voice barely above a whisper.

"The third part of the symbol?" asked Derek.

My thoughts were spinning fast now, my heart pounding like mad, and my mouth barely able to keep up with what I was thinking. I faced Derek and tried to pretend Dr. Eccleston wasn't there. "All right, okay—what if . . . listen, I know how this sounds, but just think about it . . . let's say for a second that somebody, through, I don't know, some kind of advanced technology or something, found a way to *extract* a soul from a human being? The third symbol stands for distillation or separation, right? What if the combined symbol stands for a process of physically separating a soul from its body? And then *binding* that soul to the earth."

Derek stood silent, dread filling his eyes.

I nodded slowly, my eyes big and fearful. "A disembodied soul."

Derek shook his head as if clearing away cobwebs. "You're saying that someone out there did this on purpose. To Jordin and maybe Carrie? And they could be doing it to more people right now?"

I wasn't sure I was ready to commit to endorsing this altogether, because it sounded ludicrous. But it fit the facts. So I took a deep breath and said it out loud.

"What if somebody's found a way to *create* a ghost?"

———————

It was getting late, and our heads were dizzy with many thoughts of what all of this could mean. More than likely, it was just nonsense, so we agreed to turn in for the night and consider it all again with fresh perspectives. But before parting ways, we decided that our next avenue of investigation had to be finding Jordin's journal.

"I've looked everywhere," Derek told me. "Her dorm room, her condo downtown. Everywhere she normally hangs out. No one's seen it. You suppose it could still be somewhere up in Martha's Vineyard, since that's where she disappeared from?"

I nodded, thinking. "Maybe we should take a ride up there. Do you know where Jordin and her friends were staying?"

"Jordin owns a vacation home up there," said Derek.

"Of course she does," I said wistfully.

Going there ourselves might be the only way we would ever discover what path had led her to wherever she now was—or whatever she had now become.

I still don't think Derek believed me about that, even after all that'd happened. I decided to put it aside until tomorrow as I crashed in a sleeping bag in my old roommate Jill's room for the night.

I wasn't asleep yet when my phone vibrated, thanks to a very unexpected caller.

————————

"You said in your email that you have a friend among the missing students," said *Boston Herald* reporter Pierre Ravenwood, playing it cool and turning his paper coffee cup slowly in his hands as he talked.

In the rush of hearing from Jordin, I'd forgotten to expect his call. He'd made his way down from Boston and we arranged to meet in a popular coffeehouse just off campus. It was almost midnight, so the place was packed with students in need of a caffeine fix for study purposes, but we located a tiny table off to one side in the crowded room and spoke in hushed voices.

I had arrived first, but Pierre followed in less than five minutes. He was on the short side, with dark, straight hair that he wore a little longer on top than was currently in style. But he had on designer jeans, a crisp button-up shirt, and black sunglasses with lenses that were nearly clear inside the building.

I could see from the way he carried himself that Pierre was going to keep his cards close.

"At the time, I did," I replied. "Now I know *two*."

"Two," he repeated.

I nodded. "And I know for a fact that both of them experienced something very, very odd shortly before they vanished."

Pierre shifted forward in his seat a hair. "How odd?"

"Odd enough to defy conventional explanation," I told him. "I even have photographic evidence."

He took a moment to absorb this, and I saw a multitude of thoughts whiz through his brain. He pierced me with his dark eyes and said, "I'd like to see this evidence."

I interlaced my fingers and placed them on the table. "Tell me what you know. About the disappearances. And about Durham Holdings. And I'll give you the exclusive—including my photo."

I expected an argument, but he merely leaned back in his seat and considered my terms, not changing his facial expression a single tic.

There was something about watching him think that I found captivating. Everything about him seemed so even-keeled, confident, thoughtful. I wondered if he ever played poker.

He displayed several qualities I admired, and . . .

Well . . .

He was kinda cute.

"How old are you?" I asked, not caring about how brazen the question might come across.

"How old are *you*?" he fired back without missing a beat.

"Twenty-one," I replied.

"You look older," he noted, and I couldn't tell whether he was intentionally trying to provoke me or if he was just socially inept. "I'm twenty-six."

"Hmm, an older man," I remarked before I could stop myself.

I should probably interject here that whenever I meet a guy I like, I have a tendency to be a little too forward.

Okay, more than a little.

I was about to ask him if he was currently seeing anyone when he reeled the conversation back in, having decided to accept my terms.

"The disappearances have been going on for more than a year," he said. "The rate at which it happened started very slow, with just one or two students vanishing from a couple of colleges in a single state over three months' time. But it built and according to my research there's over three hundred students unaccounted for. Not very many from one place, but the total is frightening. I don't know if I was the first to pick up on it, but I was the first to write about it."

"Why isn't this all over the news? There should be Amber alerts and all that."

"Well," he said, leaning forward again and growing a teensy bit more animated, "whoever's doing this knows how to be discreet. Every person that's vanished has had a good reason for not drawing a lot of attention to their absence. Many of them are young people who are estranged from their parents for one reason or another. Others have no immediate family to miss them. Sometimes they even go to the trouble of leaving notes behind for roommates and friends to find, claiming the 'need to get away' and 'find themselves' and so on."

I let out a long breath as I considered this. I knew how the stresses of college life could get to people; I saw it every day. It wasn't inconceivable that someone out there could be taking advantage of that.

"So how did DHI fall onto your radar?" I asked.

He threw me a dark, threatening look, a nonverbal communiqué that he'd find a way to chop my head off if I repeated to anyone what he was about to say. "I have an inside source. A few days after I published my story, I started getting anonymous emails from someone claiming to work at DHI's corporate offices in Copenhagen. I doubted its veracity, of course, but over time, this person convinced me that they were legit. But DHI's security makes Fort Knox look like a day care—this company is not just vigilant, they're *paranoid* in every sense of the word—so my source has to be very, very careful.

"I still don't know anything about him or who he is. I don't know if he is a he. But I know they're scared out of their minds by something that's going on inside the company. And that something is directly related to the disappearances, or so this person's told me. Meanwhile, DHI is impenetrable. I can't even get them on the phone, and my editor thinks I'm getting paranoid, so she won't pay for a flight to Denmark. I've been trying to hire some locals in Copenhagen to do some snooping around for me, but so far I can't find anyone willing to go anywhere near these people.

"Now. I've been more than generous in what I've told you— mostly because I'm at a dead end and in desperate need of something to justify continuing this line of pursuit to my editor. So if you can connect these dots for me, let's hear it."

"The connection," I replied, "is Ghost Town."

"That amusement park?"

"Yes. I don't know how, but Ghost Town is at the heart of all of this."

From there, I told him what I knew, leaving out the heaviest paranormal bits because he didn't seem the type to swallow it. I told him about Jordin and what we knew of the circumstances surrounding her disappearance. And I told him about Carrie Morris, and how she'd vanished from Columbia literally overnight.

Pulling my cell phone out of my pocket, I said, "I don't know if I can connect every one of those dots for you, but I can show you what one of them looks like." I handed him the phone, which had the picture of the symbol on its screen.

"What is that?" he asked, taking the phone and examining the image up close from behind his heavy-rimmed rectangular glasses.

"It appeared on Carrie Morris's neck the morning before she disappeared."

He looked up at me with a strange expression, like he was trying to figure out if I was putting him on.

"There's more," I said. "A lot more. I think I know what DHI is up to, and I have a pretty good idea of what's become of all those missing students."

He eyed me carefully. "And what's that information going to cost me?"

"A willingness to believe in the impossible," I replied.

———————

By the time our meeting ended, I couldn't tell if Pierre was humoring me or if he was simply dazed at such an outlandish hypothesis. Either way, I knew I'd given him a lot to think about.

As I walked through the brisk New York night, my thoughts returned to Dr. Eccleston's discovery and our theory about what was behind all this. *Manufacturing* ghosts? Were Derek and I grasping at the implausible just because we were desperate to solve this mystery?

To my great relief, it occurred to me that Dr. Eccleston had shown no interest in my and Derek's possibly crazed musings on the mechanics of fashioning a ghost. He'd heard everything we'd said, of course, but remained far more interested in the origins of the combined symbol, and promised to let us know if he discovered anything more about it.

I returned to Jill's room and passed out almost the second my head hit the pillow.

———

It was after four in the morning when I woke up. Someone was shaking me by the shoulders.

"Maia!" the voice shouted.

I opened my eyes reluctantly, unwilling to give up my rest. Jill was leaning over me with her hands on my shoulders.

"You were screaming," she said with a worried expression. "Were you dreaming about what happened to you the other night?"

My head was still swimming in the dream I'd been having, which was definitely *not* a dream about the attack I'd suffered in my dorm room a couple nights ago. I sat up slowly.

"Yeah," I lied. "Just a bad dream. Don't worry about it. Sorry I woke you."

Whatever last vestiges of sleep that pulled at my mind were

erased as I realized that my sleeping bag was stuck to me, because I was covered in sweat.

As I lay back down and smiled reassuringly at Jill, my heart skipped a beat as my mind revisited my dream in vivid detail. In it, I was alone in a murky, empty place, running in abject terror from a dark, terrifying figure that was uttering a single phrase, over and over.

I ran a shaking hand through my hair when I was sure Jill was no longer watching me.

The nightmare is coming, the phrase passed through my mind, like fingernails on a chalkboard.

The nightmare is coming true.

USS North Carolina

Commissioned: 1941
Retired: 1947

hard work, but totally worth it!

TWELVE

Docked in its own dedicated harbor off of Cape Fear River in Wilmington, North Carolina, the USS *North Carolina* was a great metallic beast of a ship. The old warhorse did not welcome our arrival; her one hundred thirty-seven cannons and guns were a harsh, threatening reminder of just how intimidating this vessel had been in her day. Much of the seven hundred twenty-eight feet of her gray hull and her enormous towers loomed high over the shoreline, and those cannons on the deck were pointed outward in an unspoken warning.

Her teeth were bared as our car neared the welcome center. But she didn't smile.

The ship was visible long before we got close to her, and

Jordin whistled at the sight. I told her what I knew of her history while we approached the visitors center, and she took copious notes. She grew very hushed when I warned her about the small, confined spaces we would find inside the ship; I'm sure I saw her swallow. But I was genuinely happy to be there.

This was going to be a special treat. The USS *North Carolina* had always been one of my favorite places to explore, having investigated it on four separate occasions with my parents. It was more than just the ship—there was a dear friend I was looking forward to seeing here, as well.

I'd really stacked the deck for this investigation, knowing it would be the final stop on our week-long trip through the South. I'd used my connections to get special permission for us to roam far outside the visitors' tour, so we could explore every nook and cranny at will.

"It was only in service for six years. . . ." Jordin mused as I continued my rundown of the ship's past. "So how many people died on board?"

"Only ten are on record. But the ship was a part of every major naval offensive of World War II. And she survived. So I suppose you could say death has surrounded her since her birth," I said in a quiet voice.

Good grief, Maia. Over the course of all this, I'd somehow turned into a hackneyed tour guide, getting my kicks by giving goose bumps to sightseers.

And it actually annoyed me that Jordin kept referring to the ship as "it" instead of "her." I knew it was stupid, but it just got under my skin.

The sun was beginning to set behind an overcast sky as we parked in the tourist lot adjacent to the dock and began the long trek through the gigantic visitors center and across the causeway that ran out across the water to the ship. Our hands were full of duffel bags and backpacks, because I'd insisted that we bring along every piece of investigative equipment we had. I'd even talked Jordin into stopping at an electronics shop and buying a slew of new digital video cameras so we could disperse them throughout the ship.

And I *was* interested in putting the new equipment to use, but truth be told, I also hoped that the extra "eyes" would minimize our need to move around so much during the trip. I'd done everything I could over the last two days to shove thoughts of my weak heart aside, but it was always there, lingering on the edge of my mind. It was the last thing I thought of before sleeping at night and the first thing to come to mind in the morning. I just couldn't escape it.

There would be time to get fully checked over when we got back to New York. For now, I had one more investigation to conduct. I'd just need to try and keep from overexerting myself. It was a perfect time to let Jordin step up to the plate a little more.

She had really surprised me this week. Jordin's annoying enthusiasm never wavered, but neither did her dedication. And she had proven to have solid instincts, which was one of the most useful tools a paranormal investigator could have.

"What is that?" she asked, looking out over the edge of the bridge into the river.

"Alligator," I replied with a glance.

She recoiled slightly. I think the idea of spending the night in the claustrophobic spaces onboard the ship suddenly sounded better than staying outside.

We were met at the far side of the causeway by Carl Swift, an elderly gentleman in a navy dress uniform. Though it wasn't the first time I'd seen his medals, I couldn't help but allow my focus to slide down his chest to land on the purple heart affixed there beneath a dozen other badges and medals.

"Maia!" he shouted, though I was only a few feet away. He was a kind man with a big heart, but an old-school navy man, too, who tried his best not to show too much emotion. I'd known him for ages, and he felt like part of my family—only with none of the baggage. "Good to see you, young lady, good to see you! How are Malcolm and Carmen?"

"They're great," I said with a grin and forced him into a bear hug. I really adored Carl. "They send their best, and promise to come back to shoot a new episode for next season. Apparently there have been quite a few fan requests for another investigation here."

"Well, what do you know about that," he said in a conspiratorial tone. It was the closest Carl ever got to sounding playful. If he'd been anyone else, he would have been winking and smiling at me right now. And I knew why: those "fan requests" had probably been arranged by the old codger himself.

"This is Jordin, the one who asked for the private tour," I said. It was only partly true, since Jordin had had no idea what our three destinations would be on this trip, but she *had* asked to visit the most haunted places I could come up with. I had to stroke Carl's ego a bit, because he was so proud of the *North Carolina* that my parents called her his mistress. Which might as well have been true since he was unmarried and actually lived in a stateroom on the ship as her primary curator and historian.

He offered a tight-lipped smile. "Pleasure to meet you, miss," he said, extending his leathery hand. "Just listen to Maia tonight and be extra careful while you two are poking around. She's a smart one, this girl." He put his arm around me as if to emphasize his point.

She offered a captivating smile in return, no doubt giving the old man a little flirting for what she thought was his concern for our safety. But it wasn't *our* safety he was worried about. He just didn't want us breaking anything on board.

"And if you get anything good, I expect you'll get me a copy, young lady," he said, turning back to me. It was the same arrangement as with my parents; we could investigate, but always had to provide a copy of any ghostly audio or imagery we captured. The tourists who visited the ship just loved that stuff. The Battleship Commission, the group that owned and oversaw the ship, had even begun giving monthly "haunted tours" based on the growing number of paranormal enthusiasts who'd begun making inquiries.

I nodded and reassured him that the agreement between him and my family still stood.

Carl was about to take his leave when he stepped forward as if about to impart some great secret that only the two of us should hear. "You both take great care belowdecks," he said. "A lot of strange things have been happening lately—even more than usual. See that you don't lose your heads."

As he walked away back along the bridge that led back to shore, Jordin asked, "He didn't mean that literally, did he?"

It was long into the night before things got interesting. We spent over an hour placing our newly acquired high-def/low-light cameras in eight paranormal hot spots all over the ship.

They were motion-sensitive, so they would only record if they detected movement.

Then we set up our sleeping bags and other essentials in crew quarters just off the main deck. We'd planned to set up our little home base out on the deck itself and enjoy the cool night air, but the threat of rain changed our minds.

Our tour began in the boiler room, deep belowdecks. The most interesting areas of the ship were naturally the ones that were hardest to access, but I decided it would be easiest—especially for my health needs—to start at the bottom and work our way up, so we wouldn't have to backtrack, and we'd end the night back in our crew quarters.

Having barely set foot through the hatch to the boiler room, we both nearly gagged.

"Oh man!" Jordin moaned, trying to cover her nose. "It smells like an outhouse down here!"

The pungent odor was strong and offensive, and it saturated our sinuses. I suggested we take a look around, see if maybe an animal had found its way down there and left a little something behind. But ten minutes of shining our flashlights into every corner turned up nothing but pristine steel catwalks. Nothing else happened in the boiler room, but the smell was so strong it seemed to follow us as we left.

"I feel like I need a shower," Jordin said.

I didn't want to be a wimp and say it out loud, but I'd been thinking the same thing. The smell had left me feeling completely soiled.

We trudged on.

————————

We were up in the mess hall when we picked up cold spots all around the room. I had brought along a handheld temperature meter I still had from the old days, and discovered a handful of spots twenty or even thirty degrees cooler than the rest of the room. And they weren't moving. In my mind's eye I could almost see the residual ghosts of navy crewmen sitting at the old tables and eating their meals.

"Okay, I have a question," said Jordin softly.

"Shoot."

"The shadow person we saw the other night was hot. He showed up as a heat source on the thermal camera. So why are these—whatever they are—so cold?"

I had no answer for her. It was one of the many mysteries of the paranormal. Sometimes ghosts were hot, sometimes they were cold. I'd heard theories about temperature being related to temperament, where the entity's light or dark character could affect how they manifested. But as with everything else, there was a frustrating lack of hard facts on the matter.

One of the spots literally gave us a charge.

I was feeling the cool air in a cold spot at one of the tables when I suddenly yanked my hand away. "Whoa. Hey, come here. You gotta feel this."

Jordin, who had been across the room doing EVP work, came over quickly and looked as I pointed at the empty cold space. "This one's different. Put your hand in there."

She obediently stretched her hand out and felt the air where I showed her. Nothing happened at first, but then she pulled back with a start. "Ow!" she said, but then stuck her hand out again. "Oh wow . . ."

"I know!"

"Is that . . . ? It almost feels like static electricity," she observed. "You ever encountered this before?"

I nodded. "Just once. It's a very rare phenomenon, from what I understand. My dad told me that sometimes positively charged ions are found in certain cold spots. It feels like a weak electrical current in the air. Dad said it was almost certainly a sign of an intelligent haunt."

"Wow . . ." Jordin took out her digital camera and snapped several shots of the cold spot while I talked. She held out her digital recorder and asked several questions, like "What's your name?" and "Did you die on the ship?"

I snapped my head around quickly, looking into the far corner of the room.

Jordin spun as fast as I had, searching. "What?"

"I guess it was nothing," I said. "I thought I saw something out of the corner of my eye."

But there was nothing there. I couldn't help wondering if this heart thing was making me paranoid.

For a few hours, we wandered through the onboard hospital, the machine shop, a rec room. We scanned for EVPs and took plenty of video, but the old ship seemed quiet tonight. I wondered if we'd finally found ourselves a haunted site where the deceased just weren't in the mood to come out and play.

We passed by a set of stairs leading back down into the ship's bowels when Jordin screamed. I spun to see her land on her back.

I ran over and knelt down. "What happened? You okay?"

She looked up at me, startled and confused. "That wasn't you?"

"I was in front of you, Jordin." I helped her up to a sitting position. "What happened?"

Her mouth hung open, and she leaned around me to look down the corridor ahead. Her complexion was paler than I'd ever seen it.

"Somebody—something knocked me down," she hissed. "Like, *shoved* me out of the way!"

My eyebrows went up at this and my heart thumped, but I was careful to take deep breaths to keep calm. "Did you feel a *hand* push you, or was it something else?"

Jordin glanced down the hall again, searching for the words. "It was just like somebody was running down this hall, and I was in their way, so they kind of . . . pushed past me. It might have been *shoulder* first, I don't know. . . ."

I saw it again. In my peripheral vision, something dark moved. My head spun in its direction, and my eyes landed on the stairs going down.

The sound of shoes on metal reverberated up the stairs, and then came to us from farther away.

Okay. This was too good to be true. Which meant it couldn't be.

Somebody was messing with us. Had to be. Someone had snuck onboard the old ship tonight and was having fun at our expense. I pulled out my phone to give Carl an earful about his lackluster security. I had my thumb on the *Send* button when Jordin jumped to her feet.

"Listen! It's underneath us!" Jordin whispered. "It's under us right now!"

Despite my better judgment, I followed her to the stairs, flashlights and cameras in our hands. We paused there, looking and listening, and sure enough, we heard it again. I swept my flashlight back and forth down the stairs but couldn't see anything.

This was a bad idea. A real person was here trying to play with us. Things could get dangerous very fast. I needed to find a way to keep Jordin from pursuing this, but I didn't want to freak her out by sharing my suspicions that we weren't the only living people on the ship.

Jordin took a few steps down the stairs.

"Stop, what are you doing?" I asked.

"Going toward the stuff other people run away from," she quipped and continued down the stairs.

"Jordin, I don't have a good feeling about this," I whispered. "I think we should call it a night."

"Something's playing with us, Maia." Her expression told me what she thought of my desire to leave. "It's intelligent and it knows we're here, and it's all but invited us to follow it. This may be our best chance of getting solid evidence tonight. Isn't this *exactly* what we're here for?"

She turned and continued to the bottom of the stairs, and then disappeared down a corridor.

It was too late now. My heart was thudding madly, and though I was trying to keep my composure, I was sure I felt it skip a beat or two.

So I ran. I caught up with Jordin and we chased it down a long corridor and then stopped, listening. We heard it again down another set of stairs to our right, and we went again. There was no sign of it at the far end of the next hallway, so we froze, repeating the pattern of listening for signs of its presence and scanning the area with our flashlights.

I took deep breaths, clearing my mind and trying with all my might to relax, to force my heart to calm itself. In all likelihood, we were just chasing some punk kid who would later be having a lot of laughs with his buddies over the two girls he scared in the middle of the night.

I looked into a large room to our right marked "Post Office," and against the far wall I saw something dash impossibly fast to the left, and out of sight. I couldn't tell for sure what it was—it wasn't quite black enough to be a shadow person, and I think it might have had some detail and definition to its form.

But it moved much too fast to be a living, breathing person.

The sight of it sent my heart into random sputters. It forced me to double over.

"I saw it! In there!" I gasped, pointing to the words "Post Office" that were now over my own head.

Jordin—who seemed to think I was just out of breath—stepped past me into the large room, flashlight raised in one hand and video camera in the other. "We know you're here," she said in a nonthreatening voice. "Could you please talk to us?"

I was having trouble breathing, barely aware of what Jordin was doing, and sank down to my knees. I clutched at my chest and rubbed the beads of cold sweat from my forehead. My heart was pounding so fast it actually made my rib cage hurt with each strike. I backed up against the bulkhead, still in the hallway outside the room Jordin had chased the apparition into, and lowered myself slowly to the ground.

"I see it!" Jordin hissed in my direction, still inside the post office. "It's running, Maia, come on!"

"No!" I called out. "I can't—I need to go back!"

"Are you nuts!" Jordin didn't even bother to look back in the room. "We can catch this thing! I just saw it run through another door! Come on, Maia, let's go!"

"I can't, I need some air," I said, the world spinning around me, barely able to choke out any words. My voice was failing me, as well. "I need . . ." I croaked.

"NO!" roared Jordin with a shocking level of anger in her voice. "I have to do this! If you won't help me, I'll do it by myself!"

"Wait!" I tried to say, though it felt like there was an obstruction in my throat. I was holding my chest with both hands and seeing spots in front of my eyes. "Jordin!"

She never answered.

———

I fell into an abyss.

Something had its rock-hard fingers clenched around my heart and dragged my whole body down into the void with it.

Not literally, but that's what my mind pictured while I felt these strange sensations surge through my body, rendering me all but powerless.

It was what drowning in a stormy sea must be like. Fighting an endless battle against nature, trying to keep my head above the water only for another massive wave to crash down on me, all while the entire ocean spun around me like a waterspout. And the worst part was knowing that every time I might catch a moment of rest, that hope would vanish with the next wave of nausea and fear. The terror seemed as if it would never stop coming, and knowing I was defenseless to keep it from happening immobilized me completely.

Where had Jordin gone? How could she just leave me?

I suppose it was partly my fault for not outright telling her about my heart problem, particularly now when I was having this . . . attack, or whatever it was.

I tried calling out to her a few times, but I was so weak that I couldn't raise my voice.

I focused on breathing. If I could just get some deep breaths into my lungs, maybe I could relax enough to get a handle on this and drag myself back up topside for some fresh air.

Slowly, the dizziness came to an end, but not until after I threw up. Afterward, my skin felt clammy and tingly, and I knew my face had to be ashen white.

I thought of my pragmatic father, and tried to imagine what he would do in a similar situation. It didn't take long to come up with the answer—he would never have allowed himself to get into a situation like this. He would have prepared better than I did, packing walkie-talkies for Jordin and me in case we got separated. It had never occurred to me to bring coms of any kind, because Jordin and I had always investigated together.

I thought then of my strong-willed mother and her take-no-prisoners attitude. Her feisty, quirky demeanor had endeared her to legions of TV fans everywhere. She would never let a little thing like a weak heart slow her up.

Okay, Mom, this is for you.

I shined my light around the dark hallway, searching. I crawled in a circle to the door to the post office and grabbed the handle that opened it, hoisting myself slowly up.

Getting on my legs again seemed to help the blood flow, and

the world quickly righted itself. I was still sweating, but my heart was resuming normal operation, as well.

Cautiously and with exhausting effort, I worked my way back down the hall the way we'd come, and ascended the stairs. It took a good ten minutes, and by the time I reached the next set of stairs, my strength was spent. I caught the slightest whiff of the glorious North Carolina coastal sea air, drifting through the upper decks of the ship. I thought I heard the sound of rain tapping against metal. But I was powerless to reach it.

Just as the darkness was taking me again, I thought I saw a tiny bright light shining in my face and a familiar voice saying, "Now what have you gone and done to yourself, young lady?"

Never had I been so happy to smell dead fish.

That was my first sensation when I awoke in a bright room where a man was sitting next to me.

"Carl?" I rasped.

I blinked and noted the tiny cot I lay on, and the stark surroundings of the small metal room I was in. It was bright from several lights that were shining in the room, and I could hear the rain coming down just a short distance away. I was inside on the main deck.

My crusty old friend was staring me in the eye, his expression unreadable.

"Thirsty," I croaked, my tongue and throat dry. "How did you find me?"

Carl held up a single hand, and inside it was my phone. "Almost had to get the jaws a' life to pry it out of your hand."

I understood. Before Jordin ran off, my finger had been right on the phone's *Send* button, with his number already input. I must've mashed it sometime during the chaos that followed.

"Where's Jordin?" I said, still having a hard time getting my voice. But I noted with relief that my heart was beating normally, and the sweats and pains I'd felt earlier were gone.

"Your friend?" Carl shrugged. "Must still be belowdecks somewhere."

"I better go find her—"

I tried to sit up, but Carl gently forced me back down, and I was surprised at how much strength the old seaman still possessed. "You ain't going nowhere till you tell me what happened."

My mind scrambled, trying to think of an excuse. I didn't dare tell Carl what was really wrong with me; as much as I appreciated his care and concern, I knew he'd take the information straight to my parents. And I wasn't ready for them to know.

"I forgot how hot it can get down there," I lied. "Must've gotten dehydrated."

His eyes narrowed, and he stared me down. "Then why did you call me?" he asked, producing the phone again, and this time handing it over to me.

I sighed. "I thought someone was on the ship—a real, live person—other than us. I thought somebody had snuck onboard and was pranking us. But then I saw the thing we were chasing, and it definitely wasn't alive."

Carl seemed to sense the truth in this part of my story, at least. "I run a tight ship. Nobody gets onboard without my knowledge, you know that, Maia. Why were you all by yourself when I found you?"

I shook my head in frustration, or almost anger. "Jordin ran off after the apparition. I tried telling her I didn't feel well, but she was already gone. I should've brought some walkies. . . . Just didn't think about it."

Carl seemed to deflate a bit. I read this to mean that all of his questions had been answered to his satisfaction.

"Something's happening, Carl. Something's wrong," I said, at last vocalizing a dawning comprehension that had been bugging me all week. It had nothing to do with my little heart problem. That was just my own personal stuff, and one way or another, I would handle that myself. There was something else going on here that was much bigger than me.

He sat back in his seat and looked at me.

I took a deep breath. "Every single time I've gone investigating with Jordin, we've encountered paranormal phenomena. Every time. One hundred percent success rate. That . . . that's impossible. It just doesn't happen."

Carl crossed his arms in front of his chest and frowned. "Honey, you know I don't know much about the ghost business. I'm just an old sailor who never lost his sea legs. Why are you talking to me about this, instead of what's-her-name?"

I smiled, with a hint of desperation on my face. "Because you're here." And because he was my friend. Though that went without saying.

His eyebrows rose as he resigned himself to being my sounding board. "Well, when you're at sea and you wind up somewhere you didn't expect to, there's only two possible explanations. There's a problem with the weather or there's a problem with the boat."

I pondered this. "So . . . either the paranormal itself is . . . I don't know, *changing*, like the weather, which doesn't make any sense. Or there's something wrong with *me*? Am I the boat?"

He stared me down. "You're *driving* the boat, Maia. But you're not the only passenger on it, are you?"

———————

It was over an hour from the time I passed out until Jordin emerged from belowdecks. Carl had left me to get some rest twenty or thirty minutes ago. He made up some excuse about needing to check the ship's moorings because of the weather.

In that time, I'd left his quarters and returned to the crew bunk Jordin and I had selected, curling up in my sleeping bag. My strength had improved tremendously, but I was beginning to fear the worst about Jordin. What if she had fallen and hurt herself? Maybe she'd been impaled on some metal spike. Or, more likely but no less troubling, the batteries in her flashlight had drained thanks to all the paranormal activity, and she was lost down there in the dark, amid the ship's endless, mazelike corridors.

I was working up the resolve to go look for her when she ran into the room, breathless and grinning ear to ear. I wanted to beat the living snot out of her.

Instead, I played it cool.

"It went well?" I asked, yawning as if she'd woken me up.

Jordin nodded vigorously, plopping down on top of her sleeping bag and pulling out her laptop. "I think I got it on video! Can't wait to get this to a bigger screen. . . . *Man*, that thing could move."

She was hooking up her video camera to her computer when she noticed that I was buried in my sleeping bag. "Hey, you okay? I saw where you threw up back in that hallway. Did you get food poisoning or something?"

"Or something," I replied, turning over to indicate that I was going to sleep.

"Do you need to get out of here? Want me to drive you to the emergency room?"

"I'm fine," I said, thinking only about Carl's boat metaphor, and wondering if he could be right about Jordin. "Don't worry about me."

THIRTEEN

There was a knock at the door at 7:30 a.m., and I knew it was Derek. Had to be.

I decided I wasn't going to hold back from him this time. I would tell him about my nightmare, and what it probably meant.

Jill was an exercise freak who got up early to run and do yoga, so I had to get out of my nice, warm sleeping bag to answer the door. I shivered and rubbed my arms.

"I saw Jordin last night!" Derek blurted. His face was pale and his eyes were bloodshot. "She was a ghost."

"You—she—*what*?!"

He walked into the room and shut the door, probably worried

that someone outside would hear the pastor-in-training claiming to have seen a ghost.

"I was asleep . . . in my room," he explained, "and she called out my name. It woke me up, and I saw her! She was right there, beside my bed. I think she was kneeling. I was so startled, I didn't get a good look at her body—"

"There was no mist?" I asked.

He shook his head. "No, but she was definitely there. Only I could kind of . . . see through her. She was only there for about twenty seconds, and then—" Derek bit his lip and swallowed back an emotion that threatened to overtake him. "These three dark figures—I couldn't see any details, they were just like, shadows—they grabbed her and dragged her away! They dragged her through the walls of my room. . . ."

He couldn't hold back the tears anymore, but he let them sting his eyes as just two spilled out and ran down his cheeks. "It's real. Somebody's out there turning living people into disembodied souls!"

Derek's story was unnerving. I could see why it would upset him so, but it struck me as consistent with the scenario I was already imagining. She had found a way to reach him, but whoever was behind all of this caught up with her and put a stop to her efforts to communicate.

"Did she say anything?" I asked, already knowing what the answer would be.

"She said 'the nightmare is coming,' and she said something I couldn't quite make out about Howell Durham," Derek replied. "Then she just vanished."

Howell Durham, I thought. President and CEO of Durham

Holdings International, the company funding Ghost Town, and very likely the conspirators behind all this.

Derek was so beside himself, I had to ask. "Are you *sure* you weren't dreaming?"

"I'm sure!"

I let out a long breath. "Okay, all right. . . . There's something you should know. I had a nightmare last night."

"So?"

"A *nightmare*, Derek."

His eyes popped. "Oh! Wow! Are you okay? Do you have—?"

I shook my head. "No, I don't have a mark on my neck. Not yet. But both reports we've heard suggest that there's roughly a week between when the nightmares start and when the mark appears. And *then* . . ." I didn't finish the thought.

"And then," he agreed, looking at me with worry. "I guess Durham Holdings is making good on its threat to target you next. Assuming they're the ones that threatened you."

"That's what we have to find out," I said, turning to business. "And Jordin's journal may hold the key."

"The Vineyard, then?"

"You're driving."

An hour later, we were on I-95 heading north in Derek's pickup truck.

"So, uh, when you saw Jordin last night . . ." I said, trying to sound as innocent as possible, "was she wearing clothes?"

I was expecting a dirty look to be shot my way, but Derek maintained his expression of caffeinated anxiety, though there was a knowing gleam in his eye. "I don't know," he said without a trace of deception. "It happened really fast. . . . She was there and then she wasn't. She might have been."

"I'm surprised to hear you admit that," I offered in a friendly tone.

"It's what happened," he said with a shrug. "I'm not going to lie about it because it doesn't fit with my theology."

I didn't reply, but I valued his commitment to the truth.

We drove for a while in silence and then he said, "Try this one. When I was about seven or eight years old, my parents and I were living in this small apartment. This was back when Dad had gotten his first church, which was in Kansas. I remember one day at the apartment that I looked out the back door and saw a man standing there on the other side of the screen door. He smiled warmly at me through the screen, but he never knocked on the door or even waved at me. He had curly white hair and a beard and wore old-fashioned overalls and muddy work boots. He kept his hands in his pockets the whole time.

"I went to tell my mom about the man at the back door, but even though I was gone less than ten seconds, when I brought Mom back to the door, the man was gone.

"That afternoon, I told a neighbor kid about what I'd seen, and he said that it was 'old Mr. Andrews,' a farmer who had owned all of the land for miles around, about a hundred years ago, before the land had been zoned by the city for development. I thought my friend was nuts, of course, but he described the man I'd seen down to every last detail.

"He asked if the man I saw had kept his hands in his pockets the whole time. I said that he did. My friend explained that that was because Mr. Andrews died after an accident where his hands were cut off, and he bled to death in his cornfield."

Derek finished his story and we drove again in silence until he added, "I haven't thought about that in years. I told my parents once and they just sort of ignored me."

"My dad says everyone has a ghost story," I replied.

"I don't know what it was," Derek insisted. "But it was different than seeing Jordin last night. She was terrified. Something is wrong."

We were both quiet for a while, contemplating the world of ghosts and spirits and what parts of it were real and what parts were the products of overactive imaginations.

"What I don't get is the *why*," Derek said, breaking the silence twenty minutes later. "DHI or whoever's behind all this . . . what would they *get* out of creating a disembodied soul?"

I shook my head. The question had already occurred to me, and I was bothered that I couldn't come up with an answer. It made no logical sense. I couldn't imagine anything to be gained from such a scheme. "I have no idea."

"Equally troubling to me is the idea that technology to do something like that could even exist," Derek continued. "I mean, you'd need to have developed brand-new tech in a number of different fields. For starters, you'd have to pinpoint the exact physical location of the human soul. If there even *is* a physical location where it resides."

"Maybe they just found an access point," I suggested. "Like a port on a computer that they could plug into to get at what's inside."

Derek kept his eyes on the road but kind of shrugged. "Then you'd have to find a way to separate the soul from the body. To literally reach inside—maybe through that access point you mentioned, which apparently is at the back of the neck—and *extract* the soul. The thought that something like that could be possible I find profoundly disturbing, because it's *not* in keeping with my understanding of how God made us. And if it *is* possible, what becomes of the body? Can it live without a soul to inhabit it? Is Jordin dead?"

I had to agree, it *was* a troubling thought. In my mind, the thought of rending a soul from a human body was something that had to be a violent procedure.

"Then there's the whole 'binding' thing," I said, picking up the conversation. "A soul freed from its body, its mortal coil, would be, in a word, *free*. Doing this runs the risk of not producing a bona fide ghost if the spirit they free has the ability to move on to the next life. They would need to have a means of keeping a spirit tethered to mortal soil."

Derek agreed. "Exerting control over a spirit this way should be impossible. It's simply not how the universe works. If it's true, if someone has found a way to do these things . . . then they're perverting God's creation in ways that are so profoundly wrong, the word 'sin' is not big enough to describe it."

I fell silent, thinking.

"A few decades ago," I said after a few minutes, "things like genetic engineering and cloning were impossible. Until technology caught up with science fiction and made them possible. We live in a universe governed by science and scientific laws. I happen to believe that science and religion are pursuing the same goal: understanding the nature of the universe and our existence in it. Science looks for the mechanics of it, while religion seeks the meaning. But they're both looking at the same universe for the same answers. Everything we can't explain about this life—including ghosts and spirits—has a rational, scientific explanation. We just haven't found it yet. The soul is no different. If it exists, then there have to be mechanical functions behind it that make it work."

For the first time, Derek looked away from the road to glance at me. He had a stern expression on his face, as if considering my words but finding them hard to swallow. "Can't a miracle ever be just a miracle? Does it always have to have a scientific explanation or cause? The miraculous power of God himself requires no scientific basis. I don't accept that everything that happens, and has ever happened, occurs only for scientific reasons. It's like those people that try to explain away the ten plagues God sent down on Egypt for refusing to free the Hebrews, or the theory that a 'land bridge' exists under the Red Sea, and that with just enough hurricane-force winds, the Israelites may have been able to walk across that 'bridge' without it ever actually parting. Why can't it just be a miracle? What is God, if not miraculous and omnipotent?

"Science may be the glue that holds the universe together . . . but who or what caused those laws to work and gave them the power to govern the universe, to begin with? Who wrote them into being? Who made science? Science can't explain everything, and it never will, because it, too, requires a Creator."

I was quiet. Unlike our past discussions, this one hadn't left me feeling cold or frustrated toward Derek. I didn't entirely agree with his ideas, but he'd delivered them so passionately, so fervently, that I suddenly understood why he had such a bright future ahead of him as a minister.

I didn't feel like disturbing the silence he'd created with his impassioned speech. I thought it deserved too much respect to argue with.

It was Derek who spoke next, but his sermon voice was gone, replaced by a sad, lonely young man.

"Maia, how are we going to find Jordin?" he asked. "You said DHI's offices are in Copenhagen, so it stands to reason that that's where they're taking the people they abduct and doing this . . . *procedure* . . . on. They have money, resources, and mega-security. They're untouchable."

I couldn't disagree, but decided on a logical approach. "One hurdle at a time. Let's consider what we know. Someone—probably Howell Durham and his evil little empire—is abducting lonely college students and turning them into, as crazy as it sounds, ghosts. Each of these students has gone missing after three alchemical symbols have appeared on the back of their necks, which directly follows a week full of terrifying nightmares when they sleep. I can attest to this personally."

I swallowed, not wanting to linger on this point. I soldiered on. "It stands to reason that the symbol is more than just a symbol—it may be part of the technology that makes this whole soul-extraction-and-binding thing work. Jordin disappeared from Martha's Vineyard around the beginning of August. We can safely assume that she was conducting solo paranormal investigations every night while she was there, and it's entirely possible she was abducted during one of those investigations. You and I have both seen her disembodied soul, asking us for help and warning us of this 'nightmare' that's coming. Whatever that means.

"We also know that she was keeping a detailed journal of her experiences. A journal that hasn't been seen since she disappeared, and—if it wasn't carted off with her when she was taken—it could provide some clues about the circumstances surrounding her abduction.

"Then there's Ghost Town. You saw Jordin in your dorm room, but I saw her at this amusement park and I don't think that her being there was a fluke. I did some digging online and I don't believe that Jordin is the only genuine ghost to appear there. A number of tourists have reported encounters with realistic apparitions that said 'the nightmare is coming' to them."

Derek sighed. "It's a start, I guess."

Since things were going so pleasantly between us for once, I decided it was the perfect time to make a request I'd been considering for a while now.

"If and when we find the journal," I said slowly, "if you should come across it before I do . . . I want you to let me read it first. Before you do."

He glanced guardedly into my eyes. "Why?"

"I just think . . . there might be things in there that Jordin wouldn't want you to see. Inner thoughts that she never meant for *anyone* but herself to read. And I don't want whatever we may find . . . to change your feelings for her."

Derek offered a meager smile. I think he was genuinely touched. "I appreciate the concern, but I promise you, there's nothing Jordin could ever say or do to make me love her less."

I was undeterred. "All the same . . . You wouldn't have gotten any answers at all without my help, and I haven't asked for anything in return. Just let me have this."

He kind of frowned, but said, "Okay, all right. You can read the journal. I'll keep my hands off."

Satisfied, I let the matter drop.

"Here's something I've been puzzling over," Derek said after a moment. "About Jordin. And ghosts."

"Shoot," I said, warming up a bit to this nice, new Derek. We would never be best friends or anything, but I was finding it more tolerable being around him when he was playing so nice.

"Most hauntings seem localized to certain buildings, right? What is it about a piece of property or a house that can confine a ghost?"

I knew this was another devil's advocate question, along the lines of his earlier test of logic about sightings of ghosts who wear clothes. But he wasn't being antagonistic this time, so I decided to humor him.

" 'Structural possession' is the formal term," I said. "*Genius Loci*—the spirit of the place. Most investigators think that 'confinement' may not be the right word to describe it. I mean, there's no direct evidence to indicate that a ghost is strictly *unable* to leave a certain place. The more accepted explanation is that they're *unwilling*."

"Right. But Jordin *isn't* confined right now. That seems important somehow. She's able to go wherever she wants."

"That's true. I don't know what it means, but you're right."

"And I've never understood it from a logical side. If a ghost *could* choose to leave, why stick around."

He had me. There was no way I was going to wiggle free of this one. "No, it doesn't make logical sense. This is something I've always hoped to find a better explanation for. I've been to so many haunted locations where the owners or residents claim to know the identity of the dead person that's haunting them, and every time I would hear that, those claims made me wonder how they could possibly know for sure who the ghost was, when visible sightings are so, so rare. It seemed more likely to me that ghosts, as you said, would want to explore, to come and go as they please, wherever and whenever they want. *I* certainly wouldn't feel compelled to stick around a site where some terrible thing happened to me."

Derek was reveling in his small victory when I made a slight addendum.

"But then again, I've never died before."

———————

It was a five-hour drive to Martha's Vineyard, and we talked theories and debated the paranormal most of the way there. I saw the intelligence Jordin loved—and saw how much he loved and missed *her*. Derek and I still barely qualified as friends, but I think we had grown to respect each other.

We arrived at Jordin's beach house around one in the afternoon. Derek knew exactly where to find it, having been there before, and was frustrated to find the house in shambles. The furniture was dirty; the kitchen was filled with filthy or broken dishes. And by all indications, it had been this way for a while. Either Jordin's friends had been utter slobs and left the place without cleaning up after themselves, or somebody else had been here looking for Jordin's journal. Or both.

I started by turning over sofa cushions, looking under furniture, and searching the kitchen cabinets and drawers. Derek said not a word as he marched to the staircase and up to the second floor.

Twenty minutes in, I'd had no luck at all when Derek returned from upstairs.

"It's not in her bedroom," he declared.

"You sure?"

"I turned it inside out. And I know where she keeps things she doesn't want anyone to find. When she was growing up, she kept a diary hidden in her pillow cushion. I'm confident in saying it's not in that room. And if it was going to be anywhere in this house, I'm sure she would keep it there."

I sighed. "All the same, let's finish searching the house. Just to be sure."

He scowled but agreed to pitch in.

A thought occurred to me. "I think this is actually good news. If we'd found the journal here, it would mean she was taken from here, right under the other girls' noses. It would make all of this a dead end. If the journal's not here, then chances are it's still wherever she was when she was abducted. And finding it could lead us straight to her."

Derek said nothing, but had a little more spring in his step as we combed through the house.

Columbia University

New York

FOURTEEN

MARCH 18TH

I had to wait a full week and a half for an appointment with my doctor, only to be greeted by a med student when I was taken into the exam room.

The student doctor—and I'm not kidding, he was younger than Doogie—asked me a full set of questions about the trouble I was having with my heart. He read them off of a multi-page list on a clipboard while I repeatedly said no to increasingly personal questions about my family history, my sexual history, and my use of alcohol and drugs.

He listened to my heart with his stethoscope, which had teddy bears on the fabric cover—I'm just saying—and made some further notes on his clipboard before excusing himself and promising me that Dr. Hudson would be with me shortly.

Which of course was doctor-speak for *You might speak to another human being in about an hour, if you're lucky.*

I wasn't lucky, and it was actually an hour and a half before Dr. Hudson entered. She apologized for the delay and made some glib comments about her student's examination of me, and then informed me she was ordering a number of tests.

A full day of tests later—including a visit to the hospital for several of them—and I sat waiting in a different exam room for Dr. Hudson to enter and give me the news. By now, I was all set to hear that the diagnosis was dreadful. It was something my pragmatist father had taught me when I was young: *Hope for the best, but prepare for the worst.*

Only ten minutes passed between the time the nurse left me alone in the examination room and when Dr. Hudson entered.

"Well, Maia . . ." she began, taking a seat on a round stool. Two of her students filed in behind her and closed the door, standing at attention and observing closely. "It looks like you're suffering from panic attacks."

"What?"

I must've misheard her. I didn't panic.

She nodded. "This is good news, Maia. It's very treatable."

"But . . . how?" I was still struggling to understand. "What brought this on?"

Dr. Hudson gave a little shrug. "Panic attacks can be caused by all sorts of things—reaction to another drug or withdrawal from one. Heavy drinking. Most often it's hereditary. But sometimes it can be triggered experientially, and based on what you told me, I'm inclined to think that's the case for you. Your recent . . .

extracurricular activities . . . you told me you've been undertaking are going to have to stop. Any experience terrifying enough to cause a panic attack like this most recent one you had could, in extreme circumstances, cause an arrhythmia," she said. Then she added, "That's a heart attack."

"I know what arrhythmia is. . . ." My head was spinning. It was like someone had just told me that I was really half Nigerian instead of half Mexican. "I still don't understand. I'm not afraid of the paranormal. I never have been."

"It's not a matter of choice, Maia," Dr. Hudson said in her most condescendingly soothing tone. "Your body is having a very harsh stimulus-driven physical reaction that you really have no control over."

I almost felt angry—angry at myself and my own body for betraying me. How could this be happening?

"So how do we treat it?" I asked.

"Well, I'm going to give you some reading material to look over, as we find that equipping yourself with knowledge is the best preparation. And I'm going to prescribe an antidepressant for you, a newer one with antianxiety properties that we've found to be very effective. It's low impact on your system otherwise, and that's the kind of treatment we like. I'm also going to give you some Valium, but I need to stress that it is only to be used during an extreme attack, to prevent a full-on arrhythmia. It's not to be used otherwise, as it's highly addictive.

"Lastly," she said, "I have to insist—you *must* avoid situations that produce the kind of stimulus that could trigger a panic attack."

It was about a week later when Jordin rang me up and asked me to come by her condo downtown. She said she had finally finished reviewing all of the photographic, video, and audio footage we'd collected in our "tour" of the South, and she wanted me to see what she'd found. She sounded excited, so I promised to stop by after my last class of the day.

I'd been taking my new antianxiety medication for almost a week now, and felt like I was starting to benefit from its effects. I hadn't had a single panic attack since we'd returned to New York, which was pretty encouraging, though I was nonplussed to realize that I only experienced these attacks when Jordin and I were investigating. It was possible that the one thing in all the world that triggered a panic attack in me was the one thing that shouldn't bother me in the slightest: the paranormal.

On the other hand, if the paranormal *was* my trigger, then that was good news for my career plans. Cops and detectives deal with crimes committed by the living, which apparently posed no medical issues for me.

I had never been to Jordin's condo before, or even her dorm room for that matter. I found it surprisingly spartan. It was huge, don't get me wrong, the kind of open space only someone as wealthy as Jordin could enjoy. It had modern furniture and a few art pieces—but very little personality. Cold, unwelcoming, even sterile, it made me think of a mausoleum.

This place wasn't really hers. It couldn't have been. She had to have bought it furnished, sight unseen. That must've been it.

I wondered if she and Derek planned to live here after they were married. She'd introduced me to him briefly after we got back from our week-long trip, and I couldn't picture him in these surroundings at all.

Jordin welcomed me in very excitedly, and ushered me quickly to a large desk she'd placed in an otherwise unused room. It had been thoroughly outfitted with the most modern computer equipment money could buy and three huge side-by-side monitors, along with all of Jordin's recorders and other investigative tools.

She sat down behind the desk and started by playing some EVPs for me. The first few were garbled and indecipherable. She pouted when I said as much, trying to convince me that she could understand what was being said. But I didn't hear anything resembling a human voice.

Thankfully, she was just getting warmed up.

"Remember the gazebo at the Myrtles?" she said, cuing up a new audio file on her computer. "You said a soldier was seen there sometimes."

"Of course."

She clicked *Play*, and out of the computer's speakers came the loud hissing sound of static, followed by Jordin's own voice shouting, "Grab your gun and fall in!" In the silence after that, a faint male voice could be heard saying, "Leave me alone."

"Not bad," I said.

She played several more for me, including one particularly chilling recording from St. Louis Cemetery of a voice whispering that we should "lay down and sleep." I rubbed the goose bumps away from my arms after hearing it. Whatever had said it, it wasn't a friendly voice, and neither of us believed that it was all that concerned with us getting rest. And of course there was the unsettling one she'd caught at the Myrtles in the room with the painting, where a male voice had declared its preference for the blond one. Based on the face she made when she replayed it, it hadn't gotten any easier for her to listen to.

Next Jordin turned to her only still photo. She had the clear outline of a male figure from somewhere far belowdecks within the battleship *North Carolina*. It was impossible to forget the dark apparition she'd chased down there alone for over an hour while I tried to crawl up to the main deck, fearing that I was having heart failure.

It was an impressive photograph, I couldn't deny it. It was rather dark, but the distinct shape of a human-type form was visible standing in the middle of a corridor. You could almost make out its apparel, but the image was just too dark to perceive that level of detail. *I* knew and *she* knew that this was a picture of a genuine haunting, but a skeptic would easily dismiss it as a staged photograph using a very much alive stand-in.

We moved on to video, and this was where she had found the best stuff. First she replayed the video from the Myrtles for me, proving that there was a slight variation in the expression on the face of the painting in that room. Again, a cynic would say it was a trick of the light or something, because the change *was* subtle. But I knew what I saw.

Jordin had also managed to catch some video of the shadow person moving through St. Louis Cemetery, but it was a fleeting shot, and hardly conclusive. She showed me again the video of the face she'd seen peeking at us at the cemetery, and I have to admit, it still creeped me out. Whatever it was, it wasn't human—not even a deceased human. We also reviewed the thermal imager's recordings from the cemetery, which caught the shadow person a few times, but it was nothing a skeptic would accept as ironclad. She had a few other bits: some strange sounds caught on video, a door that closed itself, a picture frame on a tabletop that seemed to be pushed over facedown. As paranormal investigative evidence goes, it was exceptional stuff.

But her last find was the most striking. It was from a stationary video we'd set up in a main corridor of the *North Carolina*. I watched in astonishment as a partially closed door some twenty feet down the hall from the camera suddenly came to life, shifted off of its hinges, and seemed to *walk* sideways out of the frame. One second it was part of a hatch, the next it had tilted to one side and for all the world moved like something that took a step.

"That's unreal," I commented.

Jordin nodded.

"That's one of the best pieces of evidence I've ever seen, Jordin. Seriously, even my parents would be jealous over that one. You've done a fantastic job, with *all* of this."

I expected her to be thrilled—I wasn't exactly known for offering praise, after all—but she had an odd look on her face.

"How does it feel to have captured real evidence of the paranormal?" I asked, trying to boost her enthusiasm.

Jordin turned in her seat to face me and smiled, but there was a hesitation about her reaction. "Good. Really good."

I knew what was wrong, though I didn't know what it meant. "Even with all this . . . you're no closer to contacting your parents."

She looked over my shoulder at nothing, registering a sad, distant expression. "I've proven that the paranormal is real, to my satisfaction. I don't expect any of this would hold up in court, but after all I've seen and done . . . I *know* it's real. But that's all I know. I have no idea how to reach out to my parents, or even if I can."

I sighed. "Didn't you say your parents were Christians?"

She turned to me slowly and nodded.

"Then . . . don't you believe they're in heaven?" I couldn't help frowning, because Jordin once again defied my understanding. "I mean, I'm not an expert or anything, but as beliefs go, that's a pretty universal one for Christians. If you're a believer, then when you die, you go to heaven. Right? Don't you believe that, too?"

"Sure I do," Jordin replied. "It just . . . never gets any easier. Being without them. I guess I never really thought of heaven as a prison. It's supposed to be a reward, not a confinement."

"Got me," I said. It was a nice thought, but I doubted that most believers would accept it. "The way my mom always describes heaven, it sounds like a place so great that you'd never *want* to leave."

Before I could stop it, bitterness crept to the surface as I thought of how Jordin had abandoned me in the bowels of the *North Carolina*. She still didn't know what had happened to me down there because I hadn't told her, but I was most hurt by the fact that when we were down there, she didn't even stop long enough to make sure I was okay. She just kept running, kept chasing, kept pursuing this obsession. But I didn't know what it was like to grow up without parents, either, I told myself. I wondered if the thought of getting back someone I'd lost would be enough to drive me to such mania.

Jordin still looked far away, but she snapped back suddenly after the room had been silent a little too long. "There's something I'd like to try. It's kind of extreme, but I think it might bring me a step closer to reaching my parents."

I didn't like the sound of that. "Okay . . ."

"That inhuman face we captured at the cemetery, it got me

thinking about aspects of the paranormal we haven't got into yet, and I can't help wondering if trying other avenues of the paranormal might yield different results. . . . There's this old abandoned church in New Jersey I want to visit. It's called Mount Hope Methodist Episcopal, and locals say it's not only haunted, it's possessed by a dark spirit."

My face hardened and my muscles clenched. "Absolutely not. What you call Mount Hope is nicknamed the 'Satanic Church of New Jersey.' Actually *wanting* to go there is something I would describe as madness—especially for someone with as little experience as you've had, no offense. It could be a demonic haunt."

"I looked it up, and there's no evidence that there's an actual demon living in that place," said Jordin, crossing her arms. "It's an urban myth. And even if there is, I have nothing to fear from it. It can't touch me. I'm a Christian! Derek always says, 'I've been bought with the blood of Jesus Christ, and against that, the forces of darkness have no power.' "

My jaw was clenching involuntarily and I forced it to relax as I replied, "My mother would disagree. She always warned, 'The powers of darkness have no power except that which passes through God's hands.' Sometimes God allows bad things to happen to test you. To test *us*. To grow us and mold our character."

Jordin hesitated, thoughtful. "Okay, yeah, that sounds familiar, too. But even still, there's no way He would let one of His followers come to any actual harm at the hands of a demon."

I had an impulsive thought. "Are you telling me the truth about your reasons, Jordin? Is this *really* about contacting your parents? I mean, I know you've acquired a taste for the paranormal, and I know how addictive the thrill of the hunt can be, but—"

"This isn't about feeding some addiction," she replied.

"Then *what*?! What on earth would drive you to such an extreme as this? I can't believe your parents would ever want their daughter to go near something like this."

Jordin's expression turned grim. "If you won't take me, I'll go by myself."

"Are you crazy? You stay away from that place! You hired me because of my expertise, and my expertise *forbids* you to go there."

Her eyebrows rose, but she didn't smile. "You work for *me*. You don't get to forbid anything."

I stared her down, wanting to grab her by the shoulders and shake some sense into her. Another idea occurred to me.

"I'll tell Derek," I threatened.

"I'll withhold payment for the last trip if you do. And I would remind you that it's a triple-sized payment for three separate stops."

So that was how it was going to be. She knew all too well that the money card worked with me, because she'd played it before. And once again, my need for funds was railing against my better judgment.

"I'm going," Jordin said, closing the book on the subject. "Come with me, or don't."

FIFTEEN

Martha's Vineyard has been called the most haunted island in the world, with dozens if not hundreds of scattered sightings. Finding the one Jordin was investigating when she was abducted wasn't going to be easy, and my best guess was that Jordin would go after the most notorious places first. That was certainly her M.O. when we were investigating together. She only wanted to visit the places most likely to generate results.

Derek and I started with the most public spots we could access, assuming Jordin would have done the same. We asked around at shops, the post office, the police department, some local churches. No one remembered seeing her; there were just too many tourists fitting Jordin's description that visited the area.

After searching seven different locations, we retreated to the truck around nine o'clock to search for a place to stay for the night.

Earlier in the day we had found much to talk about, but now we had retreated into silence. Tired, hungry, and discouraged, I stared out of my side window, watching the quaint brick sidewalks speed past.

"Stop the truck! Stop!" I shouted, sitting up ramrod-straight.

Derek slammed on the brakes in a panic, and the screech was earsplitting. "What?!"

"Over there!" I pointed out my window. Something had caught my eye. Something that shouldn't have been there.

"What? The graveyard?"

Instead of responding, I opened my door and got out of the truck. I ran through an empty field toward the graveyard, my adrenaline surging. I was more sure of what I'd seen with every step.

Derek parked the pickup near the sidewalk and caught up with me where I stopped. The graveyard was surrounded by a tall iron fence, and the gate, which had doors that curved up on both sides to form an arch, was the highest part of all. I grabbed the iron bars and looked desperately through them, trying to see if I could catch a glimpse of what I had seen again.

"Maia, what did you see?" Derek asked, panting for breath. He stared at me instead of the graveyard, interested only in my answer.

I glanced at him sidelong, wondering what I should say. The edge of my vision had only caught the briefest of glimpses, from a significant distance. There was no way to be completely certain, and I didn't want to upset him.

"I saw a girl," I said.

Derek turned to the graveyard, fatigue filling his eyes. "I don't see anyone, Maia. The place is empty. Which isn't really surprising, since the sun's been down for two hours. . . . Your eyes are playing tricks on you, you're just tired—"

"It was Jordin."

Derek stopped short and twisted his head in my direction so fast I was afraid he would sprain his neck.

"Are you sure?" he asked.

"No! I'm not sure at all!" I replied, drained and not wanting to have to explain myself.

I couldn't tell him it was definitely Jordin. I had no proof, and as tired as I was, it was entirely possible that my bleary eyes *were* seeing things.

But I *knew* it. It was her. I don't know if it was some latent paranormal investigator's instinct or if Jordin had pricked my consciousness somehow to let me know beyond a doubt that she was trying to get my attention. But I knew it was her.

"I think she was trying to get our attention," I explained. "Maybe she wants to help us find the journal."

"Then where did she go?" Derek asked, examining the graveyard again, desperately looking for his love. "If she could appear enough to get your attention, why couldn't she just stand there and point out the journal's location to us?"

"It doesn't work that way," I said, still not in the mood to give any lessons in the paranormal just now. "Ghosts that manifest visibly can rarely do it for very long. It's like it requires some great exertion and they can't maintain it."

I could hear Derek breathing loudly as he considered this, still studying the interior of the cemetery. "Where did you see her?"

I pointed through the bars. "Over there somewhere . . . near some of those big headstones in the back."

The grave markers I'd pointed out were in the far left corner of the smallish cemetery.

"We need a way in," said Derek, and he was already scanning the area around us, searching for a means of getting inside.

It wasn't going to be easy. The fence was topped all the way around with black metal spikes. They didn't look sharp, but they were more than nine feet in the air, so I couldn't imagine a scenario where we might try to climb over them and not be impaled, even if they were blunt.

Despite my misgivings, Derek tried to do that very thing.

There were only two horizontal bars, one near the top and one near the bottom. They didn't provide much leverage, so Derek actually tried to climb up the fence using nothing but his hands gripping the vertical bars. It didn't go well. With the running he'd just done a few minutes earlier and now the sudden urgency he was feeling, his hands were too sweaty to get a solid grip.

Derek grunted with the effort, and the ensuing frustration. "Okay, plan B," he growled, and turned to march back to his truck.

My stomach churned. I had no idea what he had in mind, but I assumed it would be something reckless. Exhaustion was never a good companion of desperation.

I had turned back to study the interior of the cemetery once more when I heard the engine of his truck start up behind me in the distance.

When I turned to look, Derek had jumped the sidewalk curb and the truck was plowing through the empty field headed straight for me. My breath caught in my throat for a second but then I collected my wits and jumped aside. Seconds later, his truck battered straight through the huge iron gate, crashing the two doors wide open. He slammed on his brakes just in time to avoid running into the nearest graves.

"What are you doing?!" I cried as he stepped out of the truck.

"I'm not a ghost hunter, Maia, and I'm out of my depth with all this paranormal stuff. But I'm getting my fiancée back," he declared. He grabbed a shovel out of the back of the truck and started striding toward the back left corner of the graveyard.

I grabbed my flashlight out of the front seat and then had to walk fast to keep up with him. "Do you know how illegal what you're doing is?"

He threw me an ugly glance. "Do you know how much I don't care? Somebody has taken my girlfriend and literally sucked her soul out of her body. She needs my help, and if I ever want to touch her, hold her, or kiss her ever again, I *need that journal*! If I broke the stupid fence, I'm sure Jordin will gladly pay to have it fixed or replaced once we get her back in her body, where she belongs. Good grief, I can't believe I just said that."

Once again, I was seeing a new side of Derek. But I didn't know what to make of this one. He was so rigid, so polite, so straightlaced. . . . I wouldn't have thought he had a dangerous or unpredictable cell in his body. The stress and exhaustion were getting to him, stripping away his filters and boundaries.

"What's with the shovel?" I asked. "You think she buried it?"

"Makes sense, doesn't it?" he replied. "If she had time, if she was being chased or something, she would have wanted to hide it where it wouldn't be found."

It did make sense. Though in my mind, I'd always pictured her being snatched without having a chance to make a run for it. I don't know why; it was just how I thought about it.

"Maybe she was investigating here," I mused. It was an old

graveyard; I saw dates on some of the tombstones going back to the 1800s.

We reached the back corner and started our search.

"Why was all this so important to Jordin?" Derek asked as he grabbed the flashlight from me and scanned the graveyard.

I heard the pain in his question and part of me wanted to tell him what I knew. But it wasn't my place.

"She was obsessed with the paranormal, Derek," I said, taking the flashlight back. "Obsession doesn't usually adhere to logic." It was a cop-out answer, stating the obvious. I knew it. But I couldn't think of anything else to say.

Derek stopped where he was, a few rows over from me. "Why won't you tell me?!" he shouted. "I have a right to know!"

A beam of light lit up Derek where he stood, and I turned to see that it was coming from a flashlight.

A policeman stood in the cemetery, less than twenty feet from us, and he wasn't happy.

"You two partying a little too hard tonight?" the cop asked. I figured it was probably the hundredth time he'd asked it to kids our age.

"No, sir," I said. "No partying. We're looking for a friend." It was kind of true.

"File a missing persons report," he replied mechanically, "after I run you in for breaking down the fence. This is private property."

Derek tried to argue, his temper still flaring. "We've *tried* filing missing persons reports, we've tried everything we can think of, and no one will help us!"

If I hadn't seen and done the things I had seen and done in my life, I might not have noticed what happened next. The brisk night air was subtly and slowly being replaced by a bitter chill. I doubt Derek or the cop were conscious of the shift.

The cop opened his mouth to argue back at Derek, but the words caught in his throat. Choking, he put both his hands up around his neck, trying in vain to pull away invisible fingers that were squeezing off his ability to breathe. His eyes bulged, and he started to sway.

I ran, hoping to catch him before he fell to the ground, but at the last second, his arm flew straight out and I slammed face-first into his fist.

The next thing I remember is opening my eyes while flat on my back. The cop was standing above me holding his gun straight out at Derek, but I could tell from the horrified look on his face that he wasn't in control of his actions. He didn't look like he was possessed, either, though. I'd seen a few possessions and they were nothing like this.

It was instead like a powerful apparition was maneuvering him like a puppet. It had weakened him first by closing off his air supply, making the rest of his body malleable. Then it had pulled his strings, knocking me to the ground and holding Derek at bay with the cop's pistol.

I tried to sit up but something shoved me back down onto my back, hard. It knocked the wind out of me, and I was reminded again of how cold the air had become in the cemetery. I noticed I couldn't move now. I could no longer raise myself up. Something was pinning me to the grass.

I could see the cop's finger trembling as it hovered at the gun's trigger, and I prayed that in the fleeting seconds while I had blacked out, he hadn't already shot Derek.

My chest felt like a cannonball had landed on top of it,

jump-starting my heart and causing it to beat painfully hard. I couldn't see a way out of this. I had been around the paranormal all my life, but never had I been forced to *fight* it.

"Derek?!" I cried out. "Are you hurt?"

His voice came from nearby, and it was high enough up off the ground that I could tell he was still standing more or less where I'd last seen him. "Not for the moment."

"Something's here!" I called to him. "I can't move. It's holding me down. It's trying to make the cop shoot you!"

When Derek didn't immediately answer, I found my flashlight on the ground nearby and craned my neck backward on the ground, trying to spot him. I saw him standing in front of a large grave marker, but he was perfectly still and his eyes were closed.

Then they snapped open. With more power and authority than I'd ever heard come from his mouth, he strongly stated, "In the name of Jehovah the Most High and His Son Jesus Christ, you are commanded to leave this place! The Holy Spirit compels you: Be gone!"

The pressure let up from whatever was holding me down, and I saw the cop's eyes roll up into his head just before he went limp and collapsed on top of me. A warm air descended upon us and I wrapped myself in its soothing heat.

Derek appeared quickly and rolled the cop over and off me, and helped me to my feet. I could see the policeman's chest rising and falling, but he was out cold.

I looked at Derek anew, swallowing hard. "That was . . ." I couldn't find the words. "That was really good."

Derek was all business, and I was glad to see his maniacal phase had passed. "Would it be safe to say that that was not the garden-variety paranormal activity?"

I nodded.

"Right. Let's find that journal."

————————

It was less than ten minutes before we'd uncovered it. As Derek had suspected, it was buried, hidden just a few inches down in the sediment of a freshly dug grave. Derek was very careful to respectfully replace all of the dirt he had to dig up, making it appear that the ground had never been disturbed.

Per our agreement, he let me have the first look at the journal. I decided to wait until we were back in the truck and on the road before I cracked it open.

I skipped straight past the entries on our trips to the back of the journal, looking for Jordin's final entry. Two minutes later, my expression must have changed drastically, because Derek picked up on it.

"What?" he said. "Talk to me."

I stared at the pages again, still not believing the words it bore. "I don't think Jordin was abducted."

"What do you mean?"

I skipped backward in time through the journal, scanning page after page. "What's happened to her is something she *wanted*. According to this, she had a planned meeting at the graveyard with somebody who works for DHI, and she wrote in the journal that DHI was going to help her find what she was looking for. They were going to make it a reality. And a lot of her earlier entries talk about wanting to reach 'the other side,' to see it and feel it and *go there*. As in, physically. I think she meant the spirit realm. All that time she spent investigating the paranormal with me . . . what she was after was a way *in*."

Derek scrunched up his face in some combination of confusion and disgust. "Are you saying she *wanted* DHI to make her go all *Flatliners*?"

"I don't think she had a death wish," I replied. "But she definitely wanted to find a way to bridge the divide, reach through the veil, and . . . well . . . *visit* the spirit realm. There's something she felt like she needed to do there."

"What? Why?"

"She doesn't go into detail about her reasons," I said, holding up the closed journal.

He eyed me significantly. "But she told you herself. Didn't she."

I was saved by the bell. My phone rang.

"Ms. Peters?" said the male voice on the other end.

Uh-oh. I was about to receive more threats, just like the last time DHI's artificially created apparitions had reached out and touched me—when my dorm room had been destroyed.

"Who's asking?"

"It's Pierre Ravenwood."

"Oh! Right, yes."

"I'm just calling to let you know that I've been taken off of the story. My editor allowed me to pursue it as an indulgence, but her patience ran out when—in a last-ditch effort to save the story—I filled her in on your 'ghost manufacturing' theory. I was able to talk her out of firing me, but I've been assigned a different beat. I'm sorry I can't help you anymore."

My mind spun. "But what about Durham Holdings? Did you ever find anything out about them?"

"DHI's secrets are buried deep. That headquarters of theirs in Copenhagen is literally some kind of fortress. They're just untouchable. I couldn't even get anyone at their upstate office to return my calls."

I sighed loud enough that I'm sure he heard it.

Then my head popped up. "Wait, what 'upstate office'?"

"Durham Holdings has an office building somewhere in upstate New York. It was built prior to the opening of Ghost Town, but apparently it's so small it wasn't worth making a deal about. There were no press releases or announcements about it, of any kind."

My heart beat faster, new thoughts pummeling my mind and stirring up dust like an old bag of flour. "Do you have an address?"

"Sure, but I told you, there's nothing to it—"

"Mr. Ravenwood," I said, "it'll take us some time to get there, but if you can meet me at that address a few hours from now, I promise you'll leave it with the story of your career."

I stared out of my window, feeling a plan start to come together. It felt good. I couldn't stop the grim smile that formed on my face.

But when I turned to share the news with Derek, he was staring at me, pale white.

"What?"

"Your neck . . ." he whispered.

Something stung a bit at the back of my neck, and I had the sense that it had been stinging for a few hours now, but I hadn't taken the time to stop and really notice it. I didn't need a mirror to see what it was.

"You're marked," Derek said.

Mount Hope Methodist Episcopal Church

Mount Hope, New Jersey

Built: 1868

what moved in when
the congregation moved out?

SIXTEEN

MARCH 20TH

I couldn't sleep, so I cursed the name of Jordin Cole as I lay in my bed.

And not just any curses. I used the good ones—the ones my mother uttered in Spanish when she was *really* mad. The ones she knew were bad enough to require a visit to confession.

It was all Jordin's fault, after all. I wouldn't be able to sleep now. If she'd just listened to me, she wouldn't be in any danger while I lay there trying to rest. Instead, she'd completely ignored my advice and left to investigate the church in Mount Hope alone, about an hour ago.

What was she thinking? I understood obsession; my father had his own unique brand of it when it came to his work. I knew enough about the subject to perceive the difference between obsession and desperation.

Jordin was desperate. Desperate to contact her parents? I wasn't so sure about that anymore. This went way beyond an addiction to paranormal investigation. She had something much more personal at stake in all this, and only now was I beginning to see just how far she was willing to take it.

Whether it was her parents or not, apparently she was crazed enough to risk her life for it. But at this abandoned church, it wasn't just her mortal life that would be in danger.

And if my suspicions were right about her somehow attracting the extreme amounts of activity we'd observed on our investigations . . . then I didn't even want to think about what she might attract at a place this bad.

I angrily muttered something under my breath in Spanish as I threw my covers off and got out of bed.

Mount Hope Methodist Episcopal was surrounded by a small wooded area on all sides, but rather ominously, the ten or twenty feet of the woods that touched the tiny old church was dead. It was like the ground had been salted and nothing could grow there. Even the sickly brown hue of the dirt looked cursed.

I rubbed my cold hands together as I carefully walked up to the ancient little building and thought about how much I *didn't* want to go inside. Jordin or no Jordin, this just wasn't a place a person in their right mind would go. The faded wood siding was rotten. Every window and door had been covered over and sealed tight with plywood. There were no electrical lines running to the building, and there was a sign over the door warning people to stay out.

I climbed the cement stairs—which looked like they might crack and fall away from the building at any time—and shivered involuntarily as I examined the front door.

There was a small space in the sealed-up entrance where Jordin had pried open the plywood just enough to crawl through.

Abandoning all sense of self-preservation, I held my tiny flashlight in my mouth and crawled through the open space on my hands and knees. The ground was filthy and I was none too happy about whatever grime was getting all over me.

Inside, I stood and looked around the tiny sanctuary. It was a cold night outside, but the interior of the church was like a freezer. The kind of biting cold that cut through your skin down to the bone. Not only that, but I was immediately overcome with a sensation of dread. Every hair on my skin stood at attention, and the air felt thick and heavy.

What could have happened in the spirit realm to cause a one-time place of worship to become a haven for something evil? Was this considered a victory by the forces of darkness? A "gaining of ground" in the never-ending war between angels and demons that no human eye could see?

The place was not much bigger than a modest living room, with only one or two small, ancient-looking pews still standing and not much else. There was no light in the room at all, with the windows boarded up, and the sound of my feet creaking on the old wood floor was enough to creep me out. There was no sign of Jordin, but I spotted another door at the back of the room that was propped open.

Inside the door I found some wooden stairs leading down.

She's cracked, I decided. *She actually went down into the basement.*

As I studied the stairs for a moment, I heard a voice emanating from the silence below. It was Jordin's voice, but it was barely above a whisper. She sounded like she was talking on her phone. I almost thought I heard her ask a question, but I couldn't make out what it was.

I descended the stairs as fast as I dared and entered the basement, which had the same basic square footprint as the sanctuary above. I spotted Jordin sitting alone in a far corner with a small flashlight in her hands, and no sign of a phone. Her audio recorder and video camera were on the floor nearby, both with their red recording lights on.

"Did you miss the signs outside that forbid trespassing?" I said. "You're breaking the law by being here."

"No I'm not, though technically, you are," Jordin replied. "I bought the property from the city this morning. Those were your footsteps I heard upstairs, weren't they?" she asked, looking disappointed. "Why are you here?"

"I'm rescuing you!" I shot back, furious. "There's evil in this place. Don't you feel it?"

"Do I look like I need rescuing?" she said, incredulous. "I'm totally fine."

I studied her surroundings. The building looked so old that it could fall apart around us at any moment. The corner she sat in had been cleared of the rat feces that peppered the rest of the floor. The cement was cracked and splattered with red streaks of either paint or blood. The wooden planks that made up the sanctuary decking over our heads were rotted, with the wear of time beginning the process of crumbling.

"Who were you talking to?" I asked.

Jordin grinned. "I think it's the spirit of a former parishioner, possibly a deacon or a minister."

I looked around the room again, my skin crawling. I wanted to be absolutely anywhere else in the world. "You actually heard it speaking to you? The voice was audible?"

She nodded enthusiastically and grinned again. "I knew coming here was a good idea—I've made *direct contact* with the other side!"

"But contact with *what*?" I said under my breath, though it wasn't really a question. I walked out into the middle of the room, grounding and steeling myself. I wasn't very good at what I was about to attempt—I'd watched my mother do it several times—but there was no telling what kind of door Jordin had opened here and one of us had to close it. Once I was in the center of the basement, I spoke louder and with as much authority as I could muster. "Whatever is in this place, in the name of Jesus Christ, I order you to reveal yourself."

I may not have been a very good believer, but I believed nonetheless. Mostly because the command I just uttered always produced results. Nothing in the spirit realm was powerful enough to disobey it.

The room was silent, but a harsh wind whipped up outside, battering the plywood that covered the old windows in the sanctuary above. A chill brushed across my arms and I was very aware that the basement's temperature had dropped by at least ten degrees in a matter of seconds.

"Reveal yourself!" I challenged it again.

"No need to shout," a voice said in my ear. "I'm right here."

I jumped back, stumbling onto my rear end as my blood turned to ice.

The voice that replied had spoken in *my* voice. This thing was using my own voice to answer me.

In all my years of investigating, I'd never encountered anything like this before. But even a rookie would have to know that hearing your own voice come from something outside of you couldn't possibly be a good thing.

I glanced back at Jordin. She was watching me with interest, but showed no sign of alarm. I assumed this meant she hadn't heard my voice emanating from the dark room around us.

"Why are you here?" I asked it.

"I like it here," it replied in a soothing, playful tone.

I stood up again and steeled myself. Demon or no demon, I was a professional and this thing would not get the best of me.

"What do you want?" I asked.

"Who are you talking to?" Jordin whispered.

"Shut up!" I whispered back. I was so mad at her, I didn't even want to look at her.

"Maia, Maia, Maia . . ." was the entity's reply, only now it spoke using my mother's voice, and I could hear it smiling. "You already know what I want, *mija*."

"I do?"

The force of a gunshot or a sledgehammer slammed into my chest, knocking me off my feet. I landed hard on my back, and my heart skipped a few beats as I lay there in shock.

Jordin screamed.

"Sweet pea," said my father's voice from somewhere close by, "I just want to have fun."

Jordin screamed a second time as a tremendous crash came from upstairs, as if a part of the roof had caved in.

"Maia . . . ?" she cried out.

"Sweet pea . . ." I felt hot breath on my face but saw nothing as the voice of my father spoke again, though this time it was only a whisper. "I'm going to play with you. I'm going to rape you until you're dead. I'm going to burn you. And when I'm done, I'm going to carry your soul to hell in my arms."

My heart was no longer beating in my chest. Every part of me was frozen in fear as I lay on my back.

"MAIA!" Jordin shouted.

I spun my head in her direction. She had backed away from her corner and was pointing at the walls.

Now I screamed.

Streaks of dark red blood ran down the basement walls. I swiveled my head all around. The blood streaks weren't covering the walls, they were scattered about, a batch of them here and there. Very, very slowly they oozed down the cement and pooled on the ground beneath. Based on the way Jordin was wiping at her clothes, I guessed that some of it must've gotten on her.

I wanted to jump up and flee for my life, but it was as if some terrible weight was pressing on my chest. I don't know if it was the creature playing with me or if it was my heart condition rendering me numb, but I was pinned solidly to the ground.

Jordin sprang from the floor. She was quivering as she grabbed me by the hand and dragged me to my feet with all the strength she could gather. Once I was standing, the sensation upon my chest disappeared, but I was still in pain and felt sick all over, like I was in the worst throes of the flu.

We both heard a deep, rumbling growl from the perimeter

of the room, like a wild predator was about to pounce on us. I knew Jordin heard it this time because her already huge eyes grew even bigger as she turned slowly to look at me.

"Run," I whispered, and she took my hand. Leaning on her for support, I was able to make it to the stairs.

I took one last weary glance back at the room as I mounted the stairwell. The blood on the basement walls had vanished as if it had never been there. I wondered if it had ever really been on Jordin's clothes or if it had disappeared there, as well.

When we reached the sanctuary up top, the growling and snarling came again, but it sounded no farther away from us than before.

I heard Jordin gasp right before I looked across the room and saw it for myself: one of the old pews I'd seen on my way in had been flung up against the double doors, barring the building's only exit. It was suspended more than two feet off the ground.

This had to be the source of the terrible crash we'd heard only minutes ago. Our jaws hung open for just a moment as we took in the terrifying sight.

Jordin whimpered in fright, but the sound barely registered. My mind was spinning and my heart racing as we stared down the barricade before us.

"If we don't die, I'm going to kill you," I whispered.

The wind whipped up again outside and howled against the old church.

"In the name of Jesus Christ, I command you to let us out of here!" I shouted over the wind.

The wind only blew harder, and we heard the growling again. It was deep and powerful.

"You're a Christian. Now might be a good time to start praying for a little help," I remarked to Jordin.

Not amused, she closed her eyes and began to pray, moving her mouth, though only her breath came out. Still she held my hand tight and squeezed it hard as she prayed.

Since her eyes were shut, I was the only one to see the hand and arm-type shapes that protruded from the decayed wooden walls, reaching for us. It was like the walls had turned to fabric sheets and people were pressing against them from behind, trying to tear through them to get to us.

It was the most terrifying thing I'd ever seen, and I thought I might pass out from the horror that gripped me.

I tried to compartmentalize the fear, looking all around the room for some kind of solution. A boarded-up window we might break through. A loose plank we might rip free and use to pry the pew away from the doors. Something. Anything.

Jordin was still praying when I smelled it: the scent of burning wood and smoke.

I looked back toward the basement and could see the flickering light of orange flames reflecting off of the wooden steps. I put aside thoughts of how such a thing could even be possible and decided to focus on finding a way out, while Jordin kept praying. She was at it so hard she was sweating.

The fire reached the planks beneath our feet and began to burn quickly, unnaturally through them. I jerked Jordin out of her reverie, and when she saw what was happening, she pulled me toward the double front doors, moving fast. There was little time until the floor burned away beneath us, and when that happened, we would surely fall back down into the basement and be trapped there.

I wondered if anyone would ever even find our ashes in this accursed place.

We pulled on the pew blocking the doors, but it was held firmly in place by some supernatural force. We couldn't make it budge.

I spotted a loose plank nearby and saw that one end of it was on fire. An idea forming, I yanked it free and held it up to the bottom of the pew blocking the door. The flame caught right in the middle of the pew and I knelt down to blow on it, trying to coax it to burn through a cross-section of the pew.

We heard the growling again, this time right in our ears, and it was louder than ever. It was like a massive lion was breathing down our necks, about to take a bite. We both screamed at the sound, and I saw tears were streaming down Jordin's face. It was only then that I realized my cheeks were wet, as well.

Cinders rained down on our heads as the pew caught fully on fire, and I pointed Jordin to one end of the pew as I moved to the other. The floor beneath our feet crunching and sagging with every step, we heaved on either end of the pew and with a great spewing of fiery ash, it split in half.

I could hear pieces of the floor crashing behind us as we crawled to Jordin's makeshift opening and pushed ourselves frantically through.

"I'm sorry I'm sorry I'm sorry I'm sorry!!" Jordin screamed and cried as we fled together.

I put a hand over my chest to try and force my heart not to palpitate, and wiped the moisture away from my face as we ran.

I heard a throaty, cackling laugh from somewhere deep inside the church as we ran into the night.

SEVENTEEN

By my best guess, now that the mark had appeared on my neck I had less than eight hours before whatever was going to happen to me happened.

It was strange how fast the symbol had appeared. Jordin and Carrie reported multiple instances of the nightmarish dream before they ever had the mark on their necks. I had only had the dream once.

Howell Durham's apparitions that attacked us at the grave must have reported back to him. So he and his pseudoscience cronies had accelerated the process just for me.

I knew that Jordin and Carrie had both disappeared at night. Even though Jordin's journal indicated that she signed up for DHI's crazy scheme, that didn't mean she knew the full extent of it at the time, and the fact that she had come to both Derek and me asking for help meant that something had gone very wrong. As for the others, there may not have been anything particularly otherworldly about their disappearances; now that we knew real men made of flesh and blood were involved, it was more likely that these people from Durham Holdings just outright kidnapped the people bearing the mark. Maybe it acted like some kind of weird homing beacon for them.

If so, then it would be leading those same men to me right now.

But the question remained of how it got on my neck in the first place. On that, I hadn't a clue.

Then again, Jordin and Carrie both hadn't been on the move when they found their marks. They hadn't done anything to prevent what was going to happen, because Carrie had no idea what it meant, and Jordin pretty much just submitted to it.

I, on the other hand, was a moving target. If they wanted me, they would have to catch me.

Or, I thought sourly, *they could just wait until I knock on their front door.*

Why should they bother chasing me if I was headed straight for them?

———

Derek drove in the early morning to reach the address Pierre Ravenwood had provided, a heavily wooded area at the foot of the Catskills where we found nothing.

The exact address didn't exist. It was an empty lot in the middle of nowhere, with a large wooden sign proclaiming that a new strip mall was coming to the sleepy, barely inhabited area about a year from now.

The one thing we did find was Pierre, waiting for us on the side of the road in front of the parcel of empty land. He stood outside in the unseasonably frosty ground, leaning up against the side of his sedan with his arms crossed.

I instructed Derek to pull up behind him and stop.

Pierre inspected us with a sour expression as we approached. "What are we doing out here, Ms. Peters?" he said, a little louder than was necessary.

"You tell me," I replied. "This is the address of Durham Holdings' New York office, right?"

"According to the sign," Pierre replied, nodding at the billboard announcing the construction of the soon-to-be strip mall. "That doesn't tell me why I'm here."

"Look," I said. I had run out of patience. "Whatever has happened to my friend, it's preceded by the appearance of that symbol I showed you, and now it's happening to me!"

I spun in place, pulled my hair to the front, and lowered my collar so he could see the mark on my neck.

Pierre was silent, but I saw his eyebrows scrunched together when I turned back around.

"*Something* is at work here. You must know it, you can feel it in your gut. It's what led you to write that article about the college dropouts. You can either help us figure out what it is or you can go back to writing obits or whatever you've been demoted to."

A moment of silence passed as Pierre Ravenwood stared me down.

Derek chimed in. "Why would DHI fake an address? You think it's all a hoax and the office just doesn't exist?"

My instincts were saying no to that. "What would that serve? An address to an office that isn't really there?"

"So what are you thinking, then?" Pierre asked. "This address is a decoy?"

"Has to be," I replied, nodding. "The office is real, it's just not here. But I'd be willing to bet it's around here someplace."

"We passed a gas station a few miles back," Derek pointed out. "Maybe we could ask around."

Pierre let out a long sigh, but said, "I'll follow you."

"No," I said, stopping him before he could get into his car. "You're driving."

"What?" Derek and Pierre both said at the same time.

I looked at Derek. "The two of us are being hunted. If whatever attacked us at the cemetery reported back to DHI, they almost certainly included a description of the truck that smashed through the cemetery gates."

Derek reluctantly agreed.

Pierre closed his eyes and shook his head. "Just get in the car. I'll busy myself pretending I didn't hear any of what you just said."

———

The lady at the twenty-four-hour gas station hurriedly put out a cigarette butt as we walked into the store.

I looked at my watch. It was after three in the morning already.

"Help you find something?" the woman asked.

I forced a smile as I approached the counter. Her name tag identified her as Vera.

"We're looking for directions, actually," I said in the friendliest tone I could muster. "We're trying to find an office building, but the address we have took us to the wrong place."

"Lived here my whole life, sweetie," said Vera, and she helpfully pulled out a map from a rack just in front of the counter and unfolded it on the countertop. "What are you looking for?"

"Durham Holdings," I replied.

Vera was looking down at the counter but I saw her flinch. She tried to remain casual as she asked, "You always go looking for offices in the middle of the night?" The "helpful local" had dropped out of her tone.

"Just the mysterious ones," said Derek, stepping forward and flashing that charming smile of his. "Surely you've heard of it, haven't you?"

To my tremendous surprise, and a growing irritation at my entire gender, Vera actually blushed a bit at his attention. I was watching when it happened, and I was so offended that I must've opened my mouth, because Pierre elbowed me to get me to close it. The guy might have been somewhat handsome, but come on. He was going to be a minister, for crying out loud. There had to be some commandment that forbade him from using this uncanny ability to make random women swoon.

"Well, sure, I've heard of it," Vera said. She leaned in conspiratorially and lowered her voice, even though we were the only people in the building—or anywhere for miles around. "We're not supposed to talk about it."

"Why not?" asked Derek.

Even though she was still mooning over him and those Colgate teeth of his, she hesitated.

I rolled my eyes. "You can trust us, Vera. I'm nobody, this guy in the back is just along for the ride, and Derek here is a preacher's kid and has never done a bad thing in his life. The last six hours notwithstanding."

Derek threw me a look but quickly returned to Vera. He flattened out the map that she'd unfolded and pointed to a familiar spot on it. "This is where the address led us to. Is there somewhere else we should be looking?"

Vera gave Derek a half frown/half smile and slid her finger down the map to a location high up in the Catskills. Then she winked at him.

Pierre stepped forward and got a good look at the spot on the map Vera was pointing to, memorizing it.

"Thank you, Vera," Derek said, and smiled at her one last time before we left.

As we were walking back to the car, Pierre asked, "Are you two dating?"

"No," Derek told him.

"No!" I stated emphatically.

"My heart belongs to another," Derek said, all the charm dissolving into hardened resolve. "She's one of the girls they abducted and I'm going to get her back."

"Well, you two act like an old married couple," Pierre observed.

I grimaced. "We just . . . we've had to spend a little too much time together lately. Derek's engaged and I am *exceedingly* available."

"Good," Pierre said, getting into the front seat of the car. "Then if we get to the bottom of this DHI business and I get my old job back, I'm taking you to dinner, Ms. Peters."

I blinked. Then I grinned as I slid into the back seat.

We wound our way slowly through a small township and on up the mountain, passing a sign that labeled the area as "Catskill State Park."

"Why would the state of New York let a company build an office out in the middle of a park?" I mused.

"Kickback," Pierre said from the front seat. "Have you seen these roads we're riding on? They've been re-paved very recently and outfitted with reflectors and guardrails on both sides."

"Yep," said Derek. "And I noticed a brand-new-looking high school in that town we just passed through."

Pierre nodded. "DHI lined the pockets of all the right people in that tiny little town, made sizable contributions to the local economy and the natural environment, and were granted a concession in return. Your friend Vera said the locals weren't supposed to talk about the place. They've probably been asked by the bigger businesses in town to help them keep a low profile."

"But all that subterfuge just to build a little office out in the middle of a forest up on a mountain?" I asked. "Feels like an unbalanced trade."

But something had caught Pierre's eye. "Maybe the office is not so little. Look."

He pointed through the front windshield at a sight far in the distance, and it couldn't have been more out of place if it tried. Derek whistled.

The mountain forest concealed most of it, but the top few floors of what was easily a ten-story building or better stuck out above the tops of the trees. It was white, with a perfectly round footprint, and had floodlights lining the roof's perimeter, shining straight down to create *A*-shaped glows up against the building.

We were more than five miles away, maybe farther, but moving straight toward the big white structure. "Stop the car," I said.

Pierre pulled over on the side of the road, up against a thick cluster of spruce trees.

"You said they knew you were coming," Pierre said.

"Right," I agreed. "We can't drive in, we'll be spotted before we get close."

"Then we find another way to reach it," Derek said, "and go the last leg by foot."

———————

We agreed to the plan, though the extra trouble we went to added two hours to finally reaching our destination.

Pierre found a side road that looked like it led around the far side of the building, and we parked about two miles out so we could walk the rest of the way.

It was biting cold up on the mountain and all three of us had come without winter apparel. I insisted we slog through the dangerous, hard-to-see forest off to the side of the main road, and no one argued.

Creeping through the forest, yet keeping the road in sight, we made painfully slow progress. Not once did we see a sign of any sort along the road, but we did see trucks. Unmarked white trucks thundered by us, coming and going again and again. The thought of what they were probably delivering made me feel a little sick to my stomach.

Despite the dark, it was impossible to get lost, because the big white building always loomed straight ahead. It was so huge, it barely grew in our vision even after walking for more than half an hour. Oddly, we couldn't see any windows. The thing was a big white cylinder, like a missile silo for an incredibly fat rocket.

As we came to about half a mile out from the building, I felt something cold touch my nose. I stopped and looked around.

It was snowing.

We couldn't believe it. We were walking through a snow shower in a dark mountain forest at the end of summer. There was no way things could get any more surreal.

We finally drew near to the building and found it to be devoid of electronic fences or guards. Pierre pointed out that there was probably no need for them, since the building was completely unmarked—no logo even designating it as Durham Holdings International—so for all intents and purposes, it just didn't exist. Who needed security when nobody in the world knew where you were?

The three of us squatted behind some trees just on the edge of the forest and got a look at the loading dock where several of the unmarked trucks were backing in and unloading their cargo.

I hugged myself in the cold as I got a better look at the building from up close. It was even bigger than I'd thought. The lack of windows made it hard to judge, but I guessed it must have been over fifteen stories into the night. And while it was perfectly round, its white cement sides were not smooth. Hundreds or maybe thousands of symbols were carved into the cement. Every inch of the building was covered with the colorless engravings, overlapping and intertwining with one another. In no way did it surprise me to see that they bore a resemblance to Dr. Eccleston's alchemical symbols.

I had been to a lot of places all over the globe that most sane people considered to be frightening. Yet I hadn't been genuinely fearful in many of them. The behemoth of a building that stood before me like an enormous sentinel reaching high into the night sky was the most terrifying place I'd ever seen. I couldn't imagine why DHI had gone to all the trouble of building Ghost Town; if they wanted to scare people, they should've just invited them to see what I was looking at now.

"Look there!" Derek whispered, pointing to the loading dock.

A couple of workers in navy blue jumpsuits—deceptively similar to those of a paramedic, I noted—were hauling something out of the back of one of the trucks. When it emerged into the open, we could see that it was a gurney, carrying an unconscious man, who was covered with a white sheet all the way up to his neck. The two men wheeled the stretcher up a ramp inside the covered delivery bay, and we could just see the recipient. A man in a lab coat, holding a clipboard, stopped them and took custody of the gurney and its occupant. The two delivery guys waited off to one side while the man with the clipboard turned the unconscious man's head painfully to one side and took a close look at a black mark at the base of his neck. The symbol. He noted something on his clipboard and then nodded at the guys in the blue jumpsuits. They grabbed the gurney again and pushed it through a large doorway that led inside the building.

"Guess we know where they're doing the whole 'soul extraction' thing," Derek whispered. "At the rate they're bringing them in, it makes me wonder how many of them are in there."

"But what do they do with the victims' bodies after the procedure?" I asked. "I see them taking plenty of people in, but nothing's coming back out."

"There's no conspicuous landfill in sight," said Pierre.

I was glad Pierre didn't finish that thought, for Derek's sake. He didn't need to hear someone suggest that his girlfriend's body could be piled beneath a bunch of others in a big hole.

"Anybody thinking about *Star Wars*?" Pierre asked.

"Wookie handcuffs?" I guessed.

"Wookie handcuffs," he said with a nod.

Derek glanced at both of us, a mixture of eagerness and resolve. "Let's do it," he said.

Alcatraz

San Francisco, California

Main Cell Block Opened: 1912
Closed: 1963

a night I'll never forget...
it ain't called "Devil's Island" for nothing

EIGHTEEN

APRIL 22ND

It took a full three weeks of Jordin's badgering, pleading, begging, and promising never to ignore my instructions again before I deigned to even speak to her. It was another week after that that I finally agreed to take her on another trip.

I knew I shouldn't. I knew my doctor would kill me, and that it could be dangerous for Jordin if she really was the epicenter of all the activity we'd been finding. But I also knew that she'd go investigating anyway, without me, and though I hated to admit it, I felt a certain level of responsibility for getting her so hooked on this stuff. Plus, the scientist in me had an almost clinical desire to see this through, just to find out if it really was Jordin that was somehow a magnet for so much of the paranormal activity we'd seen.

I could hold on to a grudge for a long time. I got it from my mother. So I enjoyed nursing those angry feelings for Jordin as long as I possibly could.

Making matters worse between us was the fact that Jordin had lost her digital recorder and video camera in her rush to flee the church in New Jersey. These were easily replaceable, but it irked me that if we *had* to have gone to a place like that, we had absolutely nothing to show for it. No evidence whatsoever, despite the extraordinary and awful things that happened there.

Plus, my physical well-being was foremost on my mind now, since the events in New Jersey had done nothing to help my heart condition. More than once, even the memory of the things we'd seen at the church in Mount Hope had nearly forced me to take a Valium to keep my heart from racing.

When I felt like I was up to it again and I'd decided Jordin had suffered enough for her sins, I said I would take her investigating again. But I told her I would only do it on the condition that I had no more than two or three of these trips left in me. The end of the school year was approaching and we both would have exams to study for soon, so whenever I said we were done, we were done for good and I wouldn't be talked into any more of this.

She agreed with one condition of her own: that I make these last few trips the biggest and best we'd ever undertaken.

Choosing locations to fit that bill wasn't hard. The first one that came to mind was an obvious choice, but I decided to save that one for last in favor of a more immediate trip to California. My parents lived in San José, and I was eager to see them. I hadn't yet shared with them the news about my panic disorder—I didn't want to do it over the phone—and my inner child was longing for a little parental sympathy from Mom and Dad.

———————

After we exchanged tea and sympathy, I asked Mom and Dad how the family business was doing. I was hoping to find out, without giving away my reasons for asking, if they had seen an increase in the levels of paranormal activity in their investigations of late. But Dad reminded me—and I should have remembered anyway—that they were in the middle of their annual downtime, between seasons of the show. They were consumed with the business side of things—paying bills, planning where they would go to investigate next season, that sort of thing—and had conducted no investigations of their own for months.

After personal time was over, we pointed our rental car west and I informed Jordin of our next stop.

"Alcatraz?"

"Private access for one night. I promised you'd be very generous to the National Park Service."

———————

Alcatraz was an easy choice for me. I had been fascinated by the place and its storied history since before I was able to join my parents on investigations. My career interest in criminal justice might even owe some small bit of influence to my obsession with the island prison. Before this trip, I'd been at least a dozen times, mostly as a tourist, though there had been a few investigations over the years, as well. I was pretty much a walking encyclopedia when it came to Alcatraz.

It's said the island was haunted long before people ever

inhabited it. Before Europeans discovered the New World, Native Americans held to the belief that the island was occupied by evil spirits. They called it Devil's Island, and it was used as a place of imprisonment almost as soon as it was found by the living. Native American tribes banished tribal lawbreakers there for years or even the rest of their lives, depending on the severity of their crime.

Jordin rented a private boat to take us to the island and gladly paid the exorbitant sum of money required to have the place entirely to ourselves overnight. I warned her against sending the boat away, along with our park service friends, suggesting that we might want someone else on the island with us in case things went wrong. But she was growing more and more independent of late, despite what happened at the church in New Jersey, and argued the only way to control our environment was to limit human access. In the end, I agreed, and she paid each one of them to sail away into the sunset, leaving us completely alone on the twenty-two-acre island.

The dilapidated main cell house was arranged in four long rows of cells, called cell blocks, each assigned its own letter—A, B, C, and D—with a corridor running between them. The corridors were lined with cells on both sides, while catwalks above held more cells on the second level.

We wandered for hours through the terrible, fascinating old building, winding up in the primary corridor between Cell Blocks B and C. Anyone who's seen photos of Alcatraz is probably familiar with this famous hallway. The men who were imprisoned here nicknamed it Broadway.

Four hours passed without anything happening at all. At some point in that time, we grew tired of walking and decided to camp out in the center of the Broadway corridor. No matter how many times I came here, I was always impressed with the creepy feeling it imparted so easily on all who visited, and I could tell Jordin was feeling it, too.

The oppressive atmosphere of Alcatraz saturates the air like a toxin. The rusted, eroding interiors are especially eerie at night, when the island's decades of history seem to come alive in the mind's eye. It was always easy for me to imagine the likes of Al Capone or George Kelly—both of whom had made a laughing-stock of other prisons by paying off guards and continuing their illegal businesses from behind bars—languishing in a place with such extreme security as this. Its accommodations could only be described as barbaric, and they were made worse by the knowledge that no escape from this place was humanly possible.

At precisely 1:17 a.m., the silence was broken by the loud echo of a cell door sliding open somewhere in the building.

We were both on our feet at once, and I had to remind my heart to slow down. This would mark the true start of our investigation, and we had several more hours to endure. I'd never make it through the night without a heart attack if I couldn't keep this under control.

Jordin's flashlight and video recorder were in hand as she silently swept the cell block, searching for the door that had shut. But my eyes fell to my backpack on the ground and the Valium inside that could give my heart a chemically induced calm, if needed.

No. I wouldn't use it unless I was in much worse shape than this—like, only if an actual heart attack were imminent. I was young and strong, with big plans for my life, and I was not about to become a junkie.

We quickly realized that the sound was too far away to have been in this corridor, and Jordin seemed to have a hunch about where the echo might have emerged from. She motioned for me to follow and walked deeper into the facility, away from the main entrance.

Her flashlight bobbed back and forth as she scurried through the dark hallways, and she turned left at the end of the hall. I had a suspicion about where she was going, and it was quickly proven right. Two corridors down was D Block, site of the most extreme and intense punishments.

It was a segregation ward, where the most unruly of prisoners were sent for "treatment." Forty-two miniature cells spread out over two floors, thirty-six of which were made to hold just a single prisoner. The remaining six were even worse.

Five of these were collectively known as the Hole, and being sent there meant solitary confinement in what amounted to little more than a hole in the ground, with dual containment doors, and a sink and toilet. The sixth cell was a steel-encased room called the Strip Cell, and it was the worst punishment Alcatraz had to offer. Prisoners sent here were stripped naked and left inside for days in pitch-darkness. Conditions were cold, sleep was all but impossible, and the prisoner's diet was heavily restricted.

I followed Jordin at a fast trot, which was as quick a movement as I dared. Rounding the final corner to enter D Block, we soon came to a stop facing Cell 14D, one of the five "Hole" cells. 14D was infamous among paranormal investigators, but it wasn't the only cell here with an open door—some had been left open, others shut, by the park rangers before they left the island.

"Why this one?" I whispered, fishing out my own flashlight and peering inside the dank little room.

"It was closed before," she whispered back, her features set and grim.

I did a quick back-and-forth down the block, unable to determine how she could know that. We'd marched through here twice earlier in the night, but all of the cells looked largely the same to me, though the cells in the Hole had much narrower doors. Maybe that was why it stood out in her mind.

Or maybe . . .

Someone did her homework.

"What do you know about this cell?" I asked. "14D?"

"I know it's famous for high levels of paranormal activity," she replied.

"And you're sure this very famous landmark just *happens* to be the cell door we heard?"

"*You* may have been sleepwalking while we toured the building," Jordin pointed out, with just a hint of condescension, "but I memorized every detail of this place as we walked through. And yes, the fact that 14D is famous made me pay closer attention to it when we passed by. I'm *positive* it was shut."

It was good that she'd noticed, no doubt. But it also pointed to her growing obsession. Looked like I wasn't the only one in danger of becoming a junkie, only Jordin's drug wasn't one you swallow. A part of me wondered if she'd made up her mind that she was going to become good enough at this that she wouldn't need me anymore.

Whatever, then. I was ready to be done with this stuff anyway. Jordin was a big girl, and if she wanted the baton, I would pass it on with no regrets.

"Ow!" Jordin yelped, not bothering to whisper. Her cry echoed around the building just like the clanging door had. She put a hand up behind her back, flinching as she did.

"What's wrong?" I asked.

"My back!" she cried, turning in place in futility. "It's on fire!"

"Let me see."

I reached down and pulled up the bottom of her sweater, and I almost gasped but I caught myself. A large round patch of skin across her lower back was inflamed in a bright scarlet red, like a carpet burn or a welt. And that wasn't all.

"Something scratched you," I explained, leaning in with my flashlight to examine it up close. There were four marks, arranged in a parallel pattern as if a person had dug into her flesh with their fingernails and dragged them all the way down her back.

"It stings!" she howled.

"The entire area is enflamed," I explained slowly, trying to remain as calm as possible, for both our sakes. "I think we may want to consider leaving now."

"Why? What is this?" she said. "What's happening?"

I debated not telling her, because I had a feeling that the truth, which would terrify a normal person, might only spur on her obsession further. But her life was in danger, and she needed to know.

"In most cases where something makes direct physical contact this way," I said, "the person bearing the injury usually winds up with an attachment."

Jordin pulled her sweater down and turned to look at me. "What's an attachment?"

I tried to remain as even-keeled as possible as I replied, "It means some-*thing* has taken a special interest in you. It's attached itself to you, and will remain fixated on you until you leave, and possibly beyond, if the bond between you is allowed to strengthen. In a best-case scenario, it would be one of Alcatraz's less-than-charming former prisoners. Worst case? Something similar to the church."

Jordin turned away, her wide eyes examining the area around us, as if she was trying to find the spirit that had suddenly grown interested in her. "I can't decide if that's awesome or if I need to pee."

I rolled my eyes, furious now. "It is *not* awesome! Attachment cases can end in outright *possession* if they're demonic, and this one's already shown an intent to hurt you! We have to get you out of here before something worse happens!"

Jordin was about to reply when we heard a very faint sound. Some kind of tapping noise, and it was close.

She spun and shined her light into the open Cell 14D. Though I tried to stop her, she brazenly walked in and searched for the source of the sound. It took her only a moment to determine that it was coming from the left wall, or rather, whatever was on the other side of it.

The cell next door was open, as well, and she walked around into it, approaching the same wall from the other side. There was nothing in the cell that I could see that the sound could have been coming from.

"It still sounds like it's coming from the other side of the wall," she whispered. "Go in there and see if you still hear it."

I didn't want to go in there and see if I could hear it. I wanted to stop her from getting herself killed. But my feet marched beneath me nonetheless, and soon I was leaning with my ear up against the cement wall.

"Yeah, I hear it," I said.

"That's so weird!" she shouted, suddenly enthused. "What if it's a spirit *inside* the wall?"

"If it's inside the wall, it's probably just a rat," I pointed out.

Jordin was unfazed by my logic. "But what if it's not?"

My jaw clenched and so did my fists as I pushed away from the wall. "All right, enough. If you're going to call every stupid little thing that happens 'paranormal,' you're just thrill-seeking and making a mockery of this entire field of study."

"Oh, come off it, Maia!" she shouted through the wall. "Listen to that sound! That doesn't sound anything like a rat to me!"

I didn't listen to it. Instead I left the cell and swerved around to the one she was in. "We have a rational, nonparanormal explanation for the sound, so questioning what's rational can only mean you've lost your objectivity. There are paranormal things happening in this place, but that sound isn't one of them. The potentially life-threatening thing that happened to your back, however, *is*. Get your things. We're leaving. Now."

Jordin's face had drawn tighter and angrier with each word I'd spoken, and now she looked ready to crack. "And where are we going to go? We're alone on this island, and no one's coming back to get us until dawn."

"Then we'll camp out under the stars," I said. "It's too dangerous in this place; it would be better to be out in the open."

I was already marching out of the cell when she grabbed me by the shoulder and spun me around. I was preparing to rip her hand off me if she didn't let go, but when I faced her, she had an index finger to her lips.

It was only a second before I heard it, too. The sound we'd

been hearing, which had sounded so much like a tiny scratching from inside the wall, had morphed into something else while we were arguing. The scratches were gone, replaced by the sniffling and muted sobs of a woman.

I was forced to swallow my pride—which did not go down smoothly—and admit for the moment that Jordin had been right. Together we slowly approached the wall and put our ears up to it. The crying sound was coming from inside it, all right.

We left the cell in silence and walked back around to enter 14D, where the sound was even louder. It still came from inside the same wall, but it resonated much stronger in here. Jordin shivered and rubbed her arms, and I noticed that it had become cold enough that I could almost see my breath.

"Did Alcatraz have any women prisoners?" she whispered as we continued to listen.

I shook my head. "This place wasn't always a federal prison. It was considered haunted long before Al Capone and his ilk were here. And entire families lived on the island when it was a penitentiary—the families of the prison guards."

The crying went on for more than ten minutes, and Jordin recorded every second of it on the shiny new digital recorder in her hand.

_____

Despite my better judgment, the encounter with the crying woman in the walls of D Block had gotten my old juices flowing, and I let Jordin talk me into going down into the Dungeons to explore. But I made her promise we would only stay for a few minutes.

"The Dungeons" was an unofficial term for the catacombs

beneath the main cell block. They were leftovers from the island's storied history before it became a prison.

I almost immediately regretted allowing this little detour, because Jordin's unfriendly attachment shoved her down the stairs as we descended. I was up front, so she was pushed into my back and we both tumbled down to the dusty rock floor.

I tried to jump up quickly to cover my suddenly hammering heart, but lost my balance and went back down.

"You okay?" she asked, eying me suspiciously.

"Fine," I lied, trying to face away from her as I struggled to steady myself, slow my heart, and catch my breath.

We had no further incidents down in the Dungeons, but it wouldn't have mattered if we had, because Jordin was no longer paying attention. I caught her watching me sideways again and again as we walked on.

———————

During the witching hour, things got hairy.

It started when Jordin began taunting the ghosts of Alcatraz, despite my warnings.

"Why don't you come out and get us!" she shouted as we patrolled the hallway outside Cell Block B. "Come on! We're just a couple of little girls! You're not scared of us, are you?"

"Stop it!" I yelled. "I've told you not to tease or insult whoever or whatever resides in haunted places."

Jordin turned to me with a pained, annoyed face. "Maia, get real. We're talking about the very worst elements of society. These were criminals, not tragic victims. Do you seriously think that the prisoners who lived here deserve our respect?"

A tremendous shaking sound came from somewhere up in

the building's rafters. We shined our flashlights up there, along with all of our recording equipment. It was like a group of people were standing up there and rattling and pounding on the I-beams with their bare hands, though we saw nothing.

I spoke in a soft voice, my eyes still scanning the ceiling. "A lot more people lived and died here than just prisoners. This penitentiary is just one chapter of Alcatraz's long history."

"It's a big island," remarked Jordin. "Did they all die right here in this one building?"

I was about to reply when the silence was broken again, only this time by the stifled roaring of an angry mob. It was as if a hotly contested baseball game were going on in another part of the building. I knew we should be chasing after its source, but we just stood there, stunned, listening to the shouting and grunting and fighting.

Jordin snapped out of it first when the crowd fell silent. "Oh, so all the big bad prisoners *are* in the house tonight," she called out. "Where ya been, fellas? It's about time we got this party started!"

In response, a cacophony of sounds erupted up near the ceiling. Banging rafters, fierce, howling winds, shouting voices. The place had suddenly come alive, and we could *more* than hear it. We could feel it. It was the loudest example of paranormal activity I'd ever heard, like the prison was suddenly full of living prisoners again, and although I was furious with Jordin for instigating it, I was gratified that we at least got the whole thing on tape.

The thunderous sounds went on for a good two minutes before the building finally fell silent again. I had my hand reared back to smack Jordin when she let out a shout. Both of her hands flew up to the top of her head.

I turned my flashlight on her and saw three narrow streaks of blood slowly emerging from her hairline and creeping down her forehead.

"Move your hands, let me see," I said, shooing her hands out of the way.

She leaned over so I could part her hair and see the scratches. They weren't terribly deep, but they were red and angry and oozing a small amount of blood.

My face was as hard as stone when she looked back up at me. Hers was unreadable, though she still winced from the pain on her head.

"You think maybe you're done playing around now?" I asked, not caring about the harsh, unsympathetic tone in my voice.

She wasn't happy, but conceded a nod.

We spent the rest of the night outside.

NINETEEN

"You ready for this?" I asked Derek as he zipped up his blue jumpsuit.

"It'll be a miracle if it works," he replied, adjusting the ID badge hanging from his lapel so that the photo on it was partially obscured. A blue cap pulled down near his eyes completed the effect.

I lay on the gurney on my back. "It's all we've got," I told him.

I pulled the white sheet up over my body and waited patiently while they exited the front seat of the ambulance. I took deep breaths to calm my pounding heart.

The back door of the ambulance was flung open and Derek and Pierre, behaving like they knew exactly what they were doing, grabbed the back end of the gurney and pulled it out until the wheels popped down to the ground. Then they pushed me up the ramp leading to the back of the loading dock.

I was afraid that procuring the ambulance and disguises would prove difficult, but Pierre had taken the reins for that task. After hiking about half a mile back down the mountain, Pierre found a large rock, about a foot in diameter, and held it over his shoulder, waiting. About five minutes later, the next ambulance came driving through, and Pierre ran out to the edge of the road and lobbed the huge rock toward the vehicle. It was too heavy to get very far, and never actually made contact with the ambulance, but the driver saw it and must've thought it was part of a rockslide, because he swerved madly to get out of the way and ran off the road.

While the driver and his partner were still stunned, Pierre opened the driver's door and pulled something out of his pocket. The next thing we knew, he was pulling the driver from the vehicle, unconscious. I glanced in the truck and saw that the other worker was similarly knocked out.

Derek and I looked at him in disbelief. Pierre held up his tiny device—a miniature Taser—and explained, "I cover some interesting parts of Boston."

Ten minutes later, we were pulling up to the loading dock of the massive DHI building.

I played my part, keeping my eyes closed and remaining completely limp as the DHI worker at the top of the ramp shoved my head to one side to inspect the symbol on the back of my neck. He must've been satisfied with what he saw, because he let me go and we were rolling again.

I heard a hydraulic door slide open and the rush of warm air as we entered the building.

"We're alone," Derek whispered.

I opened my eyes and looked around. The place was white and sterile, though a closer inspection of the walls indicated that they were made of the same concrete as what we saw on the building's exterior, with more of the endless overlapping symbols carved into every part of their surface.

Otherwise, it was a very high-tech facility, with lots of sliding doors, armed security, and the occasional computer terminal that looked like it came out of a spaceship.

Derek and Pierre followed another gurney and two jump-suited workers about twenty feet ahead of us, assuming we were supposed to be headed to the same place they were. They entered a large elevator up ahead, but the doors closed before we could reach them.

When the car returned, the guys wheeled me inside and I sat up when the doors closed. There were about fifteen floors, but the one at the top was labeled *New Arrivals*, so with a glance at Derek and me, Pierre pushed the button.

I lay back down as we ascended.

"What exactly is the plan here?" Pierre asked.

"The plan is to get my fiancé back," Derek replied.

"Assuming that's possible," I added, before realizing how insensitive I sounded.

I closed my eyes as the doors parted but peeked out through slitted lids. I saw we were in a large, curved hallway. I imagined that we must've been on the outer edge of the building, tracing its circumference. A large set of stainless steel doors waited ahead on the left, and they parted as we approached.

I heard Derek gasp and chanced raising my head just enough to get a quick glimpse.

I couldn't stifle the similar gasp that escaped my lips, either.

The brightly lit, spotlessly clean room was a perfect circle, yet it was enormous, easily the size of the building's entire diameter, minus the outer hallway we'd just been in. The chamber was filled with hundreds of tiny cubicles that rose about five feet high, dotting the interior with only a handful of narrow corridors in between to allow access.

The walls surrounding the room were like nothing I'd ever seen. I only got a quick look, but they seemed to be on fire.

A technician in a lab coat stood just inside the door but was facing the room's interior. I saw him starting to swivel in our direction and quickly snapped my eyes shut.

"Name?" the man asked.

There was a moment's hesitation as Derek and Pierre must've been deciding what to do. Derek was the one that spoke. "Maia Peters."

Guess he figured honesty was the best way to go.

"Let's see," said the technician, consulting a hand-held computer tablet. "Peters, yes. She goes to booth 1219. Hook up her IV and make sure she gets her sedative. They'll send for her when it's time for her procedure."

Neither Derek nor Pierre offered a reply, but we started rolling again, and I could only assume that the cubicles were numbered somehow, because we found our way to an empty one after a few minutes.

I opened my eyes when we were in and saw that the gray, drab cube was made of standard, movable wall dividers, and it was barely big enough to hold my gurney and the two men. I sat up, careful not to let my head rise above the low partition walls.

"These cubicles . . ." I whispered. "Are they all—?"

"Filled with unconscious people?" Derek finished. "Yeah. Saw a ton of them when we wheeled you in."

"This is where they do it," I said. "It has to be."

"You think this 'procedure' kills its victims?" asked Pierre, oblivious to or uncaring about Derek's fears.

But I had a different thought. "If the victims die, then why would they need all these booths?"

Derek liked this line of reasoning, and nodded enthusiastically. "Maybe they have to keep their bodies alive for the whole thing to work. It could be how they keep the souls bound to the earth. Since they're never actually dead, they can't move on to heaven or hell."

It made sense. But it was also a bit too easy. I suspected there had to be more to it.

"Did you see the walls?" mentioned Pierre. "It looked like double-paned glass or Plexiglas or something, with fire burning between the panes."

"There was a symbol etched into the glass," Derek said, turning to look at me. "A familiar symbol."

"Which one?" I asked.

"The one that means *binding*."

"I saw something else," Pierre said. "It was on the far side of the room. It looked like some kind of grid, but it was enormous."

Derek nodded. "I saw it, too. It was the only part of the room that wasn't uniform. It stands out, so it's got to be important. Probably where they do this 'procedure.' But the place is so big, it was hard to get a good look at it from this distance."

Pierre frowned. "I only saw a few of those lab techs or whatever they are, but maybe we could wring some info out of one of them."

Derek looked at him sidelong. "I don't think holding one of these people at Taser-point is going to be enough to get them talking."

"Then we'll use something else," I said.

———

Ten minutes later, a scientist with a name tag that identified him as Dr. Michael Simms was standing inside booth 1219 with us. Pierre stood behind him, holding what looked like the barrel of a gun inside one of the pockets of his jumpsuit. In reality, it was a metal handle we'd pried off of the gurney, the end of it jammed into Simms's back. But he believed it was a gun, and that was all that mattered.

He was a tall man, middle-aged, with impossibly heavy eyelids. There was no emotion in his eyes, no passion, no *life*. His mouth was carved into a perfectly straight line, and you could easily imagine that he'd never smiled, even once.

Simms wore the standard white lab coat that all of the scientists in the building wore. His shoes were shined, his hair slicked back, and he carried a hand-held computer tablet, which I quickly snatched away from him.

"I have no idea how you found this place or got inside, but you'll never leave here alive," Simms said.

"What are you people doing in here?" I asked, skimming through the information stored in the tablet. "Are you sucking people's souls out of their bodies?"

"No, no," Simms replied. "You make it sound so crude. Our

scientists are doing groundbreaking work that's beyond *anything* the world has ever seen, breaching the barrier between the physical and the metaphysical."

"Then why not share your breakthroughs with the world?" I asked.

"Our work is generations ahead of its time," he said. "It's been decided that the population at large is not ready to know what we've done. Can you imagine the reaction? The human soul is *real*. It exists, and we have proof!"

"A discovery of that magnitude," Pierre chimed in from over Simms's shoulder, "carries with it significant religious, social, scientific, and even medical ramifications. You have no right to keep it a secret."

"We have every right," Dr. Simms retorted. "We have no interest in converting anyone to any particular dogma or ideology. The research and development on this work cost billions, and only by keeping the process private are we able to ever dream of earning that back. The *nature* of our work would likely be interfered with if it became public knowledge, and we are simply moving ahead to the future we believe this technology can offer."

"By ripping people's souls out?"

His expression was unchanged. "Save the theatrics. We haven't harmed anyone. As you can see from the Body Chamber—that's what we call this room—every person that's undergone the procedure is still alive and well. We have merely altered their state of being, taken the intangible parts of their essence out of their physical shells."

"Incredible," Pierre remarked, though his voice was filled with revulsion. "And the symbol on the back of their necks?"

"The glyph," said Simms. "It's the lynchpin of the binding technology. It came to us . . . from an outside source."

I couldn't believe this guy's casual disregard for what he and his friends were responsible for. "What about the people you're doing this to? I have a friend who signed up for it, but I know of plenty others who *didn't*. That's kidnapping, muchacho."

Simms's expression was dead, unmoved, unconcerned. "Without experimentation, science is nothing but theory. Trial and error. There is no other way to perfect it. Animal testing yielded no results; they have no souls to manipulate. It had to be humans. We believe the end justifies our choices."

"Why go to all this trouble to keep their bodies alive?" asked Pierre. "Why not just let them die?"

"We tried it that way at the beginning," said Simms. "The glyph couldn't maintain control over the souls without their bodies remaining alive *here*, on the mortal plane. We can't brand the glyph directly on a soul, since it has no material substance. The soul is like a boat; it wants to float free. We use the physical body as an anchor, with the glyph acting as the tether that keeps the soul attached to it."

"So what's the point?" asked Pierre. "What ends are you trying to justify?"

"The eternal plague faced by mankind is an inability to find one unbeatable advantage over its enemies. Peace can never exist in such a world. And of course governments are willing to pay extravagantly to be the power holding that advantage."

"Weapons," Pierre said. "Of course. A person for whom there are no walls, and for whom solid objects are not a hindrance . . . It's the ultimate in stealth warfare. No enemy would be untouchable, and the soldier would be absolutely impervious to harm. Assuming you can control and manipulate the process."

"But you'd need some kind of control over these ghost soldiers of yours," I said, catching on. "And I'm betting none of the people here consented to play *War Games* for you, so how can you expect them to follow your orders unless you have some way of coercing them?"

"You'd need far more than that," said Simms. "Apparitions can only interact with our plane of existence in very limited ways, most of which are unuseful for our purposes. When the technology is perfected, we intend to give our 'souldiers'—and I'm spelling that s-o-u-l—full ability to interact with the mortal world."

"And then what?" I asked. "You going to sell this technology to the highest bidder?"

Simms looked at me and Derek, not confirming or denying.

I was irked and about to press him further, but Derek jumped in.

"Jordin Cole," he said with a restrained anger. "Where is she?"

"Who?" There wasn't the slightest hint of curiosity in Simms's voice.

"Please," said Derek in disgust. "She's probably the most famous person you have here."

"The physical shell of every person to undergo the procedure is stored here, in the Body Chamber. Her soul has been extracted and is now . . . elsewhere."

I looked back at the tablet, remembering how the tech at the door had recognized my name.

"So undo it," Derek demanded, his tone cold and threatening. "Put her soul back in her body."

Though his expression remained unchanged, I got the strong impression that Simms was relishing the next statement he made. "I'm afraid . . . our efforts thus far have only been focused on the extraction technique. We have not yet taken the step of reversing the process."

This gave me an idea. A mad, crazy notion. But I couldn't help wondering . . .

I decided to keep the thought to myself.

I never saw Derek move; I just blinked and Simms's head jerked back. He sagged into Pierre's arms, and I was surprised to see Derek's arm outstretched, fist first, in Simms's direction.

"Help me," Pierre whispered, and as he and Derek put Simms onto the gurney I had formerly occupied, I began searching on the tablet, quickly finding the information we needed.

"Feel better?" I asked Derek, still amazed that he'd done that.

"Not really," he whispered back, rubbing his knuckles.

"Never seen a minister hit somebody before," I remarked. "Aren't you supposed to turn the other cheek?"

Derek was still fuming. "I'll seek forgiveness later," he said.

"Booth 930," I said.

I held up the computer. Derek nodded and was out of the cubicle before Pierre or I had even moved.

———————

Staying low and communicating only with gestures, we wound our way through the veritable city of cubicles in the Body Chamber. The most activity seemed to be happening in the middle of the giant room, so we altered course to move silently in that direction, avoiding all the workers we saw along the way.

I got a much better look at the walls, and they were just as Derek and Pierre had described them. The curved outer wall was separated from us by an equally curved pane of glass that left only an inch or two of space in between. And in that space, fire burned all the way around the room. The glass seemed to be covered in etchings of the alchemical binding symbol, as well.

About twenty-five feet from the core of the room, we found Booth 930 and ducked inside.

"Jordin!" Derek whispered, rushing to the gurney on which her body lay, hooked up to an IV and various monitors.

"She's not here," I whispered quietly. "This isn't her, Derek. This body is just an empty container."

For all intents and purposes, Jordin was no longer alive. But Derek took Jordin's hand nonetheless and kissed it gently. His tears stained her wrist, and my heart pounded in grief for both of them.

This was, in some small way, my fault. I had indulged Jordin's obsession when I should have deterred her. I watched Derek in silence. I've never been a terribly emotional person, so I stood perfectly still with no outward signs of how much his pain was gutting me.

I took several calming breaths and turned my attention out over the nearest partition wall. Just a few dozen feet away, surrounded by a bustle of lab coat–decked scientists, was the machine they must have used to extract the soul.

It wasn't what I'd expected. I didn't know what it should look like exactly, but not like what I was looking at now.

It was about five feet high on one end, only three or so on the other. Between the two ends was a big clear tube that reminded me of a hyperbaric chamber, only its cross-section wasn't a perfect circle. It was flattened, oval in shape. Everything that wasn't part of the clear tube was stainless steel. It didn't look like something used for a surgical procedure. It was more like a high-tech torture device out of a futuristic sci-fi movie.

On the taller end was an enormous control station with half a dozen screens and several keyboards and touch pads. It was all very clean and organized, fitting perfectly into the space available, obviously custom made. I imagined that this was probably the only such machine in the world, though it would only be a matter of time before DHI started producing more of them. Unlike nearly every other part of this crazed facility, I saw no glyphs, as Simms had called them, anywhere on the enormous device.

We heard a deep rumble from somewhere in the chamber, so deep it hurt my ears. I wondered if it was an earthquake, or if this was part of the extractor in operation, but there was no one currently inside the thing. Even Derek was pulled out of his personal torment by the sound. He stepped over to see what we were looking at.

As we watched, a new victim was wheeled up to the extractor on a gurney—a young man. Derek was poised as if he wanted to rescue the guy, but I put a hand on him and whispered that we needed to see how this machine worked, and that giving away our position for the sake of one person wouldn't help the hundreds of other victims. Including Jordin.

So we remained silent as the clear tube split in the middle and slid open. The unconscious young man was disconnected from his IV, hefted from his stretcher, and laid inside, the tube immediately sealing around him. I noted that despite all of the complex monitors and keypads, the entire process appeared to be more or less automated. A technician standing at the controls checked over various settings but then hit a single yellow button.

The machine buzzed to life, sounding like something within it was spinning hard and fast. I cringed when I saw a spiky needle extend from under the young man's head straight into the back of his neck—piercing the center of the symbol that was branded there. I couldn't tell how deep it penetrated.

Every muscle in his body clenched tight, like an electrical current was searing through him. I saw the scientists nearby shield their eyes, and then as the roar of the machine grew deafening, a series of dangerously bright flashes seemed to fill the tube. It was as if the entire thing had become a fluorescent light bulb, only the illumination it created was brighter than lightning. It flashed several times in a row, and then there was a cracking sound like localized thunder.

The machine suddenly wound down, and I could see the young man in the tube had gone totally limp. Two technicians quickly appeared and pulled his lifeless body out of the extractor and put it back on a gurney. They worked quickly, hooking him up to his IV again, along with several other medical devices, ensuring that his body remained technically alive, even though it was being kept that way only by machinery.

"Dear God, save us," Derek whispered. "How can this be real?"

There were no words. We had just witnessed the most profound violation of nature anyone had ever conceived. I felt sick.

"Look," Derek whispered, pointing toward the far end of the room.

There we could see the huge gridlike structure Pierre had mentioned in greater detail. It almost looked like a cage, with crisscrossing metal bars, but whatever was inside the thing was obscured by some kind of deep, black darkness.

A man stood outside of the cage—a man I recognized from a photo I'd seen on the Internet.

"That's Howell Durham," I whispered.

Pierre answered first. "Really? What's he doing?"

It was a fair question. Durham seemed to be pacing back and forth next to the large cage, and inexplicably, he was talking and gesturing wildly. He didn't look like the perfectly presented, well-built silver fox that I had seen in the corporate press materials. His hair was a mess, his eyes were big and wild, and his cheeks were flushed. I think he was angry, and we could almost hear him shouting from so far away.

Durham looked up, and so did we, as the room's bright white lights turned red and an alarm began to blare through the Body Chamber like a battle Klaxon.

"I think that's for us" came Pierre's terse whisper. "Simms must have woken up!"

Before either of us could respond, the entire building began to shake, and the low rumbling sound we'd heard before returned, growing in strength and volume. It was the worst sound I'd ever heard, nearly making my heart leap into my throat.

Then as the room pitched and swayed, the giant cage at the far end of the room exploded open. A horrific creature came tearing out of it, huge—more than ten feet in height—and absolutely monstrous.

Scientists and technicians abandoned their posts and fled for their lives screaming, running from the room en masse. The creature growled and roared, blew hot steam out of its snoutlike nose, and then grabbed Howell Durham around the waist. Before any of us had time to react, it squeezed Durham like a grape, and the old man popped.

I knew two things as I watched these nightmarish events: something terrible and beyond all reason had just been unleashed, and this might be my one chance to carry out the crazy idea I'd gotten while listening to Dr. Simms talk just minutes ago.

"What *is* that?" Pierre asked.

Derek gave a slight shake of his head, not taking his eyes off the beast.

Thinking fast, I whipped out my phone and glanced at it. "No bars," I muttered, putting on a perfect performance. "Let's see if we can get reception outside—we need to call someone!"

Derek and Pierre both nodded and I motioned for them to lead the way.

Once they were out of sight, I ducked around the cubicle in the opposite direction and made straight for the extractor while the building shook and crumbled and the ghastly creature roared. Its footsteps landed like lead on the cement floor, and I prayed it wasn't moving in my direction.

The entire chamber's lights were flickering as I mashed the buttons the same way I'd seen the technicians do it, opening the central tube. Derek rounded a corner twenty feet away, but Pierre wasn't with him.

"What are you doing?!" he shouted.

"I'm going to find her!" I glanced at him only for a second but didn't give him a chance to stop me, knowing that this was it. Now or never.

I hit the *Activate* button, ran around to the side of the tube, and slid in just as it was closing around me. The horrifying sounds of the giant creature were quickly drowned out by the whirring of the extractor, and I lay perfectly still, waiting. Derek caught up with me and started pounding on the side of the glass tube, trying to break it, but it was made of something much stronger than standard glass. He looked at me like I'd lost my mind, but I looked upward. I knew exactly what I was doing.

The needle pierced the back of my neck, and the flashing lights illuminated the pod like a tanning booth on acid.

Then, I fell.

Gettysburg, Pennsylvania

TWENTY

The calm, serene town of Gettysburg, Pennsylvania, imbues all
visitors with a sense of sadness. Though its battlefields are now
reverentially quiet, the enormity of the loss of life is remembered
via endless historical markers and monuments that dot the landscape across acres upon acres of land.

Over a three-day period in 1863, more than fifty thousand
men lost their lives in Gettysburg, staining miles of its fertile farm
soil red. But these were not slow, painful deaths stretched out
over days like those on record at other haunted locations. Many
were instantaneous deaths of terrible violence that cut short the
lives of young souls who had much to live for.

Gettysburg has to be the most haunted place in America, but

it's a lot more than that. It's considered by many to be the most haunted place in the world.

After the near disaster that was Alcatraz, I'd driven back to San José alone so I could visit my folks again. I'd opted to not take Jordin along, needing a break from her special brand of crazy. After a couple days of sightseeing in San Francisco, she flew back to New York to begin processing her evidence.

As soon as I returned, she called me, ecstatic to show off her findings, which I had to admit were impressive. But I was just relieved that the spirit that had attached itself to her seemed to have lost interest when we departed Alcatraz Island the next morning.

She was ready for our final trip immediately, but when I accused her of neglecting her studies, she got angry and didn't speak to me for a few days. Which was fine by me. I was tiring of her secrets and demands and her increasingly sour attitude.

We quickly regrouped and scheduled our last trip—which I promised Jordin would be the best of the best and the most haunted destination we'd ever visited—over a four-day weekend in early May, just before finals. I arranged for us to spend not one night but three, knowing that there was enough to investigate in Gettysburg to take more than three times that long.

I booked our multinight stay at the Cashtown Inn, one of the most infamously haunted places in the world, and a major hot spot in Gettysburg. The bed-and-breakfast was so well-known for its paranormal activity that I planned for us to spend our entire first night in Gettysburg investigating just the inn itself.

I was particularly psyched for this leg of the trip. I'd been to Gettysburg several times, but somehow never found time to visit the Cashtown Inn—much less stay there overnight as a guest.

Jordin, true to form, had never heard of it, so I had to brief her on its history as we made our way through the old town after having driven down from school.

"It's unknown exactly when the Cashtown Inn was built," I explained, circling the car through the doughnut-shaped road in the center of Gettysburg, "but it's been here since sometime around the year 1800. It got its name because the original owner demanded cash payments for lodgings at a time when most establishments accepted bartering. Like everything else in Gettysburg, it's most famous for its role during the Civil War. The Confederate Army used it repeatedly as a respite. Confederate officers visited often, trading information, filling their canteens, and buying liquor. Even Robert E. Lee himself is believed to have spent many a night at Cashtown Inn."

Jordin stared at the sights of Gettysburg as I spoke, and I could see her eyes dance at every location we passed that advertised itself as haunted. The Farnsworth Inn. The Jenny Wade House. Even Gettysburg College, which boasted an excess of regular ghost sightings.

"So what kinds of ghosts do people see there?" Jordin asked without turning her attention away from her window.

"All kinds," I replied. "Confederate soldiers are seen in guest rooms, walking through the hallways, and venturing up and down the main stairs. Several rooms are infamous for sights and sounds that are *very* out of place, though virtually every inch of the place has had endless activity for centuries. The Cashtown Inn just never rests."

The inn was a bit out of the way, several miles to the northwest of Gettysburg via Highway 30. But I reassured Jordin it would be worth our time.

When we arrived, it was much more inconspicuous than I'd imagined. I'd seen photos of it for years, of course, but it sat almost in the middle of nowhere, with no special fanfare or loud signs letting us know we'd arrived. Just a small, rectangular wooden placard hanging over the door that looked like it had been there since the place was first built.

The Cashtown Inn was a decent-sized two-story brick house, with a wraparound Cape Cod porch. Four vintage wooden rocking chairs were perched there. I took special note of the five upstairs windows, at least one of which had been photographed hosting ghostly figures staring out at passersby.

We walked through the lovely front door with its rounded window arch above, and were welcomed by the friendly staff. They assigned us to the upstairs room that I had requested and led us to it. There were only seven guest rooms at the inn, so even though we weren't the only people staying there, the place was hardly overrun with anyone who might get in our way.

Making our way to our room, I almost wished I was just a visitor. The rustic simplicity of the stately old residence, with its framed artwork and antique furniture, reminded me of the Myrtles, but it wasn't as busy or colorful. We passed by a gorgeous common living room that I would've loved to have settled into, with striped carpet and comfy-looking wing-back armchairs. Meanwhile, dozens of framed photos adorned the walls, high-lighting the unique history of the place.

Our room was warm and welcoming. It had an A-frame ceiling with exposed beams, hardwood floors covered with well-worn braided rugs, and a mixture of furniture comprised of antique tables and more modern accommodations like floor lamps and sofas.

Jordin mentioned how sweaty and sticky she was when we got to the room, so I let her have first dibs on the shower. I was still unpacking when she got out, but only moments after I heard her turn the water off, the bathroom door opened and she shouted, "Maia!"

Fearing she'd slipped and hurt herself somehow, I ran for the tiny room. But she was fine, one towel wrapped around her torso and another—which I hoped wasn't mine—circling her hair. She opened the door wide as I approached, and let me in. The hot steam filled my pores almost at once, and I couldn't immediately tell why she had called out to me.

"Look at this!" she said, reducing her voice to something a little above a whisper. She pointed to the mirror over the sink.

My heart hammered out of the blue. Why did it have to be a mirror?

I could see where she'd wiped the fog off of the mirror, but left behind was a very visible handprint off to one side of the glass.

"What'd you do that for?" I asked, feeling relieved that there wasn't a creepy figure staring back at me from inside.

"I didn't," she replied. "Look closer."

She unwound the towel from her head and wiped down the mirror again. It became dampened, but the handprint remained exactly as it was.

I stepped up to the sink to get a closer look. I placed my own hand against the mirror, overtop of the lingering print, and that's when I saw it. The handprint wasn't *on* the mirror. At least, not on this side of it.

"Whoa," I noted, feeling goose bumps on my arms. "Look at that! It's on the other side of the glass. . . ."

I ran and got my camera and took several shots of it before the falling humidity in the room caused it to disappear.

We spent the better part of the night investigating every nook and cranny of Cashtown Inn, but that handprint in the mirror was the best evidence we captured.

The dead, it seemed, were still reaching out to Jordin.

Our second night was spent at a very well-known area of the battlefield known as Devil's Den. The huge outcropping of craggy rocks atop a steep hill made it a perfect sniper's position during the war, and there were tons of reports suggesting that a Civil War marksman might have never truly left.

In addition, a famous apparition was frequently sighted there: a scraggly, war-weary frontiersman soldier believed to be from the First Texas Regiment, which had taken heavy casualties at a skirmish near Devil's Den. The soldier was usually seen barefoot, and he would sometimes appear to offer tourists directions and pointers, but then disappear into thin air.

We wandered around the Den, climbing and descending the hill, inspecting the crevices between the rocks—which, sadly, were strewn with tourists' litter—with all of our recording equipment and the thermal imager going the whole time. We tried to record some EVPs but wouldn't know until later if we were successful.

We made our way over to a rise called Little Round Top, which was directly across a huge clearing from Devil's Den and was the main site the sniper had trained his weapon on during the battle. One of the biggest historical monuments in all of Gettysburg stood there, and we took our time, strolling around it, calling out to any ghosts in the area and generally capturing as much footage of the area as we possibly could.

It was a quiet night until about two.

Jordin and I had returned to the sniper's lookout at the top of Devil's Den and were sitting inside the small natural rock alcove where the sniper often appeared. Our equipment had functioned flawlessly all night, but suddenly everything went dark. Every camera, recorder, the thermal imager, even our flashlights. We sat in the near pitch-black—the only light coming from the dim haze of the moon behind a gray cloud—and said not a word, knowing that something big had to be up.

"Look!" whispered Jordin.

I could barely see in the dark that she was pointing out over the plain toward Little Round Top, and in the trees off to the side of the large monument there, a series of tiny lights blinked. They were scattershot within a specific twenty-foot area of the woods, flickering to life like a group of fireflies, and then the whole forest went dark again.

After only a second, a sound traversed the distance to reach our ears. It was the sound of muffled musket fire, and its rhythm matched perfectly the random lights we'd just seen blinking.

"Oh man!" I whispered, my heart speeding up. "I think it's the regiment!"

"The what?"

"The phantom regiment. It's one of the most famous ghost sightings in Gettysburg. It's a regiment of Civil War soldiers, dressed in dirty period-perfect uniforms, marching in formation through the fields. They disappear almost as soon as they're spotted. It's a residual apparition, but one of the most impressive, because there are like a dozen of these soldiers and they're always seen marching together. I've heard a few stories that sometimes they break formation and engage in a battle out on the fields, but I never thought it was true!"

Jordin was grinning. I couldn't see it, but I could hear it. "And what do you think now?"

"I—"

I stopped when we heard a loud clamor. Small bits of metal brushing up against metal, and it was getting closer.

We stood and looked down into the valley below, certain the sound was coming from there. How I wished our equipment's batteries hadn't drained!

As we watched and listened, we never saw a thing, but we heard plenty. The heavy, perfectly timed clomping of boots marching in step. The clanging sound we'd heard earlier, which we figured could be equipment dangling from soldiers' belts. We even felt the stirring of a freezing-cold wind as the regiment—if that's what it was—marched past us, right down the middle of the valley below.

From the sounds of it, I had to guess that there were more than a dozen of them. It sounded like an entire battalion was parading right past us, and I could almost see them in my mind, mud-stained uniforms, rifles set against their shoulders, grim faces thinking of some battle to come. I smelled gunpowder wafting through the air.

There were never any voices, no orders called out into the night by an unseen commander. They just marched.

The almost total darkness and the chill of the air made it too dangerous for us to climb down the hill to chase after them, but I was sorely tempted to try it anyway. Even though the night kept us from seeing them, we slowly followed their approximate location as they moved, rounding the valley and following a trail—which was now a paved road—off to our right.

As the sounds of the disturbance were fading from our ears, I thought I caught a quick glimpse of the rear of the group, their dark backpacks shifting back and forth as they trudged.

I could barely see the enormous whites of Jordin's eyes as she turned slowly to face me, unblinking, but even in the dark it was easy to guess the look of anticipation and excitement on her face.

———————

Our third and final night was spent out among the battle-fields. I took Jordin to the little-known Triangular Field, which is very active with paranormal activity but hard to find, because it's rarely on any maps. We smelled rotting flesh there, and thought we saw a campfire a few hundred yards away, but when we went to investigate it, it'd vanished.

I'd decided by this point that it was true—Jordin really was a magnet for paranormal activity. There was no other explanation. I'd never seen so much activity on a single trip as I had this week.

Around one a.m. we were wandering to the southwest of the main battlefield, and we made our way to the famous Sachs Bridge, a very historic and very haunted covered bridge that's open to foot traffic only.

As we walked, Jordin spotted something and ran without warning toward the small pond beneath the bridge.

"What?!" I shouted, running after her.

"I saw something! In the water!" she shouted back, not slowing down.

When she reached the pond, I was shocked to see her ditch all of her equipment on the shore and dive straight in.

"*Jordin!*" I screamed.

I arrived at the edge of the pond and shined my flashlight into its dark, murky waters. There was no sign of her.

A full minute went by without so much as a ripple in the water, and then suddenly her head popped up out of the water for a fraction of a second. Just long enough for her to take a gasping breath and scream, "*Help me!*" Then she dunked back down and vanished again. I couldn't reach her—she was at least ten feet out beyond the edge of the water.

Knowing what I had to do, I quickly shed my electronic equipment, muttered something horrible under my breath about Jordin's gene pool, and crossed myself. Then I dove.

The chilly waters of the pond were fierce and unwelcome, but I pushed the sensations aside.

I found her quickly—the pond wasn't all that big—and yet she was pulling away from me, deeper, like something was dragging her. She stretched out her arms in my direction, but I couldn't reach her. I kicked with all my might against the water, giving chase as she slid away from me, and finally I got close enough to grab her hand. I pulled toward the surface but found that she was surprisingly heavy. I wondered if her leg had gotten caught on a branch or something.

We'd drifted closer to the bridge while underwater, and when we crawled out of the pond, we were at the mouth of the old wooden landmark.

Sopping wet, Jordin got to her feet and turned back to the edge of the pond, searching desperately for something I couldn't see.

"If you jump back in there, I'm not helping you again!" I warned her, furious.

"I'm not going back in!" she replied.

"What were you doing? And why would you dive in when you're obviously such a terrible swimmer?"

"I'm a fantastic swimmer, Maia," she retorted angrily. "Something had a grip on my leg! It was pulling me under!"

I frowned, not liking the sound of that. "Then what made you dive in, in the first place?"

Jordin looked back at the water again, searching its calm, smooth surface. "I saw a person!" she said. "Or maybe a body! It was floating on the water."

"You almost drowned because you were looking for a body you think you saw floating on the water?" I cried.

She spun and glared at me. "I don't *think* I saw it, I *know* I saw it. It was there! I just wanted to touch it—"

"Why?!" I screamed. "Why are you willing to risk your life for this?"

She looked at me with a mixture of hesitation, fear, and defiance. "I told you, my parents—"

"NO!! Don't give me that again!" I shouted. "There's more to this, and you know it! For crying out loud, *just tell me*, Jordin!"

"You won't believe me!" she shouted back.

"If anyone in this world is prepared to believe you, it's me. Did you ever think of that?"

"My family is cursed," she blurted out, tears spilling out of her eyes.

I was sure I'd heard her wrong.

I turned her loose and took a step back as she took a long, steadying breath.

"A few years ago, an uncle of mine told me that the women in my family were cursed a long while back by some kind of Haitian witch doctor. My great-great-grandparents lived there as missionaries, and my great-great-grandmother did something to offend a local tribe. I don't know what. So a priest placed a curse on her, that every female descendant she had would die either right after she got married or after the birth of a child, so they would never know the fulfillment of what it truly is to be a woman."

She'd gone off the deep end. If that was seriously what all of this was about, then Jordin was certifiable. I couldn't help feeling a hint of amusement that if the two of us were at a party, suddenly I wouldn't be the one that everybody pointed at and whispered about.

Jordin spotted my lopsided smile before I could conceal it. "Go ahead and laugh. I didn't want to believe it at first, either. But it's *real*!"

"Jordin," I said, trying to be rational without making her sound as crazy as she obviously was, "I've never heard of a real case where anybody has been cursed to die. There have been claims, but proof has never—"

"I *know* it's true!" she replied, almost shouting now, and trembling with emotion. "After he told me, my uncle gave me a box of old records. Newspaper clippings, handwritten love letters, birth and death certificates. A complete record of every one of my female ancestors going back to my great-great-grandmother— my mother, grandmother, and four other women in my family between them. *All* of them died at unusually young ages, all within a few years of getting married or giving birth. And all under very odd circumstances."

Okay, I was a little intrigued now. "Odd, how?"

"Freak accidents, like the way my parents died."

Jordin's parents had been gruesomely killed by a runaway train engine that jumped the tracks and slammed into the back of their limousine.

"You know how my parents' deaths were all over the TV and stuff?" she went on. "It was the same with the rest. Mostly newspaper articles. I saw them all. It was one horrific, outlandish death after another. Being attacked by a wolf up north. A house catching fire and burning down because a tiny meteor hit its gas line. Getting washed into a sewer drain during a flood and drowning in sewage."

I didn't want to hear any more. "Okay, I get it. . . ."

"These deaths were real. They happened—you can look them up at the library to confirm, and I have. Not one of them lived past the age of twenty-seven, Maia. Not one."

I couldn't think of anything to say.

"You may think it's crazy, but I want to marry Derek and live a long, happy life with him. I want to have children with him. And I don't want any of the crazy things that have happened to my family members to happen to me. Or to *him* because he's near me. Or to any of our children!"

"Okay, okay," I said softly, resigning with my hands up. "I understand. I get it. What I don't get is how your obsession with ghosts is going to help you undo this supposed curse."

Jordin let out another long, heavy breath. "My uncle found a diary that belonged to my grandmother. It was the reason he came to me about all this in the first place. He said that in her diary, my grandmother had written not long before her death that she found a way to remove the curse. A Native American shaman told her that a curse is like a physical, tangible mark on the soul. And the only way to remove it is to *rip* the curse from the soul."

My ears were burning as I stared Jordin down. This story of hers explained every bit of her motivations and behavior, but it was preposterous.

"*This* is what you've been after all this time? You've been trying to find a way to physically touch your own soul? Jordin, it's madness."

"I know," she moaned. "I just thought . . . if I could *catch* an apparition somehow . . . maybe I could use it. It's part of the spirit world, where souls live, right?"

I shook my head in dismissal. "Ghosts are intangible, Jordin, you can't *use—*"

I stopped talking as we heard heavy, clomping footsteps echoing off the wooden planks of Sachs Bridge.

A dark figure walked into view at the far end. It stood there as we watched, blinking open a pair of glowing red eyes. It watched us silently.

A searing pain struck my chest and I clutched it, sinking to my knees.

"Maia!" Jordin shrieked, ignoring our intruder for the moment. "What's wrong?"

"My . . . heart . . ." I gasped, finding it hard to breathe the suddenly freezing air and even harder to speak. I thought of the Valium. "Pills . . . in my bag . . ."

But Jordin couldn't understand my mumblings. "Hold on! I'll call 9-1-1!" she cried, panicking at the sight of me pale and weak and in pain.

I could see past her shoulder down the tunnel of the covered bridge, and what I saw made my heart beat even heavier. "Jordin!" I hissed, raising a weakened arm to point behind her.

She turned and saw what I saw. The shadow figure was moving.

It was striding or gliding—I couldn't tell which—in our direction, right down the center of the bridge. As it walked, it passed into the ambient moonlight shining through the slats in the bridge walls, and we both gasped as we caught glimpses of it in the dim light. There, it was no longer a shadow person. It looked like a Confederate soldier, its rifle raised and pointed at us, and it had dark black circles around its eyes. Yet it wasn't fully solid; we could partially see through it.

Those eyes were locked onto ours, and it was marching forward slowly, as if planning to take us prisoner or take us down.

Jordin looked back at me. "Can you walk?" she asked, frantic.

I was still holding my speeding heart, unable to look away from the ghostly soldier bearing down on us. I shook my head in response to her question, while simultaneously wondering if this was what a heart attack felt like.

Jordin reached over and tried in vain to heft me up in both of her arms, but I was just too heavy for her. I was a good twenty pounds or more heavier than she was, and she wasn't exactly a body builder.

"Is it residual?" she whispered.

I shook my head, certain from the way the ghost had its gaze locked onto the two of us like we were prey that this was not some event from long ago merely replaying itself.

"Intelligent," I whispered through wheezing breaths.

I watched her eyes dart back and forth in thought, weighing options. She glanced over her shoulder and saw that the ghost was getting close now; it had spanned more than half the length of the bridge already and would be here in seconds.

"I don't know what to do!" Jordin cried, her voice echoing through the tunnel bridge.

The sounds seemed to give her an idea, so she stood to her feet and turned to face down the ghost, then screamed at the top of her lungs. It wasn't a frightened scream; it was a challenge. A primal warning to *stay back*.

The ghost did nothing to acknowledge her. Jordin looked back down at me and saw my eyes growing wider as the ghost drew near. I didn't want to increase her panic, but I couldn't help it. I was having some kind of cardiac arrest and this thing was behaving like it posed a genuine danger to us.

I saw Jordin breathing faster and faster, and without warning, she turned and let out a roar as she ran at breakneck speed straight into the tunnel, aiming for the apparition.

In seconds she reached it, and I watched in horror as she passed straight through it. I couldn't believe my eyes, having clearly seen the ghost envelop her completely.

I heard Jordin let out a horrendous gasp as she emerged from the other side of the apparition, and she immediately hugged herself, shivering, and dizzily fell to the ground.

I wanted to go to her, but I couldn't move. I could see her, though, and her face was whiter than I'd ever seen it. She was shaking as she looked up. Our eyes met, and the two of us watched the spirit vaporize and vanish into the air between us.

We stayed there, just outside the bridge, for the better part of half an hour. It was a good five minutes after the apparition disappeared before Jordin was able to pick herself up off the wooden bridge and feebly walk to where I sat.

She tried repeatedly to call 9-1-1, but her phone kept going dead, and when it did work, she couldn't get a signal.

What she had felt and experienced when she passed through the ghost had left her undone. Her countenance had changed drastically, her usual pretenses replaced by something much more somber and emotionally transparent.

The only words that were spoken were some she mumbled about having felt the ghost's feelings when she touched it. She kept repeating the words "no hope" and "worst fears." It was like an assault upon her senses, and it overloaded her.

I improved greatly after the spirit disappeared. Deciding that I hadn't had a heart attack after all but just the most severe panic attack ever, we sat tight for a while until I felt like I could move again.

When my strength returned, Jordin helped me stand.

We hiked the half mile back to the car slowly, mostly in silence, though once we were seated inside the vehicle, Jordin softly asked, "Why didn't you tell me?"

I was too spent to lie. "I only found out the full extent of it a little more than a month ago. It was personal. And scary. Like your curse, I suppose."

Jordin nodded without offering a reply as she started the car's engine.

Neither of us said anything else that night. We merely returned to our room at the Cashtown Inn, moving like zombies.

———

The next morning, I met Jordin downstairs at the checkout counter. Her bags were nowhere in sight, but I assumed she had already taken them to the rental car, because I could tell from the state of our room that she had been up for hours before I awoke.

Everything about her was different now. After last night, her disposition toward me was one of absolute honesty. Like I had seen her as naked and exposed as humanly possible, and she simply had nothing to hide from me anymore. Her arrogance, her chipper silliness, even her energetic resolve had all been dropped.

She didn't smile when she saw me descend the stairs, but her countenance wasn't cold toward me at all. She just felt no need to pretend about how she felt.

After she paid the bill, she pulled me aside in the tiny foyer, and her sad eyes darkened her usually sunny good looks. "I'm not leaving," she said.

"What do you mean?"

"You're going home," she explained. "I'm staying awhile longer. I want to poke around Gettysburg some more. Then I was thinking of heading to England to check out the Tower of London—"

"I'm not going to just leave you here—"

Jordin held up a hand. "I understand why you didn't tell me about your heart thing. But you're placing your life in danger every time we do this, and the truth is, I don't need you anymore. You taught me well. I'm ready to go solo."

Her resolve was absolute. Her announcement sounded as if she'd rehearsed it.

"Jordin, I think something is wrong with you!" I blurted out desperately.

"What?" she said, curious but not alarmed.

"I think you're attracting all of this activity somehow. The amount of stuff we've seen—it's not normal. I think you might be some kind of paranormal focal point."

Jordin scrunched up her face, like she'd just smelled something repugnant. "That's not even a real thing. Is it? Have you ever met anyone who was a . . . 'focal point'?"

"Well, no . . ."

"Maia—"

"If I'm right, then you'd be insane to investigate alone! You could be risking your life!"

"If I let you come with me, I'm risking *your* life. I'm not willing to do that."

My temper flared. "Jordin, you hired me to help you, and after last night, I will not let you do this alone! You're going to get yourself killed!"

Her expression hardened. "A boarding pass is waiting in the passenger's seat of the cab outside. For your own sake, Maia, *you're done*. If Derek or anybody else asks why you came back without me, just say the trip ended badly. We'll say we had a big fight or something and we're not friends anymore."

"Jordin, you can't do this—"

"Go home, Maia," Jordin said simply but compassionately. "You're fired."

She turned and ascended the nearby stairs, leaving me to watch her go in staggered silence.

TWENTY-ONE

The scales were torn violently from my eyes, and I entered a new world of majesty and terror.

The atmosphere around me drained away, water flowing out of a tub. But it wasn't just the air. Everything faded—the light and the temperature and the water in my eyes and my throbbing heartbeat and the blood pulsing through my veins. . . .

Everything, sapped from my being.

Even though my eyes had been open when I passed through the veil, they opened anew now. Everything had an intense clarity, as if my vision had gone far beyond 20/20 to 20/10 or something infinitely better.

I could see for the very first time.

But that was only after the pain subsided.

I felt my soul being ripped away from my physical body, and it was an agony I've never known. The fabric of everything that was *me* was cleaved in two, and I felt my essence being pulled away from my skin, heart, organs, bones, and even my blood.

I understood now why death was often viewed from the outside as such a peaceful thing; with the body and all of its parts dead, there was nothing to anchor the soul, to keep it trapped within. Its separation from the body must be akin to the shedding of dead skin. Painless, easy, even invigorating.

The process I endured felt like being smashed by a steamroller and the me inside my body squeezed out. Only worse.

When it was done, I was no longer in the Body Chamber. My soul had been yanked down several stories in the building into what looked like some sort of repository. I was kind of standing or maybe floating in a cylindrical capsule that glowed white on all sides. As I tried to see out beyond the glowing walls, everything faded from my memory.

I had no idea who I was or how I'd gotten there. My essence was a numb haze, a puddle of thought and sensation. I felt my consciousness drift inside the capsule, billowing with an imaginary breeze. Self-awareness left me; I had evaporated.

My bright, glowing surroundings slid down and out of sight, and I saw impossible things I couldn't begin to describe, though I wasn't truly aware of what I was seeing or feeling. I glided out of the tiny pod I'd been contained in and was shunted out into some kind of large space where there were hundreds of others like me, billowing unconstrained in a sea.

But each soul was different. Some were bright and radiant, others disgusting and vile. A handful of them seemed to have a small but bright light radiating inside them. . . .

I was taking in my surroundings without any real interest or concern, when something grabbed me. I don't know how long it was until I realized that another spirit was holding on to me, their face leaning into mine.

"Maia Peters!!" the spirit shouted. "Do you hear me? Maia?! *You're Maia Peters!* Come back!"

I had a flash of awareness and suddenly everything came rushing in. I was Maia Peters. This was some kind of facility in New York owned by Durham Holdings International. I'd come here with Derek Hobbes and Pierre Ravenwood, hoping to find—

"Jordin!" I said. "Jordin, you're here!"

My voice sounded different, just as Jordin's had. It still sounded like me, but it reverberated with a fuller, richer sound.

"Maia . . ." Jordin was awash in relief, but then she did a one-eighty and turned harsh on me. "Do you have any idea what you've done? You shouldn't have crossed through the veil!"

"Jordin . . . I had the symbol," I explained. "On my neck. This was going to happen whether I wanted it to or not!"

"There's no way to get back!" she cried. "Once you've crossed to this side of the veil, you can't go back into your body."

"We'll see about that," I declared. "I have an idea. . . ."

My attention shifted to the wonders of the world around me. I was still inside the DHI building, of that much I was certain. The pristine white walls were unmistakable, as was the wide-open round room that was almost the same size as the Body Chamber above us. And I knew from the falling sensation that I had passed through several floors after the procedure was complete. But without windows or some other frame of reference, I had no idea what part of the building I was in.

I could see every part of the mortal world, even though I was no longer a part of it. It was sharp and distinct in ways I had never imagined the world could be. I saw textures and colors that I had never before known to exist. And I could look at objects all the way down to the molecular level if I chose. It was effortless and it was incredible.

Yet there was no air that I could find, nor was there any need for it. We were ensconced in a thicker atmosphere, almost fluid, like milk.

I looked down at myself and saw that I was an indistinct solid, more or less human in shape with a head and shoulders and body. But few details.

Then I discovered that my appearance was malleable. I was made out of energy, wrapped in thought. I held out a wispy hand in front of me and watched as it responded to my thoughts, dissolving into nothing but mist. I thought of it re-forming into something more solid, and it did. I looked down at my body and transformed it into a translucent smoke, and then resolidified it into a solid representation of how I looked on the mortal plane. I even had on the clothes I'd been wearing before I underwent the procedure.

This giant room was a little different than the one above. The walls were solid white, and though they had the same symbols etched into them as the rest of the building, they weren't on fire.

Another thought occurred to me. "You know . . . I don't see anything affixed to you. Like a curse, for example."

Jordin threw me a knowing look but tabled that conversation for more pressing concerns. "Carrie!" she shouted, looking out into the ghostly crowd. "Carrie Morris!"

I looked around, as well, and couldn't see Carrie anywhere.

Jordin shook her head, sending tendrils of smoke and mist curling off into the thick atmosphere. "I lost her again. . . ."

I watched Jordin's actions with curiosity. "Lost her?"

"It takes tremendous strength of will to keep from losing yourself here."

"Why?"

"The ones who still have something to live for are the ones that seem to be able to hold on to themselves. It's a magnification of the condition of the heart at the time of death—or in our case, at the time of the procedure. Those who were wicked and unrepentant appear here as vile, sickening beings. The pure, good hearts become more . . . luminescent, you could say. The ones like Carrie, who were lost in life, are even more lost in death. Carrie lived a very frivolous life, a life with no substance, so she has none here. I remind her of who she is all the time, but she keeps forgetting. She just can't seem to cling to what makes her Carrie."

I thought of my observations of apparitions as a paranormal investigator, and how so many ghosts seemed stuck in one place, unwilling or unable to leave. Derek had just asked me about this very thing recently. I wondered if something similar to what Jordin just described was the reason so many ghosts seem to linger in one spot. Were they simply unable to remember who they were and why they were there? Doomed to roam around their old stomping grounds, searching for a life they can never fully recall?

"What is this place? What are we doing here?" I asked.

"This is where they keep us. Corralled like cattle, until they have need for us."

"Need? Like what, scaring people at Ghost Town?"

"DHI sends us there sometimes, and other places, too," she replied. "They use us to add extra chills to the rides and such. It's a way for them to observe and record the extent of what we can do, how we can interact with the mortal world. I had no idea you would be at the park that night. I was as surprised to see you as you were to see me."

"They can *make* you do things?"

"Some things," she said. "They give us directives, and then leave us with some free will in choosing *how* to do it."

"But Derek saw you at his dorm. . . ."

"I had to fight their control pretty hard to get to him that night, but it's not perfect. Still, I couldn't hold out for long before *they* came for me."

" 'They,' " I repeated slowly.

Jordin pointed to one side of the room, where a group of spirits much darker than the rest of us stood and watched. They were dark gray, almost like shadow people, but I could see some details in their forms, which were burly and clearly meant to inspire fear. "They're the prototype 'souldiers' DHI has been working on. They're spirits just like us, but they're not victims. They're volunteers plucked from various military outfits."

They were the ones that attacked me in my dorm, I realized. And they probably came after me and Derek at the cemetery.

"Why do they look different?"

"They've been given enhanced strength on this plane," Jordin explained, "making them more powerful than the rest of us."

"How is that possible?"

"It's that symbol, the glyph," she told me. "It's evil. Seriously, I think it originates from inside hell. It has power, and it's the key; without the glyph, DHI couldn't do any of what they're doing."

Thoughts that might never have occurred to me before came very naturally and easily in this place. I could almost see visible connections between this and that, lines connecting one thing to another.

"What if we took the symbol out of the equation?" I asked. "Destroyed the glyph on our necks somehow?"

"No!" Jordin cried. "The symbol tethers us to the earth, remember? If the symbol's broken, then you'd better be ready to meet your maker. Literally."

I looked around this crazy, hyper-real space. "There has to be something we can do!"

The building continued to tremble around us, though it was nowhere near the intensity it had been on the top floor, where that abominable *thing* had been unleashed. As I glanced around at the sea of spirits floating through the giant room, the lights flickered for just a moment. When the lights went out, I saw words written on the darkened walls in a terrifyingly bright shade of blood red. The words were splashed onto the walls like graffiti, and they read, "The nightmare is coming."

The words were everywhere in that split second—not just all over the walls, but on the ceiling and the floor, as well.

"Jordin," I said slowly, my words coming out in that strange, hollow way that all sounds reverberated here, "how do we get out of this room?"

"We don't. There's no way out unless we're let out. It's those symbols plastered everywhere. They're derived from the same language or whatever as the glyph, and they have power. Wherever they appear, we're under their control."

"We have to get back inside the Body Chamber," I said, scanning the exits.

"I've been trying to get there for weeks," Jordin said, "but it's like it's shielded or hidden from those of us on this side of the veil. I was unconscious when they brought me to this building, and I woke up like this. I never actually saw the chamber. None of us did. That's why we're trapped here, why we can't go back to our bodies."

"Well, I *wasn't* unconscious when I was brought in. I know exactly where the Body Chamber is. We just need to get out of this room. . . ."

With another sickening groan from the building, our prayers were answered when the power flickered twice, and then stayed out. The mass of souls seemed to read the opportunity for what it was, and rushed the exits. The souldiers tried to stop them, viciously grabbing them, tackling them, throwing them around like rag dolls. But math won out in the end. There were more of us than there were of them.

We followed the crowd out into the outer hallway, and I blindly headed for the elevator before Jordin grabbed me by the shoulder. She grinned and pointed up at the ceiling.

Of course. What need was there for elevators when gravity had no hold on us?

Following Jordin's lead, I allowed my body to float up until I passed through the ceiling. It was exhilaratingly simple.

I lost count of how many floors we went through before we finally arrived at the top, but I knew we were there, because we could go no farther. The strange symbol-inscribed walls kept us from leaving the confines of the structure. The sound of the monstrous creature grew as we ascended, and so did the horrible shaking that threatened to level the entire building.

We moved quickly around the outer hallway outside the Body Chamber until we came to the entrance, and peered inside. The dozens of scientists working within the great room had fled, from the looks of things, leaving only the hundreds of empty bodies and—

"Derek!" Jordin cried.

He was still near the middle of the room where the extractor was, but he was slowly inching his way toward the horrible creature. The beast marched around opposite us on the far end of the circular room. It was stomping around angrily, and I had the disturbing theory that it was mashing the dead form of Howell Durham into the ground, grinding its feet into whatever was left of Durham, like it was enjoying killing a bug. The monster was enraged, on a power high, snarling and breathing hot air so loudly that the sound reached us like tornadic winds.

Remarkably, despite this horrific action the creature was relishing, we could still see Derek carefully moving closer and closer to the thing, like a tiger stalking its prey and preparing to pounce.

What on earth was Derek doing? What was he thinking?

At least the creature hadn't noticed him yet. It was still having its own fun dancing on Durham's entrails. I was glad I couldn't see any more than the top half of the thing. With its every step, the whole building shook down to its foundations.

"Is that what I think it is?" asked Jordin, eying the gruesome creature with fear.

"I don't know," I replied.

When I spotted Derek, I did a serious double take. I could

see not only the solid matter of his body, but his luminescent soul within, as well. But it was different than any other soul I'd seen. There was a bright spot glowing in his center mass, and as I looked closer I saw that it was a burning flame, and it made his entire form flicker and burn bright. If he'd been standing in a crowd, he would have been easy to pick out by any ghostly observer.

I was so startled I glanced at Jordin, and she returned my gaze with a knowing smile. Whatever I was seeing, she saw it, too, and she actually seemed . . . proud? Was that the right word?

That was when I noticed that Jordin, too, had a light glowing in her center, yet hers was so much smaller than Derek's, it could have been microscopic. It was barely there at all.

The fires were still blazing in the glass walls that stretched around the room, and when Jordin and I tried to enter the Body Chamber, we ran into something invisible that held us back. I looked up and saw that the entrance was only a six-foot-high opening, topped by more of the glass/fire walls. The circular wall was complete. No breaks in it anywhere.

"It's those walls," I said. "The symbols, the fire within. It's got to be some kind of . . . I don't know, a mystical security system or something. Must be meant to keep us from trying to reenter our bodies."

"If we could put out the fire, you think that might do the trick?" Jordin asked.

The building shook hard as I looked closer and shook my head. "That fire-inside-glass trick—it's a perfect circle, all the way around the room. We might not need to destroy the entire circle, just break it. Do we have the ability to do something like that?"

I hoped that Jordin's weeks of living inside this realm had given her enough experience and knowledge to help us now.

"Sure," she said, scanning the immediate area. "We just have to use something from the other side of the veil, from the mortal world. We can't get inside the room, but maybe we could throw something tangible in there from here."

I looked down at my billowing form, sure there was no way I could possibly touch anything solid on the other side of the veil, much less manipulate it. "But we're powerless. How are we supposed to—?"

"We're not powerless," she explained reproachfully. "You just have to believe."

"I don't . . ." I hesitated. "I'm not sure I understand. . . ."

Jordin grabbed me by the shoulders and looked at me intently, urgently. "You have to believe, Maia. This isn't theory anymore. It's not religious studies classes or your parents' television show. The human soul is real. That should mean everything. But for right now it needs to mean you have utter faith that you can touch the physical world. If you have any doubt at all, you won't be able to do it."

"My whole life has been about living with doubts. I don't know—"

Jordin was undeterred. I'd never seen her with so much certainty, and I thought I saw the tiny little flame inside her flicker as she spoke. "You believe in God, right?"

"Yeah," I said and nodded quickly.

"And you believe we're more than just bodies? There's something crucial in each one of us?"

I glanced at our surroundings. "Duh."

"Then decide, here, now. *Trust* that in this place, in this form, you're *more* than you ever were in the confines of your human body. Have *faith* in what that means, *who* it makes you. And *who* made you."

Jordin spotted a piece of rebar on the ground that had fallen out of the crumbling cement ceiling. She leaned over to grab it, closing her tendril fingers around the thick piece of metal. I watched her concentrate hard as she worked to heft the thing, but she only got it to move a few inches off the ground.

"Come on, I need your help!" she said. "We don't need to move mountains, Maia. Just some metal."

I worked hard to focus, closing off everything around me. *I can do this. I can believe. I can believe. I believe. I believe. . . .*

I followed Jordin's example, carefully and intentionally focusing on the rebar. I formed two distinct hands at the ends of my billowing arms and clutched at the metal bar with both of them. . . .

And I had it! My surprise made me lose my grip for half a second, but I recovered before the metal bar could fall.

The two of us lifted the rebar and carried it as close as we could to the entrance.

"Don't think of this as working your muscles," Jordin said as we lifted the bar high enough to hurl it. "It's not. Concentrate on getting it far enough across the room to smash into one of those glass wall panels."

That didn't sound easy. The curve of the circular room was wide, and getting a clear shot to one of the panels from this door meant hurling the rebar more than a hundred feet.

Again, I focused on calming myself and concentrating on what we wanted to do. Jordin counted to three, and at the end of her count, we lobbed the rebar through the air and into the Body Chamber.

I bore down as Jordin did the same thing next to me, and willed the big piece of metal to keep going until it moved far enough to stick into one of the glass wall panels.

The panel and all of its etched-on symbols shattered into thousands of pieces. I had no idea how, but the fire inside was extinguished in an instant. It started with the broken panel and then snuffed out in a fast succession, all the way around the huge room, until the fire was no more.

The invisible barrier keeping us out fell away.

TWENTY-TWO

Demon.

It was the only word that entered my mind, and the only adequate description of what Jordin and I stared at across the darkened room, beyond the endless aisles of gurney-filled cubicles.

A real demon was living, breathing, moving, and killing in the mortal realm. Which was impossible, because angels, demons, and spirits were the inhabitants of the spirit realm. As a rule, they didn't get to cross the veil into our world. They could interact with the mortal world, but they couldn't live in it.

But then, I was a disembodied soul, so I guess most rules didn't seem to be holding at the moment. And I was fast coming to understand that there was a lot about this I didn't know. Not as much as I thought I did.

The room quaked when the beast's enormous feet slammed into the floor, leaving indentations in the white cement. It continued to grind the last remaining vestiges of Howell Durham into the pavement, and it let out a half growl, half laugh as it did.

Now that we were inside, we moved closer, and I turned my full attention to this grisly creature, getting my first good look at it. It was black all over, and my first thought was that it was covered in tar. But then I examined it closer and saw that its coarse leathery hide was burned. Charred and ruined, it was impossible to see what it might have once looked like.

Its obsidian hide was some kind of hard, scaly substance, but there were black craggy bits of burned carcass in every crevice, hanging from its hands, ears, even its chin. It was a hulking mammoth, standing more than ten feet tall upon its two feet. Its frame was more like an ox or plow horse than a man. Yet its movements were agile and fast.

Its head was defined by sharp angles, like a skull. It had beady eyes glowing the color of fire, and they showed only contempt and hatred. Its one inhuman facial feature was its nose, which had enormous nostrils that flared every time it let out a breath. It reminded me of a bull's nose, mostly because it was constantly spewing air so hot that you could see the steam. I wasn't sure if the creature was truly breathing or if this was just its way of expelling the volcanic heat that seemed to constantly burn under its smoldering skin.

"Derek!" Jordin shrieked.

I saw him, too. Derek was stepping out from behind the last cubicle partition separating him from the demon, and now took a bold stride forward. The distance between them was less than thirty feet.

The demon noticed him immediately, shifting its gigantic frame around to face him. Amazingly, Derek didn't flinch—not at the sickening attention now focused on him from the demon nor at his proximity to the incredible amount of heat pouring off the creature.

I was sure that if I'd still had a stomach, in Derek's place right now I would have thrown up.

"What is your name, demon?" Derek asked. "In the name of the Most High God, I command you to tell me."

The demon looked at him for a long moment, considering this.

"He's *challenging* it?" I asked, incredulous. "What's he expecting to happen?! It's not like he can cast it out. It's on the mortal plane now—it's a *physical* being, not a spiritual one!"

"He can't face it alone!" cried Jordin in a panic. "We have to help him!"

I wondered if she'd heard me but didn't get the chance to ask. She was already moving toward her fiancé and the abomination.

A thought struck me. If the demon was tangible now, then that meant it had no purchase on *this* side of the veil, where Jordin and I were. Which could give us an advantage. At the very least, it meant the creature probably wouldn't be able to see or hear us.

"I see the light of faith in your eyes," the demon said to Derek, its voice deep and hollow, yet silky smooth. "Come closer so I can pluck them out. I could use a snack, and there is nothing tastier or more satisfying to devour than a believer."

I took special note of what it had said. Why would the demon need Derek to come closer to *it*, in order to harm him?

Did the symbols around and throughout the building affect more than just the apparitions inside it?

Derek stood his ground, the picture of restrained strength. "You are nothing but a servant to a pathetic poser with delusions of superiority. *I* serve He who is greater. And in His name . . . I command you to leave this place."

The demon bared its black opal teeth. "Where should you like me to go?" it asked.

"Crawl back in the hole you came out of!" Derek shouted.

"No," replied the demon, and its simple refusal was like a punch to Derek's stomach. "I have no desire to leave."

Derek took a small step backward, saying nothing.

"You and your God have no control over me," gloated the demon. "Not here, where you cowardly mortals live in your precious flesh. Durham thought he could control me, too. He had such vision, such intellect. But his mistake was believing he could contain me."

I looked behind the creature at the boxlike object behind it, and saw now that it was some kind of large, complicated cage.

"You don't belong here, demon," Derek said again, glaring at the monster with stern disgust. His eyes never blinked or wavered as he stared it down. "I command you to tell me: how did you get here?"

"Save your commands," the demon replied. "I seek answers myself. It was three of your years ago. Something punched a hole in the veil, the fabric that separates our realities. It's a very rare occurrence, and it was only for an instant. The tear started to collapse almost as soon as it appeared. So I went through it."

Jordin and I moved closer, slowly, carefully, watching the creature.

Derek appeared skeptical, and I saw him take a quick glance at the rubble from the shaking building at his feet. Was he looking for something?

"What could possibly punch through the veil?" Derek asked. "Who but the one true God, Jehovah, has that kind of power?"

The demon flinched when Derek said the name *Jehovah*.

"Who, indeed?" the demon said. "It is the greatest of mysteries. Minuscule tears have punctured the veil a handful of times in recent times, and will likely do so again in the future. We know only that some profound event happened that has created a slight instability in the veil.

"Almost as soon as I emerged into this world, I could feel my side trying to pull me back. The sensation grew in strength over time, the tugging becoming stronger and stronger, and I knew I wouldn't be able to resist it for long. So I used certain . . . *elements* . . . from this side to fashion a way to keep myself anchored to this reality." The demon reached back inside its broken holding cell and pulled out a small metal cube, less than six inches across, and held it in the palm of its beefy, charred hand. It looked like a child's toy block in his enormous hand.

I broke away from Jordin, who continued on her careful path toward Derek. I moved closer to get a good look at the demon and this cube it had produced. I wondered now if I was wrong before about the creature's ability to sense me. It was still a supernatural being, regardless of where it was currently located. Did it already know I was there? Would it turn on me any second?

The cube it held in its hand was a solid, thick thing. It had been sloppily hammered together, or maybe it had been poured into a mold as a liquid and cooled. I couldn't tell, but it was crude and imperfect. There was a raised mark on just one of its six sides. A small, roundish but highly detailed symbol . . .

Derek had taken in everything about the cube, just as I had. "*That's* how you do it? You mark these people with *that*? Or DHI does?" Derek gestured at the bodies throughout the chamber.

"I did not construct the cube for their benefit," the creature replied. "Not at first. As I said, I made it to tether myself to this reality. To keep the other side from pulling me back."

The demon bared its barrel-like chest, and for the first time I noticed—as I'm sure Derek did—that right in the center, where a human's breast-bone would be, was the same glyph that Jordin and I bore on the back of our necks. Or rather, our physical bodies did.

Seeing it there, I had the best idea ever.

But Derek was revolted. "But you have no soul to bind, demon," he seethed.

The creature bared its teeth again. "No, *He* did not see fit to imbue us, His *first* creations, with souls. Nonetheless, I required something to keep me from being pulled back to the other side. Howell Durham was the one to see the potential for a different use for my little trinket."

Derek took another bold step forward, and I pulled up less than ten feet from the demon, waiting to see if it would notice or acknowledge me. I thought I heard something scraping on the ground as Derek shuffled closer, like he was pushing at something with his toe.

"You were partners in this?" Derek asked. "Why did you kill him?"

The demon's body language suggested that it desperately

wanted to take a step forward, toward Derek, but it couldn't seem to move far beyond what was left of the cage it had broken out of.

I got the impression that it was freely relating its story to Derek the same way a fisherman lures a fish to his rod. Derek must have thought that by continuing to inch forward, he was demonstrating a lack of fear in the face of this grisly beast. But I was suddenly afraid that the demon was playing him, working him carefully with its truthful words in order to reel him in. It was a seduction, a dance, taking place between the two of them, and the demon was winning.

"Howell Durham was a world-class game hunter," the demon said, like a storyteller settling in to tell a good yarn. "He was following a game trail in the Amazon valley when he came upon me, wandering across this hard, cold rock you call home, trying to find my way to civilization. He assumed I was some previously undiscovered animal, some leftover from an ancient era, like a rediscovered ape or dinosaur. So he used his fancy equipment to capture me. That's what I let him believe, anyway.

"He took me in my little cage to Copenhagen, where he was shocked to discover that I was intelligent and could speak to him. And I was no mortal animal. I was from the other side of existence. He sensed an opportunity, so he proceeded to 'use' me to his profit. It took years of trial and error on the part of his scientists—working off of metaphysical concepts I gave them— to construct the device he wanted. Durham wanted two things: a device that could free a soul from the confines of its pathetic human body, and a means of keeping that body from reaching what you call the afterlife. I already had that second item, in the form of my little cube here. But the extractor device took a great deal of time to perfect, because Durham insisted on being in full control of it every step of the way. Our agreement was that I would maintain control of the cube, while Durham kept his machine. One would be useless without the other.

"But Durham never understood me well enough to know the depths of his own arrogance. Those of us on my side of the veil are infinitely patient beings. We have existed since before the beginning of what you call time, so I had no difficulty watching as Durham worked, waiting in that accursed cell for my chance to be rid of him and enact a plan of my own. Something far grander than anything even a visionary like Durham could think up."

" 'The nightmare is coming,' " Derek suggested, taking another step forward and glancing at his feet.

The demon had tendrils of something resembling saliva dripping out of its mouth in nauseating strings, and they flew everywhere when it spoke.

"*I. Am. Coming!*" the demon thundered.

Derek held fast, though a roaring hot wind escaped from the vile creature's mouth and blasted into him like a super-hot furnace.

"You pathetic humans believe yourselves to be the indigenous species on this planet. But my kind was here first, and *we want it back*. We are at war against the ones who still follow . . . *Him* . . . and the prize is the one thing He treasures most: you. The eternal, undying souls of man, His most precious creations. The other side fights to protect you, we fight to defile you. But there is only one way to life everlasting. Only one. Just as there is only one way for a soul's path to end in hell. It's a choice between two possibilities. Believe, or don't believe. Surrender yourself, or live in selfishness. But that time is over. I have finally found a way to cheat the game.

"I will use the technology in this room to circumvent that human choice, and physically *drag* every soul on this planet straight to hell. And once there are no souls left for either side to fight over . . . we win the war."

The demon ended his story with a flourish, carefully depositing the cube on a metal table off to one side of its damaged cage.

It was horrific. The perfect plan, the ultimate act of spite against God. For the first time I was thankful to be without skin or blood, because they would both have been ice cold right now.

The silence was broken by the sound of desperate whispers. I turned and saw Derek on his knees, his eyes closed and his mouth moving with barely any sound coming out. There were beads of sweat all over his head and hands; he was trembling so hard that he almost lost his balance at one point.

Derek was praying, and I recognized his words as Scripture. " 'In this world you will have trouble. But take heart! I have overcome the world.' "

"Get on your feet, boy," the demon taunted. "Believe me . . . *He's not listening.* He has abandoned this place and all who come inside it. It's mine now, and I will grow it to engulf this entire wretched world."

Derek slowly, weakly stood back up. "If that's true," he said, his voice low, "then why haven't you killed me already?"

The demon's red eyes narrowed into slits, but it had no reply.

Derek had something in his hand—the thing he had been

kicking across the floor—and he raised it before him, with his arm outstretched fully in the direction of the monster.

It was two intersecting pieces of rebar, welded together in the middle. Together, the two metal rods formed a crude but unmistakable cross.

"You can't touch me," Derek said, hefting the cross high. His voice gained strength with every word. "You can't harm me. You have no power over me. I do not fear you!"

With a move so fast it seemed impossible, the demon spun, grabbed its metal cage with its gigantic, gnarled hands, and tore the thing apart with a howl of rage.

Then it spun again, and two things happened at once.

The demon hurled a large crisscrossing section of the metal rods from the cage in Derek's direction.

And just before the flying metal made contact, Derek was flung violently onto the ground.

Jordin. I'd lost track of her in all this. Her spirit now stood in the exact spot Derek had been occupying a second ago, her arms thrown straight out. She'd somehow worked up the strength of will to make physical contact with Derek and push him out of harm's way. And it didn't escape my notice that the demon wasn't able to see her apparition standing there glaring at it.

The demon was furious, and grabbed more pieces of the broken cage to hurl at Derek, though Derek was now on the ground. I saw his fingers still clutching the rudimentary cross, and his lips were moving again. I was about to call out to Jordin when she started moving away, out into the middle of the chamber, on a mission.

I couldn't see if Derek was hurt or not, but I didn't spend a long time staring from my vantage point behind the demon. As it threw metal rods and other bits in a hot fury, I drew closer, as fast as I dared, still afraid that some unsuspecting interaction of mine with the mortal world might tip the demon off to my presence.

I moved around behind its enormous legs, noting the horrendous stench and incredible heat it was giving off—though neither had any effect on me—and with all of the concentration I could muster, I reached out my indefinable hand and grabbed the object of my desire.

The demon was still flinging things toward Derek when it stopped short at the sight in front of it. Thanks to yours truly, the metal cube bearing the glyph was floating right in front of its charcoal body.

I lunged, and the cube was shoved forward toward the demon's chest, but its reflexes were too fast. It stopped the cube with a single hand and snatched it away from me.

"A ghostly rebellion, eh?" it muttered, straining to see me but unable to.

But while it was speaking, I was already in motion. My strength of will was fully maxed out as one of the metal rods from the creature's cage flew into the air. Its sharp broken-off end scratched a deep cut into the demon's chest, and in that instant, the entire room shuddered.

The demon dropped the cube and the metal bar was torn free from my hands, but it didn't matter. I stood slowly in triumph, gazing at the gash I had made across the demon's chest—carving straight through the glyph that was branded there.

The demon's eyes swelled in horror when it saw that the symbol had been broken, and it scrambled about, searching the floor beneath it for the cube.

But I already had the cube in my hands once more, and I tossed it toward the center of the room, where the extractor lay, my body still resting inside it.

The brightest glow I ever saw burst into being all across the ceiling above us, and an entire legion of beings of light flew into the Body Chamber at breakneck speed. I couldn't get a good look at them because of how fast they moved, but they were more dazzling than the sun. A thousand suns.

They grabbed the demon, kicking and screaming, and the vile thing turned inside out until it vanished from sight. The angels, likewise, faded in a single powerful instant that was punctuated by a clap of thunder.

———————

Amid the silence that followed, I made my way to the center of the chamber and directly through the extractor's clear tube to slide into my physical body. The mortal world came flooding back, my dull but familiar human senses taking over as I opened my eyes and took a long, deep breath.

Jordin was already back. She was supporting Derek's weight as they stood side by side just outside the machine, watching and waiting for me to emerge. Derek looked terrible, bleeding from a gash on his head and ready to pass out. He had a broken wrist from where Jordin had shoved him to the ground. And Jordin was pale and looking rather weak herself.

She pushed a button on the extractor's controls and the clear pod slid down away from me. I realized how weak I was myself as I tried to stand on my own and my knees buckled. My trusty heart began beating faster and harder, and for the first time, I was oddly happy to feel the sensation.

As Jordin and Derek helped me to stand, the three of us heard murmuring from throughout the vast room. Other souls trapped here in the building had found their bodies and were returning to the land of the living.

The three of us never spoke, never charted a course or laid out a plan.

We stepped up to the extractor as one. In our respectively weary states, we worked methodically and tirelessly, prying free keypads and monitors from the extractor. I reached inside and tore out the needle that had punctured the back of my neck during the procedure.

As others awoke and exited their cubicles, our feeble efforts grew into a movement as dozens of us worked in silence to dismantle the extractor down to its circuits and wires, never uttering a single word between us. Pierre eventually returned and whispered to me that the authorities were on the way, and though I knew he had to be thinking about how the extractor should be preserved as evidence, he finally chose to join the group in tearing it apart.

I left them to continue the work, and went off in search of two things. I returned to the center of the room when I had them both.

Derek and Jordin looked up to see me holding the demon's cube in one hand and the rebar cross Derek had held aloft in the other. They watched silently as I placed the cube on the ground and then reared back and jammed the rebar cross straight through it.

Again and again I did this, and when I was done, the cube was crushed beyond recognition. And the glyph it bore, with it.

EPILOGUE

ONE WEEK LATER

The *Boston Herald* was proudly on display, covering a large portion of our dining table. Pierre Ravenwood's exposé of the astounding, horrifying work of Durham Holdings International took up the entire front page, and continued onto a second. The *Herald* exclusive had been picked up by all the major news networks and outlets, making its way all around the globe.

Pierre was being called "a bold new voice in investigative reporting" by some, and he had appeared on half a dozen news broadcasts—with eight more already scheduled—to tell our incredible story. Derek, Jordin, and I turned down all offers for interviews, referring everyone to Pierre instead.

Tonight, the four of us enjoyed a nice dinner out at Pierre's expense. He said it was the least he could do for the three of us helping to fast-track his career. I sat next to him—which was a bit awkward but also kinda nice—while Jordin and Derek leaned against each other and frequently looked at one another with longing, maybe just to make sure they were both really there and together again.

While we waited for our food to arrive, Jordin spoke up. "There's one thing I still can't figure out," she said, looking to me. "When you and I were investigating . . . why was the paranormal activity so unusually high? Am I really some kind of paranormal focal point? Or do you think it could have been—"

"The demon's presence in the mortal realm? Or maybe DHI tailing you while it tried to lure you in to take part in its experiments?" I sighed, but not in a tired way. "I don't know. Everything we experienced was in keeping with what I've observed about the paranormal in the past. My feeling is that it was all real, though I'm sure at least one person at this table would disagree about that."

Derek smiled a rueful smile but said nothing.

"It was just the frequency of it—the tremendous amount of activity everywhere we turned—that was odd," I concluded. "Ultimately, it's something you'll have to decide for yourself. I know what I think."

"Fair enough," Jordin replied with a thoughtful, unworried smile.

Now it was my turn. I had a question of my own I'd been waiting for the right moment to ask. "Will you tell me something?" I said. "Why did you go to that church in New Jersey when you knew a demon would probably be there?"

"Demons are more powerful than humans," she explained, not trying to hide how foolish she felt now. She shrugged a useless shrug and shook her head sadly. "I hoped to barter something with the demon if it would open the veil and let me in. I know how ridiculous that sounds now. I was . . . obsessed. Now it feels like it's lifted. I had a lot of time to think after they abducted me, and the question that kept echoing in my head was what the angel said to the women at the tomb on Easter morning: 'Why do you look for the living among the dead?' "

Derek put his arm around her and held her tight. The two of them had had a long week to reacclimate and talk out everything that had happened. It looked like they were going to survive the experience.

"So do you still feel the weight of the old family curse?" he asked, without a hint of humor or judgment in his voice.

But Jordin grinned. "It wasn't there. There was no blemish or mark on my soul. It was never there. It was clean. I should have known it would be. That's the promise after all—but I didn't have faith. I know now how short life is in this world regardless of when we leave it, and I'm not going to spend what little time we have here living in fear."

I liked that answer. I also wondered how much of it she had heard from Derek and had adopted and repeated as her own.

It didn't matter. I could tell she believed it.

"You know," Pierre chimed in with a bit of a flourish, "as long as we're tying up loose ends . . . There's a question I still haven't gotten an answer to. And this question is for you, Ms. Peters."

I smiled sheepishly at his cheeky use of my last name. "Yes?" I said in faux sincerity.

"What happens when we die?" he asked.

I couldn't stop myself from glancing across the table at Jordin, recalling our first meeting and how I had demanded that she come up with that very question on her own, before I would agree to help her. We exchanged a brief glance. Even Derek looked my way for a moment before smiling warmly at his fiancée.

After all we had been through, after actually entering the spirit world and experiencing the freedom of not being constrained by a feeble, flawed human body . . . After everything that had happened, I finally understood.

I turned back to Pierre. "It's the wrong question," I said. "I've been asking it myself for so long . . . but it was always the wrong question to be asking."

Derek and Jordin watched me with keen eyes as Pierre spoke again. "Then what's the right question?"

"The right question, Mr. Ravenwood," I replied, mimicking his use of my last name, "is 'What happens when we *live*?' "

FROM THE AUTHOR

Do I believe in ghosts? I imagine this is the question I will be asked more than any other once *Nightmare* is consumed by readers.

It's a provocative question, one that captures some part of childlike imagination in all of us, because regardless of whether ghosts exist or not, the question speaks to a world beyond the one we know, and a life beyond the one we live today.

These are the facts: the kinds of events depicted in this book happen. They don't happen to everyone, and they don't happen every day, but they happen. The paranormal, ghosts, apparitions, whatever you want to call it: they're real. They exist. But what they are exactly is open to debate. Or to science, should it ever find a way to explain it to us.

I believe that there are all manner of supernatural things happening in the spiritual realm at all times. And I believe that the spirit realm exists parallel to the mortal world we live in, and the two overlap in ways we can't and won't fully understand until our time here is over.

Disembodied souls wandering the earth have been reported almost since the dawn of time, and the majority of people alive today either claim to have encountered a ghost or at the very least believe in them.

But . . . do *I* believe in ghosts?

I'll give you this much: I've never seen a ghost in person (and frankly, I'm not sure I'd ever want to). And though I keep an open mind when it comes to the paranormal, my view of the world tends to look a lot like Derek's.

But there's enough legitimate evidence for the reality of the paranormal that I can accept that *something* really is happening in many haunting cases. And as Maia points out in the book, I'm not at all convinced that that "something" can *always* be chalked up to demons. Having reviewed thousands of reported hauntings in preparation for this book, even if only a fraction of them are legit, there's still way too much evidence for them to simply be dismissed.

I wrote this book as a way of challenging you to make your own conclusions, and I hope you will do just that.

———————

In no way should this story be considered an endorsement of taking part in the field of paranormal investigation. The story depicted herein is just that: a story. It's not meant to be absorbed as anything but fodder for contemplation, conversation, and entertainment.

While I'm fascinated by the work of paranormal investigators, it cannot be overstressed that touching the paranormal is inherently dangerous. I would no more recommend it than I would recommend swimming with sharks or sword swallowing. There may be people in the world who can do it safely, but that doesn't make it a smart idea.

Every location visited by Maia and Jordin in this book is real. These locations exist exactly as they are described here, and each one of them has had countless reports of paranormal activity, and continue to. Nearly all of them are listed on the National Register of Historic Places.

Though dramatic license has been taken in the number and frequency of paranormal events that occurs at each one of these places in the book, every instance of paranormal activity depicted herein is based on events that have really happened at one haunted location or another, all of which have been verified by recordings and/or multiple eye-witness accounts.

It should come as no surprise that the fire that burns the abandoned Mount Hope Methodist Episcopal Church to the ground, as depicted in chapter 16, is a bit of fiction on my part; at the time of this writing, the church has never caught fire and still stands (though just barely) within the very dead woods that surround it, where no plant life of any kind has grown for decades.

ACKNOWLEDGMENTS

To my family, most especially my wonderful Karen and my adorable little Evan and Emma: I love you more than you will ever know. Thanks for letting me be a dreamer, and for dreaming with me.

To my Lord and Savior, Jesus Christ: You are mighty to save, and always faithful and true.

To you, dear reader: Thanks for taking this ride with me. Let's take another one soon.

PHOTO CREDITS

My deepest thanks to the talented photographers who are responsible for the incredible photos of the real-world locations seen in this book (with the exception of the Devil's Den photo in Chapter 20, which is credited to yours truly).

Waverly Hills Sanatorium (Chapter 4)
Kristin Sauls
Sweet World Photography
www.sweetworldphotography.com
kristin@sweetworldphotography.com

The Stanley Hotel (Chapter 6)
Jacob Duncan
jacob@jduncandesign.com

The Myrtles Plantation (Chapter 8)
Amee Sorensen Photography
3119 N. Sage Loop F6
Lehi, UT 84043
www.ameesorensenphotography.com
ameesorensen@mac.com

St. Louis Cemetery #1 (Chapter 10)
Carolyn Allmacher

U.S.S. North Carolina (Chapter 12)
Chris Wage
www.chriswage.com

Mt. Hope Methodist Episcopal Church (Chapter 16)
Heather Shade
www.lostdestinations.com

Alcatraz Island (Chapter 18)
Sharon Starrett
starrett_7@live.com

Cashtown Inn (Chapter 20)
Kristi Hale
www.6whitehorses.com

Sachs Bridge (Chapter 20)
Carol Starr
www.chestercountyprs.com

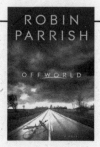